BAD IDEAS FOR LIVING

Bad Ideas for Living

A novel

by

JON RUBINSTEIN

Adelaide Books
New York / Lisbon
2021

BAD IDEAS FOR LIVING

A novel

By Jon Rubinstein

Published by Adelaide Books, New York / Lisbon
adelaidebooks.org

Editor-in-Chief
Stevan V. Nikolic

For any information, please address Adelaide Books
at info@adelaidebooks.org

or write to:

Adelaide Books
244 Fifth Ave. Suite D27
New York, NY, 10001

ISBN: 978-1-954351-40-0

Printed in the United States of America

To Suzzanne, my love

What comforts us is that, after we make ourselves crazy enough,

we can let go inch by inch into just being here; every so often, briefly.

–Anne Lamott

Chapter One

I was sure Hierro Acero had a huge dick. It wasn't visible under his skintight workout shorts. There was a suspect but unarticulated lump front-and-center. I guessed it was a jock, or a cup, or a dance belt that he used to hold his hefty junk in place. But he seemed like a big dick guy.

It just made sense given his size and the way my brain was programmed to believe in proportion; I'd expect big tires on a big truck, and small wheels on a skateboard. Acero was well over six feet and disturbingly ripped, and as he bounded across the vast Javitz Center stage, puffing his chest like a Disney prince, his muscular bulk shook the grey-felted AC/DC-blasting speaker towers. I felt like a miniature horse gazing at the winner's circle.

The *Ram Hardy: Give Zero Fucks* banners quivered with each of Acero's footsteps.

Acero's immense body and outsized charisma had their own gravitational field; around him, threats of violence calmed like pots of water taken off a flame. He made me want to lift weights, to suck in my gut and hide my sagging neck. I'd never been fit, but being around Acero reminded me I was approaching forty. I could see what was to come and I didn't like it.

I'd turned up to the weekend a skeptic, hoping I'd at least get my money's worth, but Acero's pull was undeniable. Even Andrea liked his movies, and she hated everybody. If those were the kinds of results you got from Ram Hardy seminars, they were worth the price.

"This! Is! It!" Acero shouted, the trademarked vein on his head threatening to explode with excitement, zigzagging down his temple the way he parkoured through Paris and Hong Kong in film after film.

Guitars buzzsawed through the khakied mob. The men writhed and wrestled with glee. Avi clapped his callused hand on my back. His chunky rings stabbed my spine, but when I pulled away, he gripped my shoulder like a steering wheel and held me in place. His other hand was raised in a fist like he was here to see Acero wrestle for the belt. Avi shook it in the air like he was looking for a fight. Spittle sprayed from his mouth as he howled approval in his coarse Israeli accent. I wiped my cheek with the back of my hand and scanned the room for the exits, but Avi pulled me towards the stage, slapping my back again and again. I winced. I wasn't going anywhere, anyway. Not after what I'd spent, money I didn't have.

At work, Avi was slow and calculated. I sat across from him at the agency and watched him pause and breathe before opening his mouth every time he spoke to a client. He sounded like a rabbinical scholar, even when he was talking about a midwestern tour of *Phantom*. Here at the Javits Center though, it was as if he'd been slurping espresso. He was on fire.

I'd resisted his entreaties for weeks until he backed me into a corner in our drab Hell's Kitchen office and made me hand over my last working credit card. *Come on*, he'd begged, punching the numbers into his phone. *I can't do this alone.* I'd scowled at him for the rest of the day, but I was glad he'd forced the issue. I'd wanted to be convinced.

Avi knew I needed help. He knew my bookings were in the toilet. Everyone's were. The agency had once been respected, at least in the theater world. These days it was just a notch up from representing sideshow freaks, and it was clear from the look on Gene's face when he handed out our commission checks that mine were smaller than most.

And, Avi knew I'd been sneaking away from work for long, unexplained lunch breaks. But he didn't know the extent of my woes: I'd blown $19,000—our entire savings—at strip clubs and massage parlors. I'd been hiding it from Andrea, but she'd shown a lot more interest in our finances as of late. My secret would inevitably be exposed. It was just a question of when. Our only talk outside the therapist's office was functional: *Where? What time? How much?*

On top of losing our savings, I'd amassed a ton of credit card debt she didn't know about, and I'd been scrambling to make $300 and $400 minimum payments. I'd been able to hold onto my job, at least, and I hoped Ram Hardy would kick my ass into gear and solve my money woes before Andrea found out. I needed a small scale miracle: not an impossible cancer remission or a raise from the dead, but more of the water-into-wine variety that could put me in the black.

Acero stood glowering on a riser, empty save for a mic stand and stacks and stacks of speakers like an early eighties Van Halen concert. There were no chairs for us. We'd all paid the same $1,245. We were soft-chinned, ruddy-cheeked, baldspotted or headshaved. A few of us bore thin beards like hopeful teenagers. Our Oxford shirts were pitstained and unraveled at the back, but no one restuffed his tails.

All of us looked like we needed our asses kicked.

I'd heard the bitching while we waited—complaints, blame, noise. *My boss. My wife. The subway. The weather.* They were all blamers, my Mom would have said. *Cheer up!* was her refrain in the face of any complaint. *Beats being dead*, she'd told me. My younger sister Sarah and I lip synched the words whenever they came out of Mom's mouth. Mom had developed a game plan for disappointment early on, and she stuck to it like it was inscribed on stone tablets.

We all shut up when Acero started talking. He was a Big Fucking Movie Star and the center of attention anywhere he went, and he'd gotten where he was by listening to Ram Hardy's advice. We all wanted results like Acero had gotten.

Ram was the master. We all knew about Acero's ascent from parking attendant to pro wrestler to movie star. It was the stuff of Ram Hardy Legend. Ram's crowd chanted Ram's chants, bought his merch, and watched his videos. They shouted *Give Zero Fucks!* and *Stop Being Such a Pussy!* I'd seen more than a couple GZF tattoos. It was culty, for sure—his devotees sounded like a bunch of vegans—but Ram got results. Look at Acero! He was winning! How could he *not* have a monster dong? He was the size of two men, easily, and deserved double the dick. I knew that correlation was not causation, but hell, I wanted a dick like that, too. That would be worth the $1,245 I'd spent. And I wouldn't have had to hide the cost from Andrea.

Acero yelled into the mic as he flexed his signature flex and busted open his shirt sleeves. "Are y'all ready for this?"

The horde let out a pent-up roar, nine hundred plus nametagged straight white men, a smattering of blacks, Asians, and Latinos, the doughy and the fit, dressed from the Men's Warehouse sale rack or bought with Macy's coupons. I shouted along with them, swept along with the fury. Avi kept pulling me towards the front and away from the door, like he was afraid I'd leave.

The chant started at the room's far perimeter, among a handful of diehards posed under the tall vinyl banner that read *RAM* in bold, sans-serif font. The name was superimposed over an image of Hardy's halting blue eyes, his craggy crow's feet faded into shadow. Ram Hardy looked like a drill sergeant, and that was the source of his military methodology. *Drop and give me twenty!*

Ram was all toughness, all fight, all balls. Wake up early, kick ass, repeat.

Vulnerability? Fuck that. I yelled some more. I was done being feeble, done lying to get by. I was tired of struggling to make sixty grand, tired of driving to Boston and New Haven to see middling actors in Ibsen and Chekhov, tired of post-show gushing, pretending to be *deeply moved*, pretending to be *inspired.*

Voices cycled through the sweat-drenched flock, as they rattled and shuffled in anticipation, and the rumble became words. Acero barked into the mic and shook his fist, as the bass thudded underneath crunchy power chords. *Give Zero Fucks! Give Zero Fucks!* Acero's voice boomed from the stageside boxes as the crowd tore into a frenzy.

Abruptly, Acero looked up and stopped, responding to some signal we could not see. The men fell to a hush. The music silenced and Acero stood solemnly at center stage and stepped into a subtle backlight. "I had nothing but a dream," he growled. He stared out at us. The sound system gave off a low hiss. "I was parking cars and sleeping on my brother's couch. I'd been busting my ass for ten years with nothing to show for it."

Assent murmured through the mob. Acero let the mic drop to his side. He eyed the sea of bald, angry heads and clenched his jaw the way we'd seen him do in the movies. He dragged the mic back to his mouth.

"Did I have connections?" he asked.

No! the men roared.

"Did I have rich parents?"

No!

"Then what did I have?"

Nothing!

Acero nodded and flicked sweat off his brow. "That's right, I had *nothing.*" He looked at us again, and we collectively waited for what we knew was to come, as his eyes meandered among us, the sea of sweaty, hopeful faces. I'd seen videos like this, where Ram Hardy's biggest success stories showed up and kicked off his seminars. Acero said in interviews that he did them for free, out of gratitude to Ram. Watching them on You-Tube, they were easy to dismiss. But here, among a thousand fans, I was on edge, like a teenager with a hard-on.

Acero's gaze landed near the front of the throng, on a veiny-nosed man in a greying brush cut, his pleated suit pants belted tightly under his bulging gut. "Jerry," Acero whispered, reading the name tag magneted to Jerry's lapel, "every day was the same. I'd get up, eat some food, park some cars, smoke some weed, jerk off, and go back to sleep. Does that sound familiar?"

Avi checked to make sure I was watching.

"Fuck off," I mumbled. Avi shrugged and turned back.

Jerry nodded in response to Acero, and his pudgy chin bobbled in the flesh around his neck like a marshmallow in a pudding cup.

Hierro Acero stepped down into the crowd, and held the mic close to his face. A perimeter formed around him; no one dared come too close. Acero stood at one end and stared at the middle-aged man a few yards away. "Jerry," he said, "can you go on living this way?"

Jerry shook his head quickly, embarrassed.

Acero lowered his voice and stepped closer. A chill ran along my arms. "Tell me the truth, Jerry. Can you go on like this?"

The man quivered. He looked behind him, as if searching for an escape route. "No," he said. *Me either, Jerry.* How did I get to this place? Crushed by debt, disconnected from my wife, slogging through a mediocre career? It had to stop.

Acero stepped up to Jerry, and straightened to his full height; I realized Hierro had been hunched over to minimize his size, but facing the older man, with only a few inches of space between them, he looked like a cartoon beast towering over its prey. Jerry was frozen in terror as if he was about to be eaten.

I held my breath.

"Jerry," he whispered. "Tell the truth. Can you go on like this?"

The speakers popped and resumed their hiss.

"No?" Acero asked, his voice barely audible. I gasped in a tiny bit more air.

Jerry shook his head more vigorously. "No," he said, resolute. He was standing his ground. I steeled myself on his behalf. Jerry didn't deserve this, to be singled out in front of the whole room. Acero was a star. Jerry was an easy target; it was just mean.

Acero's voice came like a jolt as he barked. "No?" he asked. "No?" Hierro Acero shook his head and bounded back onto the stage. The room shook as his boots hit the riser. "You're a fucking liar, Jerry."

Jerry looked up at him, bewildered, and opened his mouth to respond. No words came out. I let out everything in my lungs and sucked in a deep breath, shocked. I mouthed a silent *fuck you* in Acero's direction.

"Don't look so fucking surprised, Jerry. You're a liar. You lie!" he yelled, pointing. Jerry wobbled as he stepped back. He seemed to be growing smaller with each word from Acero's mouth.

The movie star went on. "You are a bullshitter, Jerry. You *are* okay with it. You are no different than I was, when I was smoking weed and jerking off and going back to bed. I mean, look at yourself!"

The men surrounding Jerry turned to look at him. A burly guy in a cheap suit smirked, and a few others followed suit.

"I am talking to each and every one of you!" His voice reverberated throughout the hall. Acero stood there in silence for a moment. The smug men looked down, admonished. "Look at yourselves! You may not like it, but you *can* go on like this. You *will* go on like this. You can spend the rest of your sad lives like this."

Fuck him. Fuck that piece of shit.

A low pulse rumbled through the sound system, a throb of bass that seemed to come out of nowhere. Acero kept yelling and the beat grew louder. "But I have good news, Jerry!" he said, nearly screaming, and he held the mic above his head as the speakers blasted an impossibly loud crunch, distorted guitars and drums that knocked me back and into Avi, who clutched my shoulders. "I have some good fucking news, gentlemen! You don't have to keep living this way!"

Staring up at Acero, a slow grin formed on Jerry's face. Hierro Acero jumped back into the crowd and grabbed Jerry's meaty shoulder, patting it like he was praising a Labrador. Jerry's grin broke into a buttery smile.

Around me, red-faced men began to chant. *Give Zero Fucks! Give Zero Fucks!* Acero joined the voices, holding the mic out into the swarm to amplify the mantra. *Give Zero Fucks! Give Zero Fucks!* I gazed around me and gave in to the mob, screaming along with a thousand men. Fists pumped in the air and sweat poured as the volume grew.

"You don't *have* to keep living this way," Acero shouted again. And then a new voice came over the sound system. It was one whispered word, but its power silenced the room, and froze Hierro Acero in place.

Stop.

Ram Hardy stepped out from behind a curtain. He was polished, a compact ball of muscle, like a featherweight boxer in a bespoke suit. His face was a leathery grimace, a nearly seventy year old man with an agelessly harsh visage. Even still, he looked like someone we should be afraid of.

And we all were. Beside him, Hierro Acero turned in awe. In Ram's presence, Acero was just another fan. He had stepped aside to make room for Ram, and Ram ignored Acero as if he'd been hired to sweep the floors. Acero had brought an edge to the room with his voice and his stature, but it was ancient history; all eyes were on Ram.

Avi stared, slack-jawed.

Ram Hardy scanned the room, the panting, expectant faces, and brought a mic to his lips. His voice was unexceptional, neither deep nor high, but it carried a twinge of something numinous, and with that, we were riveted.

"Let's get started."

When she died, my grandmother left me five thousand dollars and her favorite crystal ashtray. In my memory, it was always full of grey detritus and Parliament butts, one cigarette still smoldering as she brought another to her fuchsia lips. The money was long gone, but the ashtray still made me smile.

Andrea cocked her arm back and whip-cracked the crystal relic at me. I watched it hurtle toward my forehead from across the bedroom as if in slow-motion. It grazed my brow and sliced open a gash before I knew what was happening. Blood dripped into my eye and I wiped it away quickly, watching the unbroken glass slide across the floor and thud against the wall. I was momentarily relieved that it looked intact. Then my head began to throb.

"Fuck, Andrea," I yelled. "I'm sorry!" A coffee mug whizzed past my head and hit the door frame before shattering. I shouldn't have listened to Ram Hardy after all. What a dumb idea—a *clean slate*. Lying was a far safer bet. And I hadn't even told her about the strippers or the handjobs or the credit cards.

"*A whole new start?*" she said, mocking my words. "That's what you got from your fucking two thousand dollar seminar?" Windowed envelopes and bank statements fluttered to the ground around her.

"It wasn't two thousand—"

She grabbed a paper from the floor in a clutched fist and wagged it at me, red-faced. "Shut up," she yelled. "You want me to *forgive* you? You blew our entire savings on fucking *garbage*—" Andrea threw the crinkled page on the floor and scanned the room for something else to throw. "That was our down payment. Ten fucking years we talked about buying an apartment."

I cowered, worried she'd restart the volley, and warily ran my fingers along the ridged cut on my head. "Maybe I have a problem," I said. "We could talk to Doris." Doris was our couples' therapist, who'd obviously been doing a bang-up job.

Andrea ignored my plea. "You bought fucking *coke?* Who are you, Charlie Sheen?" She wiped her sweaty forehead with a sleeve.

"And some weed," I said, hoping to soften the blow. I saw from the look on her face that my logic was failing. "I just kept bingeing. Buying dumb shit. Steaks." I paused, watching for her reaction. "You were traveling so much," I said, putting a twinge of sadness into my voice. "I'm sorry. I feel terrible."

"You feel terrible?" She grabbed a chipped coffee mug and tossed it in my direction halfheartedly. It bounced off the bed and clunked landed on the floor, intact. "Nineteen thousand dollars," she shouted, her voice growing raspy. She pointed her finger at me. "Get the fuck out of here before I fucking kill you."

For once, I listened.

I felt guilty so instead of the usual service, I hit up a nasty Chinese place in Sunset Park, up some rubber-treaded stairs above a store that sold lamps. There was no sign on the door, just some neon locksmith stickers and an index card with a few Chinese characters written in Sharpie. A fluorescent tube fluttered with grayish light.

I'd been there once before, when Andrea was on a three day back-and-forth to Myrtle Beach. I'd failed to get anything more than a lap dance from the girls at Pumps and, with little cash left, found the massage spot on Craigslist from the cab home. All the girls were busy, but the middle-aged owner had offered to fuck me for sixty bucks. I split, grossed out. I'd just come for a handjob. I wasn't *that* kind of guy.

Lying on the massage table atop a crinkly sheet of exam paper, I stared up at an acupuncture diagram taped to the grey wall, a cartoonish outline of a man riddled with lines and Chinese characters. The left side of his body was transparent, showing his bones and guts. His face—round, blank-eyed, clean-cut—reminded me of my father, or at least of his image from photos. It had been decades since we'd seen him in person.

The overhead light was harsh and white. A thin towel covered my groin. The girl knocked at the door and came in. She was wearing a loose fitting dress, patterned in orange and yellow leaves, and she took it off and dropped it on the metal chair in the corner of the room. Her underwear looked like it came from a multipack.

"That's more of an autumn dress," I said.

She smiled like I'd given her a compliment. A whisper of a vein curved down her left side, passing underneath her breast. She washed her hands in the stainless steel sink. Her ass was sprinkled with faint acne scars. Andrea had the same thing. The girl dried her hand on a white towel hanging from a hook, just like the one covering my dick. I wondered how many other dicks had touched these towels.

This probably wasn't a job she wanted, I thought, as she pulled her bra off. I felt my dick stir and I reached up and touched the bandage on my forehead. She ran her hand along my leg.

I gestured to the poster. "Do you know much about acu-puncture?"

She smiled again, the same way.

"I hear good things," I said. "My mom can't quit smoking." It was true. Since Grandma and Pop died, I rarely saw her without a cigarette in her mouth.

The girl pumped some lotion into her hand and wiped it on my legs like she was petting a cat. I'd paid her boss fifty bucks in the waiting room. I'd thought I'd feel better, spending less.

My jeans hung from a hook on the back of the flimsy door. They were a little long, and the cuffs had frayed where they'd caught under my heels.

"I need new jeans," I said.

She took some more lotion and slid it onto my thigh. Her lips were pressed into a thin, rigid smile. "Shhh," she whispered, pressing into my skin.

I should have known better. Ram Hardy's advice might have worked for some people, but money had always been a huge sore spot for me and Andrea; neither of us had had any of it growing up, and we both lived in the same constant state of financial panic. Of course we were broke. We did the kind of shit broke people do, starting with our jobs.

Andrea had started as a flight attendant for a regional airline in Western PA soon after graduating from Penn State. She'd previously moved to Brooklyn to manage rock bands, or do stand up comedy, or make biscuits and sell them at food fairs.

But then the job came up—her high school friend Jeannie, who had an Associates Degree in Customer Service and was rumored to have a third nipple, worked for the airline—and suddenly Andrea was living with Jeannie above a machine shop in Whitney, a few miles from Andrea's parents. They rode together, back and forth to the Latrobe airport in Jeannie's Kia Sportage, and they flew to Myrtle Beach clad in polyester skirts. We had just started dating when she moved. "I can't keep living like this," she'd said, as if she could keep living like *that*, on twenty-nine thousand a year in the heart of nowhere.

By the time she left for Pennsylvania, we'd only gone out three times and slept together twice, but after a sexless month I began commuting bi-weekly to Whitney and Myrtle Beach to keep seeing her. It became a comfortable routine, though she never seemed particularly happy to see me. It was more like, *sure, come*.

Momentum, inertia. The airline shut down down the Latrobe run and Andrea got transferred to LaGuardia. She moved in. My hairline receded and grayed, my belly grew, and tendrils strayed from my nostrils onto my upper lip. Andrea grew thinner each year, as if life's strain was taking its toll. Her hair began to thin, too, which I learned never to mention again.

The masseuse was vigorously working on my dick, making sexy pouts and little moans like she was enjoying it. She rolled her tongue around her lips and touched a nipple with her finger. Someone must have told her to do that, that men found it sexy. Maybe she'd been trained that way, like a customer service rep in a call center. *Your session may be recorded for quality assurance.*

Her hand hustled along my semi-hard penis, like it was being timed. I tried to relax. Over her shoulder, I saw a handwritten sign fluttering next to the sink, stuck to the wall with curled masking tape. A line of Chinese, written in pencil. I tried to guess what the characters meant. *Employees must wash hands*, maybe. I hoped it was something more inspiring. Andrea had once bought a book of inspirational quotes in a Myrtle Beach bookstore and left it on the back of the toilet in our apartment where I couldn't miss it. *Wheresoever you go, go with all your heart.* Maybe that's what was on the sign.

When Andrea first took the job she liked to say she was "paying her dues," that eventually she'd be with one of the majors, jump-seating to Vail for ski weekends. But those rumblings had long quieted, like she'd accepted the obvious: there were no Singapore/Rome/Lima jaunts on her horizon, no clink of Champagne glasses and insignia-stenciled china. She was wearing L'Eggs and slinging PopChips to mouth breathers.

As for me, I'd grown tired of waiting tables and had a friend who worked at a fourth-rate talent agency. They had needed someone who knew how to type. I could type. I got the job, and eventually, a promotion.

At first, it seemed glamorous. I wrote off movie tickets on my taxes and got good seats on Broadway. Mom proudly introduced me as *a Hollywood agent*. Andrea and I got engaged, argued with our families over dates and locations, and slipped off to City Hall in frustration, with the promise of a future fête that never materialized. Dad had heard through the family grapevine and sent a postcard from Iquitos—an aerial view of the winding Amazon, dense and fecund, with *Congrats! Love, Dad,* scrawled on the back in blue ballpoint ink. We still had it stuck to our fridge, but it was no longer funny.

Meantime, I could tell the girl was getting frustrated. Her hand pumped harder, and she ran her tongue over her lips like she was in a hair-metal music video. It felt as sexy as a hernia exam. I could hear someone arguing in Chinese out in the hall. Through the door, the rapid-fire bickering was almost intelligible. Someone had disappointed someone, that was for sure. Then, unmistakably, I heard a high-pitched fart, and a laugh.

Andrea had a right to be upset. But the money I'd taken was from our joint account. Would it be stealing if we were sharing a dessert and I ate most of it? If Andrea got up to go to the bathroom and I ate all the ice cream, leaving her melty dregs of chocolate and a spot of syrup?

It would be shitty, sure.

The Flying Ashtray Incident was a dumb mistake on my part. I should have kept my mouth shut. Still, I'd managed to keep the credit cards hidden, and as far as she knew all I'd done was fritter away our money on garbage.

The massage girl got a glint in her eye and squirted some more lotion onto her hand. She redoubled her efforts, petting my balls and further contorting her face, but it made no difference. Whatever had brought me there had faded, and all I wanted to do was leave. I pushed her hand away and sat up.

"Thank you," I said.

She looked at me, puzzled, and reached for my dick, but I covered myself with my hand.

"It's okay." I jumped to my feet and she stepped out of the way. "I should go." I grabbed my clothes and got dressed.

The girl stood for a moment, watching me, before slipping her bra over her head. She looked down at the floor and put on her dress. She ripped the paper off the massage table and tossed the towel into a laundry basket smoothly, like she'd practiced the move.

"Two points," I said. I handed her my last twenty and hoped she'd get to keep it.

Chapter Two

"Have you been hugging?" Doris asked, her eyes darting between us. Her hair was freshly cut; she wore sharp black bangs and outsized gold bracelets, and her newly manicured nails were a violent shade of red. The office was suitably neutral; watercolors hung on the walls, landscapes and plant life. A beige UFO-shaped device sat on the floor by the door generating white noise. It was the size of a small birthday cake. Its plug trailed indecorously to a nearby socket.

"What about meals?"

Andrea and I had been seeing Doris for a while. She wore fur and changed the amount she charged us each week. It was $180, or $190, or $175, but I never questioned it, just dutifully wrote out a check I knew we couldn't afford.

Doris had been giving us homework. We had a hugging schedule. We were to eat meals together and leave our phones in the other room. We were to drink less, advice we more or less ignored. I tried to meditate. I bought a matching cushions and a Tibetan singing bowl and downloaded an app, but couldn't sit still for even a minute.

Now, we were sitting at either end of Doris' computer gray sofa, both of us staring straight ahead. I checked the band-aid on my head. I'd showed up to our standing appointment, and so had Andrea. Neither of us wanted to be the one to admit defeat.

We had first ended up there after I'd pointed out that we hadn't had sex in three months. Andrea had started crying and told me she thought she might be asexual. She'd read an article about asexual people that one of her friends had shared on Facebook and she met most of the criteria on the checklist. *Is your interest in sex more scientific than emotional? Check!*

It soon came out that Andrea wasn't asexual, she just wasn't interested in *me*. I wasn't particularly interested in her, either, but her admission let me play the wounded victim card for a bit, and took the focus off my own behavior. I was pretty sure Doris was buying it.

Andrea clutched a throw pillow to her chest.

"Have you been hugging?" Doris repeated.

"We hugged on Tuesday," I said.

Andrea instantly rolled her eyes. "He's delusional." She looked at me. "Tuesday?"

"It was hug-like," I said.

She ignored me and addressed Doris. "It was a pat on the back. That was before he went to that fucking *seminar*."

"It was, like, friendly—"

"Another two thousand dollars." Andrea sniffled sharply before pushing the pillow away.

"It wasn't that much—"

"Where did you even get that much money? Was that on top of the nineteen thousand?"

Grow a fucking pair, Ram had shouted all weekend.

I thought of something else I'd heard from Ram. "Money is a conversation," I said. "It's just an agreed-upon reality."

Andrea gestured at me, while looking at Doris. *See?*

"It has no inherent value, Andrea," I said. "It's not real."

Doris shifted in her chair. "Have you been intimate this week?"

Andrea waved her hands, upset. "Doris, did you hear what he did?"

"It wasn't two thousand," I said, taking a breath.

"You have a schedule," Doris said. "We agreed on it. All of us."

"No, no," Andrea said. "What difference does it make? There was no intimacy between us. None." She spat the last few words out for emphasis.

"I'm sorry," I said. My voice was a monotone. I wanted to be the rational one. "I just, I didn't want to keep lying. Ram said we had to start telling the truth." I turned to Andrea, my hands folded on my lap. "I'm thinking about our future."

"Good," Doris said.

I sat quietly, thinking of the walletful of credit cards I was hiding at that very moment. Doris' degrees hung on the wall in heavy wooden frames. I wondered how many other sad couples had sat in this very spot, or if my parents had gone to a therapist before Dad split for Peru. What therapist could have predicted their peculiar future?

Andrea shook her head tightly. "We have not been *intimate*," she repeated. "We are not going to be."

Doris let out a curious sound, a melodic, skeptical *hmmmm*. "Why not?"

I felt my face flush. "I've been willing."

Andrea was staring at the floor.

"You have to make an effort, folks," Doris said. Her voice had a bit of annoyed edge. We were a problem. "Are you willing to make an effort?"

"Yes," I said, not waiting for Andrea's response. She'd never been willing. We were wasting money with Doris, ticking off a box to make it seem like we had tried. And I had a feeling that Andrea was misbehaving in her own way. She was gone a few nights a week for work and this guy Joe from Pennsylvania kept "liking" everything she posted on Facebook. Occasionally they had little public flirtations in her comments section.

Joe: Seriously? You're posting spoilers without a warning? Shame on you.

Andrea: You're right. I need to be punished. 

I suppose she thought that doing it in public made it okay, that it wasn't really flirting if it was out in the open. And Joe, who appeared to be a walrus-sized elementary school crossing guard from his Facebook photos, didn't seem like much of a threat. But I had my suspicions, and anyway, they made my own behavior less odious. I imagined her meeting Joe for romantic getaways in unromantic locales. The Hampton Inn, the Residence Inn, the Sleep Inn. The DoubleTree, the Captain's Quarters, the Windsurfer. Joe, in the same Steelers hoodie I'd seen him wear in every Facebook photo. Andrea, in her "sexy" beige JC Penney underwear.

Andrea looked off into the distance, like she was examining the bland landscapes on Doris' wall.

"You have to be willing," Doris said sharply.

I looked over at Andrea, who wouldn't meet my gaze.

Doris touched her hair and stared at the two of us. She nodded to herself, as if affirming her own logic. "You could start slowly," she said, "like with masturbation."

Andrea jumped to her feet, her boots thudding on the carpet. "I have to go," she said. She picked up her purse from the floor.

I hesitated, as Doris stayed in her chair. "We have a few more minutes," Doris said.

Andrea reached for the door and turned back to face us. "This isn't working," she said. She looked straight at me, her face devoid of emotion. "I need some space."

"Space?" I said. "You're gone half the time."

Doris waved to her. "Andrea, please sit—"

Andrea ignored Doris. "Find a place to stay for a while, Alan."

I stood up. "That's not right," I said, addressing both women. "I pay rent, too."

Andrea pulled her purse's leather strap over her shoulder and turned to leave, before looking back in my direction. "Rent is just a conversation, Alan."

"No complaining today, *yadid*. Our clients need jobs." Avi sat across from me in his black *GZF* cap, his shirt perpetually untucked. He was hunched over and sweaty. Avi looked his age, a good ten years older than me. He'd gotten to the office early like always, in order to leave in time to pick up his kids. I tried to imagine what would have him come all the way from Tel Aviv to hustle guest star gigs on cop shows. He could be partying in Jaffa right now, dancing to house music with an Uzi strapped across his back. But instead, he was staring at his computer screen with his jaw hanging open, and I knew he was worried too. He had a wife and three kids somewhere in a New Jersey suburb and his property taxes were crushing him. "We're going to kill it," Avi said, pointing at me. "Get after it, right?"

I looked down at the laminated placard on my desk. It was in Hindi. I'd picked it out from a tableful of Ram Hardy merchandise at the seminar.

ऐसी बिल्ली होने से रोको

It meant *Stop Being Such a Pussy*. All the Ram merch came in multiple languages, although I'd seen only a few foreign-seeming participants at the event. Maybe it was aspirational. I bought the sign knowing I'd know what it meant.

We were used to complaining every day, and I was glad I had Avi to remind me not to; we were out to win. Complaints were an energy suck. *Quit your whining and get after it!* Ram shouted, every time he heard an excuse.

The office smelled like a long-ago microwaved burrito. The place hadn't been painted in years and was decorated with posters from failed Broadway shows. It had been meant to be funny but had started to hit too close to home.

I stared at the phone for a full minute, willing it to ring. Around me, a chorus of overly friendly voices were murmuring into their phones, pleading for auditions. "What are you working on?" I asked. I pulled my headset off so it dangled around my neck like an electronic choker. An empty coffee mug with a picture of Richard Nixon bowling stared at me from my desk.

Avi looked up at me, a leaky pen in one hand. A deep blue inkstain bruised his palm. "*Ani?*" he said. "A national tour would be nice."

"Don't get greedy," I said, looking down at my notepad and thought about who to call next. Avi was right—we could stick someone in a musical for a year and collect checks week after week. It was easy money when it worked out; we probably wouldn't hear from them until the contract was ready to end. Avi was good at convincing actors that weeklong runs in Detroit and Cleveland would be good for their careers.

We all had something in common: none of us wanted to be there, and we were all struggling. It had gotten harder to make money. I wanted to blame it on globalization or the internet. I was grateful for the paycheck, but word was that no one was performing well; all the big money-earners had left for greener pastures, larger agencies with nicer lobbies and elevators that didn't smell like pee. We were the little guys, left with the dregs, and it was shaping up to be my worst quarter in four years.

I had to do better. I needed a miracle. Or some TV money, at least. I knew I was on Gene's shit list. He'd quietly informed me some weeks earlier that there had been a sexual harassment complaint against me. *We gotta investigate dese tings,* he said, adjusting his polyester tie. Gene was around my age and lived with his ancient dad who'd founded the agency. His father was a bad influence; Gene wore short-sleeved dress shirts and was starting to look and sound more and more like a corrupt cop in a 1970's heist flick.

I'd been waiting to hear from Gene, or his lawyer, or an investigator, but it had been a month and I still wasn't even sure who'd registered the complaint. I hadn't done much I thought worthy of investigating, and I didn't want to ask Gene about it again, in hopes it would just fade out of existence. The investigation had become a dull ache that I'd grown used to.

It was another thing I'd been hiding from Andrea, but I was loath to tell her anything about it without knowing what there was to deny. I'd had enough things thrown at me for one week.

Avi clicked his mouse but kept staring straight ahead. His stubble was porcupine-coarse. Despite the cool office air, dark ovals of sweat stained his shirt like his body retained some kind of sense-memory of recon in the Negev Desert. "Did you see this?" He wagged his finger at his screen. I peeked over. The headline read, *CBS Casts Its Iceman.* The photo showed a square, unblemished jaw and slate-grey eyes topped by a tousle of blond hair.

"What else is new?" I said.

"A twenty year old." He huffed and looked away, drooping further into his chair. A poster for the musical *Carrie* hung on the wall behind him. "I could write these headlines in advance. Save them the trouble."

I laughed. "Quit your whining."

He threw up his hands dramatically.

I liked talking to Avi. His mild woe-is-me-ism kept my focus off my own litany, even if we did sound like a couple of old men complaining about the Mets.

A glob of drool threatened to drip from his lower lip. "My cousin Uri made fourteen million last year. Fourteen million!"

"Shekels?"

He shook his head. "Shekels, dollars. Does it matter?" He clicked his mouse forcefully, as if that would change what he was seeing. The worry that weighed on his face made him look like a much older man.

"What the fuck are you guys yammering about?" Gene's voice boomed from his office, right next to where I sat. He should have been driving a bus, not running an agency, but he was the boss. He spent most of his time with his door closed watching old *Law and Order* episodes.

When I'd first started working there, I'd thought how great it would be to have a hands-off boss. But it was sad watching a guy fritter away his life staring at a TV and yelling at anyone who made noise.

"Sorry, Gene."

Avi leaned back in his chair. It wobbled, and he caught himself. "Are you doing the Ram Intensive?" he whispered.

"You're kidding?" I asked. "I've spent too much already." At the end of the Ram Hardy weekend, he'd pitched us hard on *creating our futures*. What that looked like was signing up for another, more expensive seminar. The Intensive was one option; instead, I'd bought Ram's app and downloaded a series of pep talks, saving me over three grand.

Avi shrugged. "In for a penny, in for a pound."

"What does that mean?"

"It's a saying."

"I know it's a saying," I said. "But I don't see how it applies." I didn't want to tell him how badly I'd fared so far.

Avi adjusted his headset and dialed the phone. "I'm just telling you."

I gestured to my computer. "Maybe if I start booking," I said. "I need to bring in more money."

He nodded, understanding. "You'll start booking if you do the intensive." He leaned toward me. "Maybe get a colonic, too," he said. "You'll feel amazing. They stick a tube up your *tuchus*. It's the best."

I looked up at the clock. It was four-thirty. "I'm going for a coffee."

He raised a bushy eyebrow at me.

"I'll be back." I said.

"*Ani lo yodea clum.*" He shrugged and looked back at his screen, waving me off. "I know nothing. Have good coffee."

I popped in my headphones and hustled out the door into the steamy hallway where I began to sweat immediately. I pressed the elevator button and waited, hoping no one from the office would come in or out and then clicked on the Ram Hardy app on my phone. The screaming metal theme music pounded into my head. Its machine rhythm fluttered my heart.

My short-sleeved dress shirt stuck to my chest and back. I'd long given up on trying to look good at work. Most days I picked one of eight shirts or three pairs of jeans, along with dirty canvas sneakers I could have worn in high school. I saved suits for theater openings and funerals.

The music quieted and Ram started his drill sergeant patter. *This is it,* he said. *Today's the day you start living your fucking life. The day you stop being such a pussy.*

The elevator rumbled and the office door clicked behind me. I steeled myself and willed the elevator to come as someone stepped into the hall.

I glanced over my shoulder, as casually as I could muster. Elizabeth was one of the assistants. She was younger than me and worked with some of the other agents. She brushed past without looking at me. "Hi." I said, pausing the app. I'd strained to maintain a friendly but not overly interested tone with her since Gene had informed me that I was being investigated. Gene hadn't told me who'd lodged the complaint. I thought it might be her.

I had played it cool when she first started at the agency, her first post-college gig. She'd been a theater major at a decent liberal arts school. I was cautious around the young women we worked with, especially the actresses—I dreaded being thought of as a *creepy older guy*—but then I accidentally "liked" one of her Instagram posts, an old summer bikini shot. I'd been snooping, sure, but isn't that what Instagram bikini shots were for? I could clearly see the outline of her nipples in the shot. They were wider than I'd thought, and the detail made it easier to imagine her naked.

Zooming in on my phone, I'd accidentally double-tapped, and a little red heart appeared. My gut sank and I unliked it quickly. I went back to look again and her posts were private, and at the office she avoided my gaze. But that wasn't enough to investigate me, was it?

I stared straight ahead, listening to the click of her heels on the linoleum until they faded. I knew better. I'd mostly kept my misbehavior private. I didn't drink at work. There was no porn on my office computer. I'd never hit on a client; ours were mostly veteran character actors, and the only young women on the roster were quirky comedic types who didn't interest me.

The assistants came and quickly went, post-collegiates who stuck with us until they could find a better gig, but I was as attractive to them as a store mannequin. It wasn't my age, or my paunch, or my receding hairline. I'd complained to Avi that they didn't give me the time of day. He had an answer for everything.

"You're like a dad to them, Alan. You fade into the background until they need something." He'd laughed and patted me on the back. "Find one with a daddy complex."

Avi had been joking, of course. He was impressively loyal to his wife and kids: that's what kept him coming to work, he'd said. Those were the fucks he gave.

My phone buzzed in my pocket and I glanced at it, briefly hoping for rescue. It was a 561 number—Mom calling from Florida. I quickly pressed the button to send it to voicemail. I was in no mood to speak with her. I hadn't said a word about me and Andrea, and I was afraid I'd let something slip. Mom had a way of asking exactly the questions I didn't want to answer.

I turned the Ram app back on. *This is why you're fucking poor*, he said. *Look at who you hang out with. Start hanging around with rich people.* He'd spent an hour over the weekend, grilling us about the people in our lives. *Loser!* he'd shout whenever someone went on too long. *Kill them off! Get them out of your life!* It was harsh, sure, but it was hard to argue. I'd been spending most of my time surrounded by desperate people who were just trying to survive the day. We were grinding out a living in a depressing office off of Times Square. Ram was right.

The elevator came and I rode it down to the street. It was too hot to be outside. The pavement stank with garbage and the late afternoon sun baked into my skull. The coffee place was a block west, and I looked in that direction. Ram shouted *drop and give me twenty*. I turned off the app and headed east. There was an Irish-themed bar around the corner, a tiny spot decorated in shamrocks and green, white, and orange flags.

Bars know how to keep you comfortable: the air conditioning was an icy respite from the street and the TVs played sports highlights with the sound turned off. The place was nearly empty, except for the red-faced bartender and a battle-worn waitress who clutched an unlit cigarette as she flicked through the channels. She looked up as if she was expecting someone else. Then she turned back to the TV.

I took out my headphones and ordered a drink. "I'm just having one," I said, and the bartender slipped away and poured my bourbon. I sat on the stool, watching highlights from sports I didn't care about, and he slid a coaster in front of me, before placing the glass down. I took a sip and the alcohol burned my throat, and I quickly drank again. A faint glow filled my chest, warmth and looseness. It didn't matter how many times Ram Hardy yelled *Give Zero Fucks*. I needed some help.

I pushed the glass back and signaled to the bartender. He refilled it without a word. It's a special skill, that knowing concession to reality, that wordless lack of resistance to the inevitable. I wondered how many bad decisions had been made in the very chair where I sat. I drank the rest of the bourbon and left money on the bar.

A few minutes later I was peering at myself in the fish-eye mirror above the ATM. There was still a few hundred available for cash advances on my newest card, but things were getting tight and I knew I'd have to figure something out. The bourbon buzzed in my chest.

I knew the routine. I'd been using the same service for a while. They offered "tantric" massages, which were simply handjobs cloaked in spirituality. It was an ancient form of yogic practice, the website said. Below that was a grid of nude photos, the girls' faces blurred out.

The woman I'd called told me to call back once I'd gotten to a nearby corner, so I did that and called her from there, and then she told me to go to a particular address between Second and Third and wait for her to call me back. It was after five. People were hustling towards Grand Central and then on to their Tudors in Darien or Greenwich or Larchmont, their Sauvignon Blancs and Merlots. I thought about what I'd say if I ran into someone I knew, or what I'd tell Gene when he asked where I'd gone. A meeting, maybe. Something neutral, believable, something no one would question. Drinks with a client. No one they'd know.

A few Town Cars were lined up outside stodgy bank buildings, taillights aglow as they idled in anticipation of besuited women and men. The heat had subsided a bit, but I was again sticky with sweat after the time in the bar.

I race-walked east towards the address, past nondescript restaurants and the kinds of grey high-rise apartment buildings that I'd disdained ever since I moved to the city. I had no patience for the grisly reality of midtown living.

Farther east, the buildings grew smaller, and I picked up my pace until I was at a near-run. My phone rang and I grabbed it, startled.

"Yes?"

"Alan?" The same woman's voice answered, a trace of a European accent.

"Yes."

"Are you there?"

I looked up. It was a different location every time. Now I was in front of a medium-sized apartment building with air conditioners sagging from the windows like skin tags. Trash bins outside and faded buzzers told me it was nothing special. Through the glass door, bagged phone books and supermarket flyers lined the vestibule, curled with age. It looked abandoned, but I worried about seeing someone I knew. What would I say? No client would ever meet me here, unless they were planning a transition into porn.

"Yes."

"First door on the left," she said, and hung up.

The door buzzed and I pushed it open, and I sprinted to the interior door before the buzzing stopped. It flung open to my touch. A rickety, chipped-paint railing led up to another floor, and the patterned linoleum was flecked with muddy footprints. On the left, a gray metal door was ajar, a neon locksmith sticker affixed to the bell, a tall pry guard riveted to its edge. I pushed the door open and went inside, shutting it behind me.

How did this get to be a thing I do? I thought, as I spied the tattooed girl on the sofa eating from a white foam takeout container. She was in pink jogging shorts and a push-up bra. I suppose the mismatch was meant to be sexy but watching her eat lo mein, it was like I'd accidentally wandered into someone's crappy apartment. She looked up at me. I didn't recognize her from any of my other visits. She was pretty in an interesting way; her eyes were deep brown and framed with dark liner, and her head seemed disproportionately big for her tiny build. In a few years maybe she'd be waiting tables in one of the better restaurants in Short Hills, or maybe she was already. Or, more likely, she'd marry a Wall Street guy and he'd never know about her past until one of his buddies recognized her at a barbecue.

It was a tiny studio, one end curtained off. A fan blew in the corner, bolstering a meager A/C unit in the window. A massage table was visible past the curtain, covered in towels, and a large ceramic Buddha sat by the entrance.

"Sorry, I was just finishing. You got here fast," she said. She had a noticeable accent but I couldn't tell from where. Maybe the Middle East, or maybe Mexico. The girl wiped her mouth with a paper napkin and shut the box before standing up and facing me, and she put her hands together in the prayer position and bowed. A wooden mala bead bracelet clung to her wrist. "*Om shanti,*" she said. Scripted words were inked along her side, and a tattooed swirl of some sort—maybe a tentacle—peeked out from her waistband.

"Right. *Om shanti.*" My heart quickened like it always did. "What does your tattoo say?"

She looked down at it like she was surprised to hear she had a tattoo. "It's in Spanish," she said, as if that explained anything.

"Oh."

She grinned, revealing a gap between her front teeth, and handed me a towel. "Get undressed. I'll get ready. There's alkaline water in the fridge if you want some." She looked down at my feet and made a disgusted face, which quickly faded back into a smile. "Take your shoes off."

"Okay." I paused and she waited for me to speak. "I'm Alan," I said.

She nodded, uninterested. A fleck of food was between her upper teeth. I bared my own and pointed to let her know. She grinned and picked it out with a fingernail. "Let me brush," she said, flicking a switch before retreating to the bathroom. Vaguely sultry music played through a small speaker. Sitar and tabla gave it a pseudo-spiritual feel. "There's an envelope on the dresser."

I slipped the three hundred I'd gotten out of the machine into the envelope, then got undressed and laid down on the table, covering my butt with the towel. My heart pounded and my penis stirred as I gazed past the curtain waiting for her to return. The music had a low rhythm, a quiet thumb pop on a taut drumskin. My breath slowed as I began to relax.

"Just a minute," she said, her voice muffled by the door.

It's fine, I said to myself. I tried to picture her, this twenty-something girl from some foreign country who just a minute ago was eating lo mein, now brushing her teeth and preparing to touch a total stranger. How many men had visited her that same day? Could I ask her that? Maybe I was the only one. Maybe I was special. My mind raced with thought after thought. I took a breath and concentrated on the air streaming into my lungs, and the way my belly rose with the inhalation. Doris had taught us a simple meditation in our first session. *Keep coming back to the breath*, she'd said. *Notice your thoughts when they arise, and simply return to the breath*. It seemed absurd; there was nothing but thought.

I let out the breath and felt the columns of exhaust on my upper lip. Maybe this was freeing for her, a sexually liberated badass girl putting her way through grad school. Did she believe in the spiritual crap? What was she studying? Social work? Education? I found justifications like I had before. Society had no right to tell her how to earn a living.

Thoughts, thoughts, thoughts. I took another breath.

Was she sending money home to Mexico, or Lebanon? Maybe I had it all wrong. Maybe she had grown up in Jersey, or Long Island. Maybe her dad was a contractor. Maybe her mom was a receptionist at a dentist's office. Maybe they sacrificed everything to bring her here, for a better life. And this was how she repaid them? But what about the accent? Was it real? I felt my chest rise as it filled with air.

Had she gone to college? Her parents couldn't know how she was making a living. I wondered what she'd told them she was doing. Her father was probably a few years older than me. I hoped we'd never meet. How would I lie if he walked in right then?

I turned my face away from the curtains and let the air out of my lungs. My mind whinnied in figure eights. This would surely be the last time, I thought, although I'd thought that before. And then, a jolt of energy ran through my body as the girl touched my shoulders with her fingertips and ran them down my back. "*Namaste*," she said, and she pulled the towel away.

Chapter Three

"Ray," I shouted, tapping the meat of my fist on the bathroom door. I could barely hear it over the nonstop chatter and the bland voiceover drone coming from the TV. The condo was filled with Florida Jews. It was a familiar mix of family, old friends of my grandparents, and neighbors who'd snuck in for a free meal. The whole place smelled like stale cigarettes and Jean Naté after-bath splash.

A heavy-handed oil painting of an elderly, bearded rabbi hung in the hallway next to the bathroom. He had his finger pointed at a scroll, as if to underline his focused attention, his scholarliness. It seemed out of place, now that my grandparents were gone, and Mom wasn't exactly religious. There had been a rabbi at the unveiling who'd said a few prayers. It had felt like a courtesy, like the safety announcements on an airplane.

I yelled at the door. "Uncle Ray! Are you okay?"

Mom grabbed my arm and pulled me aside like I was a toddler. She threw her ropy frame at the door, rattling it. An ash pellet tumbled from her Parliament 100 onto the shag carpet. "Ray, open the fucking door." She had already changed from her dressy clothes into spandex shorts and a t-shirt emblazoned with Crossfit logos. Crossfit had become her latest obsession. She'd never exercised once in the years Sarah and I were growing up, but lately all she could talk about were her PRs and her Fran time.

Uncle Ray was my grandmother's older brother, the last one still alive. He'd gone into the shitter right when we got home from the unveiling, and it was close to an hour later. No one had noticed until Sarah had to pee.

Jews had unveilings, usually a year after a funeral, when the headstone was revealed and prayers were offered. Since both my grandparents had dropped dead on the same day, we were having a twofer. My grandfather would have been delighted at the savings.

Mom pressed her ear against the door. She was still wearing her gigantic hoop earrings. They clattered against the chipped paint. I placed my head next to hers and covered my other ear to block out the noise. I could hear water running, but it was probably just the toilet. It did that until you jiggled the handle.

"He's not breathing," Mom said, sucking on her cigarette. .

"You can hear that?" I asked, pressing harder into the door.

She ignored me and pounded on the door again. I jumped. "Ray!" she shouted with a cloud of smoke. Mom backed up and threw her shoulder into the door with a loud thud. She clutched at it, in pain. "Jesus fuck," she said. The door hadn't moved.

A clutch of hunched-over busybodies had formed at the end of the hall, watching us without any shame. Mom's mouth-breathing next door neighbor Marty was stuffing cold cuts into a baggie while he thought no one was looking. Sarah stood holding her phone at the front of the pack, narrating the scene for her boyfriend via FaceTime. "I think he's dead," Sarah was saying. She wore a flower patterned dress that was meant for someone far older. I'd seen a client in the same dress in a Pittsburgh production of *Our Town*.

"He's not dead!" Mom shouted, pounding the door again.

I stepped back, ready to make my own attempt at breaking the door, but I froze as the toilet's whoosh filled the hallway. A sigh passed through the crowd, followed by murmurs of explanation for those who couldn't hear.

"He flushed," Sarah said as the crowd dispersed. "I'll call you later."

Uncle Ray opened the door unceremoniously and brushed past me and Mom. The years had curved him into a question mark with ear hair.

Mom poked her head into the bathroom, holding her nose with her thumb and forefinger. "Ray, the sink is dry. Did you even wash your fucking hands?"

"I don't think he can hear you," I said.

"You need to flush twice, Ray," she shouted over the hiss of the Lysol can. But Ray was already at the table, picking through the deli tray, examining each mini sandwich between his thumb and forefinger before placing it back on the aluminum platter. He chose one, sat down next to Carol on the chintz sofa, and chewed with his mouth open.

I smiled at Carol, who contorted her mouth into a weird grimace before breaking into a smile which turned into her usual hacking cough. Carol was Mom's oddball girlfriend. Oddball in that she was completely normal. Quiet. She'd worked at the same bank for forty years before retiring, and she wore pantsuits even on her days off. She'd had the cough as long as I'd known her and was constantly at the doctor. The topic of secondhand smoke never seemed to come up.

Carol's family was the opposite of ours; they didn't talk over meals except to say *pass the salt*. Carol's mother was still alive, and well over ninety. She referred to Mom and Carol as *roommates*.

My sister got dramatic when Carol moved in. Sarah made it about Sarah, like always. She thought we should have gotten a card, or maybe an announcement. Do they make *I'm a Lesbian* cards?

Mom handled it like she handled everything else. She pretended it wasn't happening.

She misted the hallway with Lysol, waving the can like she was chasing a bee.

Mom's Crossfit coach Gwo sat across from her at the table. He was twice the size of anyone else in the condo. He was wearing a Crossfit Pineapple Grove tank top stretched over his pecs. Veins wound down his oversized brown biceps, jigsawing across his forearms and over his blurry tattoos. Gwo had arrived late and filled a plate with a stunning amount of roast beef. I watched him eat. He rolled each slice into a tube and used the crude utensil to scoop mayonnaise into his mouth.

Sarah stared at him from the living room, clutching my arm. Gwo's thick trapezius muscles clenched and unclenched as he chewed. They looked vestigial and out of place against his massive neck. Sarah leaned over and whispered to me. "Where did he get the mayo?"

"He brought his own," I said.

The apartment was still full. Around this neighborhood, unveilings were a social event; since a year had passed since the funeral, some measure of grief had faded and people could just relax. Mom had turned the Crossfit Games on the TV, with the volume up so she could hear it. Marty stared at the screen watching watching women climb ropes. I wondered where he'd hidden the lunchmeat.

Uncle Ray was still eating, evidenced by the crumbs and grease on his shirt. He sat back on the sofa and stuffed rugelach into his mouth. Mom yelled at him from the kitchen. "Enough, Ray. You're eating like you've got nine assholes."

Ray looked up and put his plate down for a moment, before picking it up and eating another pastry.

"I need to get the fuck out of here," Sarah said. She reached for the front door but it swung open before she could get to it.

"Bernice!" Mom shouted, as Bernice strolled in and twirled her greeting. She was a neighbor, a few years younger than Mom but she'd *had some work done*. She'd been widowed a few years earlier. Her husband, Max, had died during a facelift, but that clearly hadn't scared Bernice any. She reveled in her age defiance, and seemed to love the attention it got her. My grandmother had hated her, but Bernice never seemed to get the message and popped in whenever she felt like it.

Ta-da, she gestured before spying me across the room. Sarah slipped out the door as it shut.

"Alan!" Bernice shouted, pouncing. She threw her velour-swathed arms around me and pressed her hard chest into mine. I winced and pushed away with a laugh. She pouted. I forced myself to smile.

Mom took Bernice by the shoulder. "Come," she said.

Bernice waved goodbye like a diva, eyeballing Gwo as she followed Mom down the hall. Marty looked up from the TV, his lower lip hanging open. "The doctor will see me now," she laughed.

Mom kept a closetful of prescription meds in the spare bedroom which she doled out to anyone who asked. It had started with leftover Valium and later progressed to antibiotics, antifungals, sleep aids, and a handful of opioids. Mom collected leftovers from all over the condominium community. Lately, she'd bragged, she'd been getting calls from family members trying to unload a dead parent's Oxy stash. They were always looking for money, Mom had told me, but they usually settled for the good feeling that came with the knowledge that their dead mother's painkillers were being put to good use. Everyone down here was on multiple medications.

Mom seemed oblivious to the danger posed by her hobby. I wanted to think she was doing it out of some charitable impulse, but I knew she just liked how popular it made her.

We had never been givers in our family.

Gwo finished his roast beef and pushed the Chinet plate back, groaning quietly. There was no occasion too formal for paper plates in my family, but we saved the good stuff—the thick, coated plates with floral designs—for guests and Passover. He caught me looking at him and raised an eyebrow.

"Hi," I mumbled. I waved and pointed toward the door and stepped outside. *Stop being such a pussy.* Right.

The sun was beating down on us at the cemetery but a few dark clouds had rolled in from the ocean, cooling the humid air. Row after row of undistinguished condos matrixed the parking lots, which were crisscrossed by white lines demarcating each unit's space. Camrys and Buicks baked in the sun like lizards. Mom's big black Jeep was in her corner spot. She had traded in my grandparents' piece-of-shit Olds right after they died, and bought a jacked-up 4x4 with a light bar and oversized tires to replace it. It was ridiculous.

Sarah was leaning against it, smoking a fat joint in the waning daylight. She saw me and held it out in my direction as though it were perfectly normal.

"Give me that," I said, snatching the weed from her. I put it to my lips and took a hit, furtively looking around while holding in the smoke.

"Christ, Alan, you're like a fucking high schooler."

I exhaled a white cloud and hacked up a cough. Sarah rolled her eyes.

"Let's walk," she said, pushing off the Jeep and starting toward a manicured path between the buildings. I followed her.

"They're going to notice you're gone," she said. Sarah took the joint from me and hiked her oversized purse onto her shoulder.

"You, too," I said.

"They don't give a shit what I do," she said. "You know that." She rolled her eyes at me while sucking on the joint. Sarah was exaggerating, of course. Mom had always *kvelled* over her, to a degree. I just couldn't remember how, specifically, and besides—Sarah just liked being a victim. Everyone knew that was her *schtick.*

I reached for the joint. "Did you bring that on the plane?"

She shook her head and held up a finger for me to wait. "Marty gave it to me," she said, exhaling.

"Marty?"

"Mom said he's got glaucoma. He gets it legally." She took a big hit. "I let him touch my tit," she squeaked out.

"Gross."

She shrugged. "Free weed," she said. "I had to get the fuck out of there."

A golf cart zoomed up to us on the paved pathway. The driver flicked the headlights at us and we stepped out of the way and watched him go around the curve. It was an old man in a navy blue windbreaker. The word *security* was printed across his back in bold yellow letters. He glared at us and accelerated past.

"Sucks to be old," Sarah said. She reached into her purse and took out a water bottle. It had a cigar-sized rose quartz crystal affixed to its base inside the bottle. Sarah took a sip of water and the rock glowed pink as light passed through the glass.

"What does that do?" I asked.

"Crystals have mad power, Alan," she said, taking another sip. "You should try. You seem stressed."

I inhaled some more of the joint and held it in for a moment before exhaling. "I'm not stressed," I said. We kept walking. Palm trees were spaced evenly, impossibly upright, their fronds neatly clipped. Lush bushes, shining in shades of apple and juniper, filled in the gaps.

"Are you meditating?"

"Some," I said.

Sarah mouthed *some* and poked me in the rib. "You should go on a retreat. It'll deepen your practice. You and Andrea," she said. She looked at me to catch my reaction, but I ignored her.

"Did you really let Marty touch your tit?"

"Jealous?"

"You're gross," I said.

She took the joint from me. "Mom seems happy."

"I guess."

"She's busy, anyway. The gym—"

"The *box*," I said. "That's what they call it. That guy—"

"*Gwo*. I asked. It means big," Sarah said. She gestured with her hands, holding them a foot apart. "You think Mom's getting Haitian dick?"

I coughed, hard. "Mom's a lesbian."

"*Ish*," she said, patting my back. "You wouldn't be happy for her? Old Mom getting pounded from behind by a jacked Crossfit coach? *Fuck me Gwo!*"

"Fuck off, Sarah."

"She deserves a good fuck."

"Don't we all," I said.

We kept walking as the light faded. Through the trees, a lamp flickered on through sliding glass doors. A gaunt man in a yellowed undershirt served his bathrobed wife coffee. She waved her hand at him, gesturing for something he forgot. He scurried away.

"How's Jeff?" I asked.

"How's Andrea?" she responded quickly.

Down the pathway, lights glowed against the darkening sky. Sarah waited for me for a moment before pulling me away. "You're high," she said.

"You're not worried?" I asked. The path curved around, bringing us close to where we'd started. I could see Mom's Jeep in the distance. "She's dealing drugs—"

"She's not dealing drugs."

"She has a drawer full of Oxycontin."

"So does everyone else in Florida," she said.

"Everyone else isn't passing out pills to their neighbors, Sarah."

"Alan," she said, stopping. She faced me and took my forearm in her hand like I was a child. Sarah looked older than her thirty-six years, but in that instant I could see her thirty, forty years older. "*Bubby*. You worry too much. What's the matter?"

"Nothing," I said, pulling my arm away. "I'm really good. Pumped up." I gestured with my fist and then, realizing how lame it looked, made a goofy smile like it had been a joke. We walked towards the condo.

"Can't you relax? Finish that joint."

"I'm fine," I said. The joint was out. I lit it with Sarah's lighter. "Is work ok?"

"Work's work," I said, blowing smoke. "You still applying to grad school?"

She shrugged. "Thinking about it."

I thought of something Ram had said. "Performance is solely a product of action, Sarah."

She rolled her eyes. "Okay, then. I'm *intending*. The Universe will show me the way."

"Fuck, Sarah, that's not how it works. If you don't fucking do something different, you'll get the same fucking results." It came out harsher than I had wanted.

Sarah looked at me and smiled like a preschool teacher. "Alan, *bubby*," she said, in her baby voice, and then a song started playing from inside her bag. It was at once strange and familiar, oddly out of context as we stood on a dark pathway in a retirement community.

Hey now, you're an all-star
Get your game on, go play.
Hey now, you're a rock star
Get the show on, get paid.

"Sorry," she said, pulling her phone out. "It's Jeff." Sarah and Jeff lived on the Upper West Side in a bland apartment building that had two separate Starbucks at ground level. Jeff had some kind of job in finance that he'd explained half-a-dozen times, but I still didn't understand it. He was the kind of lacrosse-playing Jew I'd grown up hating. He seemed super nice on the surface—he was extremely polite, and did all kinds of work for an animal charity—but I bet he would have tortured me in middle school.

She frantically checked her hair before answering the phone. Jeff showed up on the screen, in a crisp Oxford shirt, his hair a shiny helmet. Wooden chopsticks hung from his nostrils, stuck in place over a goofy, openmouthed smile.

"I'm a walrus," Jeff shouted, laughing at his own joke. His voice was distorted through the phone's small speaker.

Sarah giggled and angled the phone so Jeff could see me.

"Hi Alan," he said, pulling the sticks from his nose. He wiggled them at the screen, snickering. "Walrus, heh."

"Hi."

"Did you like that?"

Sarah's face lit up. Even after thirtysomething years, I couldn't tell if she was faking. "You're so cute," she said. "The cutest."

"Honey," he whined, "you said you'd call."

"I was with Alan," she said. "Forgive me?"

"I'll think it over," he said, and then stuck his tongue out as if to show that he had, in fact, thought it over, and had concluded on the side of dismissal. "How's the job, Alan?" he asked.

"Same, Jeff."

Jeff struck a pouty pose and batted his eyelashes at me. It was his regular joke. "If they need someone on—"

"General Hospital," I said, finishing his sentence. "I know. I'll keep an eye out."

He laughed, and I mouthed the next words as he said them. "Keep 'em both out."

This was our routine. I wasn't even sure if General Hospital was still a show.

"Hold on, honey," Sarah said. She dropped her hand and the phone hung at her waist. Jeff's face was upside-down. For a moment it looked like his broad neck was a trunk that had sprouted from a pointed alien head, until the picture righted itself and he swung helplessly, bouncing against Sarah's floral dress.

It was hard to hate Jeff, but I did.

"I've gotta go," she said to me, "It's time for our walking meditation."

Jeff shouted from the dangling phone. "We do it every night, Alan! It's so peaceful!"

Sarah craned her neck. "Shut up, honey," she hissed. "I'll see you inside." She lifted the phone to her face and held it out in front of her like she was holding up a baby for playtime. Sarah pointed herself in the direction from which we'd come, and began to pace, placing one foot carefully in front of the other.

I watched her disappear down the path.

"Are you walking?" she said, her voice fading.

"Yes!" Jeff replied. His disembodied voice was unnaturally deep, distorted by space-time and the weed.

Sarah treaded into the shadows. Her form merged into the twilight, until I could no longer make it out. I couldn't bear to go back to the condo. Instead, I relit the joint and took another hit, veering off the pathway and onto the grass next to the building. The coarse Florida blades crunched underneath my feet as I slid along the stuccoed wall. I exhaled and watched the smoke rise up past a window screen.

Ram had talked about the *predictable future*, how we were all waiting for divine intervention, but chances were that things would simply stay the same. *You'll get more of what you've already gotten. Don't expect anything different*, he'd shouted. But my future couldn't be more of the same; I'd hit a financial wall. More likely, the house of cards would come tumbling down.

My job wasn't going to save me. Guys like Jeff took home jarring bonuses, a recompense for selling their souls. But where was *my* recompense? Even in my best year, my bonus had failed to reach five figures. These days, I knew I was lucky to still have a job, and I knew there would be no other reward at the end of the year. I had nothing of value to sell. My best bet was to find a new career.

The weed had settled in, and I leaned against the rough wall watching the trees glow in the harsh security light. There might be no new career, I knew, or it could take years of failed fits and starts. Weed often sent me down a dark spiral of unpleasant outcomes. I would be forty soon, with nothing to show but failures. There was an inherent unfairness about my piss-poor track record, an inherent lack of miracles or even good fortune. But I was glad my grandparents weren't around to see me fail, no matter who was to blame. It was too late to start law school, too late to get an MBA. And besides, who could afford it?

There were different expectations when it came to Sarah, of course. Having Jeff around took the pressure off a bit; he was a *catch*.

I was decidedly not a *catch*.

I stepped away from the building to shake off the nerves. The air was cooling but still thick with humidity, and it smelled like the exhaust from a clothes dryer. The sky was now completely dark, and as I stepped farther out onto the grass, the security lights lost their reach and I stood in a shadow looking up at the building, lit mainly by the glow of lamps filtered through vertical blinds. Some of the vertical blinds were turned shut, and others revealed their apartments' gilded decor. The residents favored metallic wallpaper and shiny glass cabinetry, like the whole place had been furnished by an interior designer who'd Rip VanWinkled since the eighties.

Andrea had to take me back. What would it take? I could never tell her what I'd done, but it had to stop. I could send her something, flowers, a sweater. Leave it in the apartment with a card for when she returned from work. She would soften. I needed something to hold onto. Ram had led us in a chant: *Who's in charge? I'm in charge!* It felt empty as I remembered it. I hoped my wants still held some sway.

I took another hit of the joint. It was almost gone. Movement rustled in the apartment directly ahead of me, and I stepped deeper into the shadows to avoid detection. I watched through the window as Bernice stepped into her tacky bedroom in a bra and panties. They were black and lacy and looked expensive. She reached behind her and unfastened her bra and dropped it to the floor. Her breasts looked like they belonged on a stripper, and her stomach was taut. Without thinking I put the joint into my mouth and unbuttoned my pants, before reaching for my dick.

I watched Bernice rummage through drawers, unperturbed, as I pulled on myself. She leaned over and lowered her panties. I stepped forward for a better view. My feet crunched on the grass, and I froze and let out a small sound. Bernice pivoted, and stared out the window, her full nakedness on display—she was neatly shaved—and I stuck my hand deeper into my pants automatically before she gasped and covered the front of her body with a towel she picked off the floor. She stepped forward, and I tried to recede into the darkness. A rustling came from behind me and I swerved to avoid detection, catching my foot on a stone that seemed expressly placed in my way for that purpose. I stumbled and fell on my ass as Bernice let out a shriek, and the beam of a flashlight swept past me before it landed on my face.

"Was it worth it?" Mom sucked on a Parliament 100 as she downshifted the Jeep and pulled up to a traffic light. The motor shuddered beneath my feet. We were in the lurid Florida sunshine, across from Bagel Twin, which was a block past Twin Bagel, which was a block past Bagel Palace. The top was down on the Jeep and Mom was dressed for the gym. Mandy Patinkin's plaintive voice sang and the doors rattled with the sound. It was *Mayn Mirl,* to the tune of *Maria*, from West Side Story.

"Was it?" she said.

I looked down at the sensible cars around us. Mom's Jeep was already tricked out when she got it—oversized knobby tires, a light bar, a red fire extinguisher strapped to the frame. *I'm not like these old ladies*, she'd said on the phone. She was out to prove it.

"Mom," I said. "Please."

She took another drag off her cigarette. "Is Andrea home?" she asked. The light turned and she gunned the accelerator, pressing me back into the seat. A cloth banner hung from the rear-view mirror, the size of a playing card, striped with the red and blue of the Haitian flag, a crest in its center. Below the flag read *Ayiti*. The flag whipped in the wind, perturbed.

"I think so," I lied. "We talked last night."

"Before the—"

"Yeah."

She sighed and shook her head slightly, crushing her cigarette into the ashtray. I watched her lips move as she sang along quietly. The sun beat down on us. I wiped my forehead with the back of my hand. Mom seemed unaffected. "Did you talk to her after?"

"No."

She paused for a second. "Probably for the best."

We charged onto the highway. It looked like a game for Mom, shifting up and down as she blasted between spaces and crept up behind cars as if to intimidate them. She seemed to look for Camrys and Buicks, cruising next to them until their drivers looked up and noticed her. Then, she would downshift and gun the gas, leaving them in a wake of sound. The Haitian flag continued to bounce in the airflow.

"Gwo is worried about you," she shouted, over the wind and the music. She reached over to turn the music down. "He said you look stressed."

I blinked back tears. "I *am* stressed," I said, knowing that was our family's natural state and would not be questioned. "Work."

"Work," she repeated. "Always, work."

Mom had worked for the synagogue for over twenty years. She'd started the week after Dad left. There was an initial week of panic and tears that sublimated into futility—but then she quickly got the job, scheduling Bar Mitzvah lessons for the Rabbi and the Cantor, and she paid our bills with her tiny handwritten paychecks. There was never enough.

We passed billboards for strip clubs and lawyers, and one for the latest Hierro Acero flick. I looked away from it as we passed, embarrassed.

I knew Andrea wouldn't be home; when we'd been on the outs in the past, she worked nonstop, and picked up every shift she could. She was probably in Myrtle Beach, or Orlando, or Fort Myers. I imagined her heels clicking on the airport linoleum, her bag rolling behind her as she strutted towards her plane. I could clean the house; she'd appreciate that.

Mom took the exit for the airport and curved around towards the Departures lane. It was packed with taxis and vans and families with sedans, arguing over who would carry what piece of luggage. Mom swept along the outside of the traffic and cut into a space near the front as an SUV pulled out. She turned off the engine and the music abruptly stopped, too. She made no move to get out, and instead took my hand in hers. Her leathery skin felt soft against mine. Age spots peppered her muscular forearms. "You should get a kettlebell, Alan."

"A what?" Horns honked as cars jockeyed for space. In the distance, plane engines roared with effort.

"I think you'd feel better. It always makes me feel better." Mom reached into the back seat and pulled out a plastic grocery bag. "Here," she said, handing it to me.

Inside the bag was a large wooden bowl. I recognized it instantly. "Mom—" I began to choke up.

"Take it," she said, patting me on the shoulder. "I never make tuna anymore."

The bowl was older than me. It appeared to have been carved out of a single piece of wood, and its interior was stained with the residue of endless school lunches. No amount of washing would change that. It was the Tuna Bowl, exclusively used to make tuna salad, to be served on spongy wheat bread and folded in aluminum foil. We had few treasures in our family, but this was one. I wiped my eyes. "Sarah's gonna be jealous."

Mom shrugged. "She can fuck herself."

A neon-vested guard peered at us, his face threatening a scold.

I stuffed the bowl back into its bag and stepped out of the Jeep with my things.

"Don't come back for a while," she said.

I laughed, clutching the bag with the Tuna Bowl like it was a precious piece of art. "Okay. Thanks."

"I'm serious," she said, shaking her head. "You're lucky you're not in jail." She made no move to hug me. Instead, she waved, and turned the key in the ignition. The Jeep rumbled to life, and Mom turned the stereo knob until all the sounds around us were lost and I could only hear Mandy's heartfelt voice.

Chapter Four

Joe is not that fat. If I'd had to guess from his Facebook photos, I'd have said two seventy-five, maybe two-eighty. Maybe it was the oversized Steelers hoodie, or the way his stupid mustache sausaged across his face, or the way his nose resembled a veiny Russet. I imagined his puffy fingers wrapped around a Stihl chainsaw's pull-start.

Seeing him in the flesh, his plush-carpeted asscheeks quivering as he gasped a load into Andrea (or, I hoped, a condom), I realized I'd misjudged him. On screen, he carried himself like a bigger man, all Carhartt and Timberland, two-pound janitor's keyring, phone clipped to the belt of his crossing guard uniform. With all of that stripped away, he seemed normal, even pathetic, like a fuzzy dog who gets wet and resembles a drowned rat. He wheezed and collapsed onto Andrea. She clutched at his meaty, tribal-tattooed arms, and looked into his eyes before catching me in the periphery.

Andrea looked away, and then I felt a wave of indifference coming in my direction. It was as if she thought that by ignoring me, I'd cease to be real. Maybe there was some truth to that. I wanted to slink out, to go back to the front door and knock, to let them dress and create plausible deniability. But it wasn't that different from how I'd felt for years, that I was at best, acceptable. My presence was tolerated.

Standing in the doorway, I was a notch below that. I was a nuisance, barely worth swatting away. What would I tell Mom and Sarah? How could I minimize this disaster? Ram was wrong; he'd said the predictable future was more of the same. This was much worse.

"Oh, Jesus, Alan," Andrea said, like I'd spilled the last of the milk, or I'd farted. "What the fuck are you doing here." She grunted and rolled Joe off of her. He rested in place for a moment before it registered that I was standing there after he'd just fucked my wife. He pressed his mouth into a nervous grin.

"Hey, Alan," he said, like we were pals who'd just run into each other at the gym. Joe sheepishly gathered his clothes, but not before wiping his dick off on the good sheets. *My* good sheets, sheets I'd ordered with a discount code off a podcast, sheets I'd paid for with commissions I'd earned helping Shakespearean actors deign to procedural television. Now they were streaked with Joe-cum, and they'd have to be burned.

"Christ, Joe. The sheets," I said.

He shrugged and mouthed *sorry*.

Worse still was the billboard-sized flat screen TV mounted on the wall past the end of our bed. It was new, at least to me. I'd long wanted one, but Andrea had vetoed the idea again and again. I guess it took crossing guard dick to change her mind.

The sound was turned down but not off and the bright remnants of an NFL game spilled into the room. Commentators gushed, alternating their excitement and concern over various morsels of footballery, each tidbit brought to you by a different corporate sponsor. It was an odd mashup: my wife being fucked by a crossing guard, men in suits and headsets palavering about rushing and blitzing.

Joe sat on the edge of the bed and slid his threadbare Fruit-of-the-Looms up over a forest of ass hair. He saw me eyeing the TV and nodded, maybe with pride, maybe acknowledging a facet of our commonality, our maleness. My throat tightened with regret. I wanted to be intimidating, I wanted him to be cringing in a corner or scrambling out a window, but he was unperturbed. Was this what it was like to give zero fucks? Maybe I was on the edge of something. It oscillated between reality and rah-rah bullshit, but my swelling irritation was giving way to curiosity. What would it take to be like that?

Andrea was lying against the headboard I'd paid for propped up against a pillow. She hadn't even bothered to cover herself; her only accommodation to modesty was the arm draped across a breast.

"Get lost, Alan. You're making this harder than it has to be."

"You got a TV?" I said.

"Christ, Alan."

"What is that, like, sixty-five inches?" I said.

Joe nodded, proud.

Andrea pulled a cigarette from out of nowhere and lit it in one fluid motion, blowing a harsh white cloud my way. "Fucking go already," she said. "It's not like this is a surprise."

"You, you smoke?" I stammered.

Watching her smoke was more shocking than walking in on her being jackhammered by Joe. She'd always hated smokers, thought they were weak. But she took a long drag on her cigarette and sat up straight. It was another *fuck you* to someone, maybe me.

Joe sat on the edge of the bed, already lost in the game.

"You know we're still married," I said. I repeated myself for Joe. "We're still married."

Joe kept looking straight ahead. He reached for the remote and turned up the volume. A commercial for a blood thinner medication was playing. A cheerful announcer listed a litany of possible side effects.

I reached for her cigarette, but she pulled it away. "Give me that," I said.

"Stop it, Alan."

"Andrea!"

"Fuck you," she repeated. Her ribs stuck out as she took another drag. She had gotten skinner since the last time I'd seen her naked. "You don't get to tell me what to do."

I paused. "I can't believe you're smoking."

"Go. I'm going back to Whitney."

A thud hit my chest. She'd derided Whitney incessantly over the years. It was a private joke between us. *Maybe I'll move to Whitney.* It was code for something she'd never, ever do. I leaned towards her and spoke quietly. "We'll go see Doris, get you a prescription."

"I don't need a prescription," she said, waving me away. "Doris can fuck herself. Stupid hugs." She forced out a laugh and Joe echoed a laugh in response, without looking away from the TV. "I told Joe about her. Stupid," she repeated, and she laughed again.

I froze. I'd seen Andrea upset plenty of times, but this was different. It was like she wasn't even talking to me, like we hadn't spent the past twelve years sharing a bed. Doris had spent several sessions talking to us about our lack of communication. *You don't listen*, she'd said. I couldn't remember the rest.

"What are you going to do in Whitney?" I sat down on the edge of the bed, the side opposite from Joe. Andrea pulled her legs away and I almost reached for them before catching myself.

"I told you," she said. "None of your business. You can have the apartment once I'm gone."

"There isn't even a Wal-Mart there."

"There is too." She was practically shouting.

"I don't think there is," I said, pulling out my phone. "Maybe it's in Latrobe?"

Joe muttered *yeah* without turning.

Andrea shook her head. "Close enough," she said.

"I'm just saying—"

"It's a five minute drive!" she barked.

"Maybe ten," Joe mumbled.

"Christ." I leaned toward her. "I thought we were making progress."

She rolled her eyes and scooted farther away. "You actually want me back, Alan? You know what that is, don't you? I can't even use the word I want to use, Alan." She crushed out her cigarette in an empty coffee mug on the nightstand. "I can't even use the word."

"The *R* word," Joe said, his eyes still fixed on the TV.

She nodded. "The *R* word," she whispered. "You are so fucking…" she paused, and then spat out the words. "…*R* word."

"Retarded?" I asked.

She *tsked* me and brushed a speck of ash from her nipple. "We don't use that word, Alan. You shouldn't either."

"What?"

"You don't use the *N* word, do you?"

"I mean, if it's in a rap, and I'm alone—"

She waved me off, and then, startled, pulled a blanket over her body as if she had just realized she was naked. "Where are my headphones?"

"What?"

"My headphones," she said. "I left them on the counter. They're not there."

"I don't know." I stood up and backed away.

Her face reddened and she stared straight at me. "You took my fucking headphones, Alan. Those were my good headphones."

Joe turned up the TV another notch.

"I didn't take your headphones."

"I want my fucking headphones," she said, close to tears. "Where are they?"

I just stared at her, under the blanket we'd bought together, with her not-so-fat boyfriend at the end of our bed watching a TV she'd never have let me have. When I opened my mouth, only a weak croak emerged. I was acting like a pussy.

She wiped her eyes with the back of her hand. "Get me some new ones. Then send them to me."

Hierro Acero woke up at 4:30 each morning to lift weights. Most days, he posted a picture of his chunky digital watch to prove it. The caption always read *GET AFTER IT.* "Buy your own fucking headphones," I spat, feeling slightly satisfied.

But she pulled out another cigarette and lit it, continuing as if I hadn't spoken. "I'll text you Joe's address. Send them there." She sucked on the cigarette. It glowed red, and she waved me away. "Now go," she said. "Your credit card bills are on the counter."

I looked down at her, a jumble of limbs and blanket and bony angles. Her hair wisped and frizzed, and skin drew taut across her face. This was how I'd remember her, I thought, half-naked and harsh, shut off tight like a cold water faucet.

I had fucked up, sure, but our life had been okay. It was as if she had forgotten all of that, as if our years together had boiled down to an unforgivable hiccup. A hiccup that superseded everything else. It seemed unfair, but what could I say? I croaked a goodbye.

She ignored me and gestured to Joe. "C'mere," she said. "Turn that shit down."

Joe looked over his hairy shoulder and smiled at her, trying to avoid my glare. He held out the remote and muted the sound, before crawling up the bed and cozying up next to my wife.

I left.

My phone rang as I climbed out of the subway. It was Sarah. "I'm still here," she said, whispering.

"In Florida?" I said. I was trudging up the hill from Fourth Avenue, heading towards the apartment I'd rented for the past few days. These streets were industrial: a candy warehouse, a beer distributor, a commercial bakery. Even at night—it was nearly ten—the air steamy with warm bread, diesel fuel, and trash left to fester for tomorrow's pickup. It was a suitably lonely tableau for my post-trauma slog, but hearing my sister's familiar whine was soothing.

"Your peeping Tom shit is the talk of the town, Alan."

"Fuck off."

"I'm serious," she said. "Bernice wants to sue. For emotional distress. And Mom asked me if you're on *the pot*."

"Seriously?"

"Alan," she said, getting quieter. "Tell me the truth."

"About what?"

"Were you whacking off?"

"Fuck off."

"I think she's kinda hot, too. Did you take any pictures?"

"Sarah—"

"I wanna show Jeff."

"Fuck off," I said. "Is that why you called? To fuck with me?"

She sighed. "I guess. I mean, things are getting weird, here."

"Weirder then dealing Oxy?"

She ignored me. "I asked Carol what was going on, but she wouldn't tell me dick, even after I threatened to out her to her mom," she whispered.

"That's just mean."

"You're missing the point, Alan." I could hear her exasperation growing. "She barely talks to Carol. Gwo is here all the time. She's like, obsessed with him. Maybe you were right."

"Okay," I said, "but who are we to interfere? She's an adult."

She paused, and I thought I heard her voice crack. "Come back down."

"To Florida? Jesus. I just left."

"Come down."

"I can't," I said. "I'm on Mom probation. Besides, isn't Jeff waiting for you?"

"He's busy with his fundraiser."

Jeff and his fucking charity. He was constantly posting photos of himself with homeless dogs. It made me want to barf.

"He's an angel from heaven," I said.

"Tru dat," Sarah said. "Anyway, the Universe told me to stay."

"Oh?"

"I called the airline, and I knew that if they let me change my flight it was the Universe telling me I needed to be here." When I didn't respond, she continued. "If you just relax and listen, the Universe will tell you what you need to know."

I farted loudly, surprising myself. It reverberated on the quiet street, a deep, staccato blast. A Rottweiler-sized raccoon scurried up a sickly tree, bending its branches. I smiled, pleased. At least I could still fart.

On the far side of the street, the local bodega readied itself for sleep, as its owner fended off a final lottery hopeful. "The Universe told you to stay in Delray Beach?"

"Look," she said. "I'm worried."

"About what?"

"Something's off."

"Like what?"

She paused, and took a deep breath. I prepared myself for the news.

"Alan," she said. "Mom has gonorrhea." She snorted with her horsey laughter.

"That's not funny."

"Who are you to say what's funny, Alan? Maybe she has HIV, Alan. A lot of shit goes around in these retirement communities."

"It doesn't work that way." I hopped to avoid a giant pile of dog shit in the middle of the sidewalk. Fuck anyone who doesn't clean up their dog shit. What kind of person could do that? I could never be that indifferent. No guru could change that.

"How do you know? I read that, like, eighty percent of the seniors in Florida have STDs. They don't have to worry about getting pregnant, so they don't bother with protection." She laughed. "Hey, that's an image for you. Old people fucking."

"Fuck you, Sarah. Mom's a lesbian."

"Old ladies eating old lady pussy. *Harder, bubbie.*" She snickered some more.

"Fuck you, Sarah."

"Lesbians get STDs. Carol's been coughing nonstop."

I cut her off. "She has bronchitis, Sarah. Jesus."

"Jesus yourself. I think she's fucking her coach."

"So what?"

"Did you notice he's black?"

"Seriously?"

"Maybe he's trying to rob her or something. It's like a *Nightline* episode," she said.

"You're fucking gross."

I turned a corner and headed up the side street where I was staying. Tiny unkempt yards faced the curb, where salt-rotten cars lined up under a patchwork of branches that formed a loose canopy.

A grey-sided frame house sagged over the street. Its sidewalk was littered with cardboard boxes full of outgrown books. A hand-cranked baby swing rested against pillows of trash. The house looked tired. I imagined its inhabitants were tired, too, from years of child-rearing, trash-hauling, working in dentist's offices or dingy local banks, on street repair crews or in diners. I leaned over to examine the titles. *Solve Your Child's Sleep Problems. The Power of Now. You Can Heal Your Life.* I wasn't the only one looking for answers.

I stopped on the street in front of the tiny garden apartment where I'd been sleeping for the past few days. The lights were off upstairs, and the building was quiet except for the rattle of an old air conditioner that dripped water from the third floor window onto the concrete. Weeds poked from between the cracked steps.

Sarah lowered her voice until it was barely audible. "Carol said she's barely ever around. She's at the gym constantly."

"The *box*," I said.

"Whatever."

"Whatever yourself. Ask her, if you're so worried."

"She won't tell me shit," Sarah said.

She was right. We'd grown up listening to Mom's wisdom, handed down from Nana and before that, from Nana's own mother, who it was said had walked from Poland to France carrying everything she owned. *No one wants to hear about your problems.* Somehow, a hundred year old passed-down maxim carried the weight of law.

Mom shared nothing with us, except to the extent that they related to us: *you worry me.* Whenever you asked her how she was doing, she always said the same thing. *"Pa pi mal,"* a phrase she'd learned from her Haitian cleaning lady. Not too bad. Maybe she was on to something, but I was too used to complaining to stop. It had become automatic, like biting my nails, or picking my nose.

I stepped down two stairs to the door. The apartment had an electronic keypad lock; renters came and went all the time, and the code changed with each new tenant. I pressed a button and the keypad lit up.

"Bring Andrea. Make a vacation out of it. She gets free tickets, doesn't she?"

I cringed at the thought, crammed into a smoke-filled Delray Beach condo with Sarah, Carol, Andrea, and Mom. And Gwo. "That's a fucking vacation." I entered the four digit code the landlord had given me and an amber light glowed, signaling I'd gotten it wrong. I hit the clear button and tried again. Same result. I jiggled the handle. "I have to go," I said.

"Don't leave me hanging," Sarah growled.

I jabbed at the keypad again but got the same result.

"I'll ask the Universe for a sign," I said.

Sarah sighed. "Why is this my problem?"

"It's not," I said, but I knew she was right. Men have to *work.* No one would have expected me to stay.

She started to argue and then caught herself. Instead, she sighed again. "Love you."

"You too," I said, and I hung up before the words were entirely out of my mouth. I stepped back to look at the house.

It was entirely dark, and I hadn't seen anyone else come or go since I'd been staying there. Still, I climbed the steps and rapped on the door to no response, and then tried the same code on the upstairs keypad. Nothing.

The street was still except for the barest rustle that came from the trees. An oversized SUV interrupted the quiet, passing along the avenue above. *4 Sale* was scrawled across its rear window in chalk. *Bachata* blared from its windows and blue neon glowed from its undercarriage.

Todo tiene su fecha de vencimiento
Y se venció mi amor por ti

I sent a text to the landlord and waited. The truck rolled past and the rhythm dimmed into the distance. I sat down on the concrete steps and looked out at the street. Something had to give. This was my predictable future. More of the same shit.

Sweat trickled down my back as I rattled through my credit card balances in my head, sorted by their minimum monthly payments. I knew all the numbers by heart, from largest to smallest, and smiled as I rounded them sums and added them. It was satisfying, even as the monthly tally climbed close to four figures. I was getting the *what's what*, a skill I'd learned from Mom before I was even a teenager. She had sat in front of her vinyl-clad checkbook and tape-spewing calculator, adding and subtracting, night after night, at our Formica dining room table. She was getting the *what's what*.

Alan, she would say, *you've gotta start with reality.* It was her way of reining in the chaos. Her stacks of receipts, her bank statements, pens, and WiteOut had given us solace in the face of our somber picture. We'd had very little since Dad had taken off, and Mom had long since stopped talking about child support. Now, all Sarah and I got were postcards at random intervals. They were stacked with foreign stamps and faced with local scenery: beaches, mountains, ruins. Dad was in Tarapoto, in Baranquilla, in Xela. The messages were uniform and generic. *Happy Birthday. Can't believe how old you are. Miss you. Sending love.* A year would go by with nothing, then two or three would come in a week, as if he'd suddenly remembered he was behind and had to catch up. Meanwhile, Mom was using food stamps to buy chicken parts, off-brand ketchup and dented cans of Le Sueur peas. She didn't need a life coach for that; her rules were simple. Work, pay the bills, deal with reality. She'd cried a bit when Dad took off, but pretty soon she was lint-brushing her polyester skirts for work at the synagogue. Worries and complaints took a back seat to *the what's what.*

I sat on the steps, my head a catalog of ATM receipts and stacks of twenties, of checks and cash advance fees and minimum payments. They were all clues that added up to my own failure and worthlessness, my own almost-certain future.

I remembered the curls of paper she'd examine and then reexamine looking for clues as to how we were going to pay our bills. Dad had left us with nothing but debt, but she'd shielded us from it as much as she could. Debt had been a concept. *In the red, in the hole, under water, up to our ears.* Now that I'd dug my own hole, I could feel the dirt under my fingernails and the pressure on my own back. It was worse when I sat still, so I tried not to. I didn't need a sign from the Universe to tell me I had to dig my way out. Sarah would have to manage Mom on her own.

A neon-lit garbage truck blasted past on the avenue, raging against the silence. A scrawny kid hung off the back, a cigarette glowing in his mouth. He held onto a rail with one hand, like a too-cool passenger on a kiddie carousel. From where I sat, he was barely out of his teens, with years of trash-hauling in his future, years of freezing rain, of maggots and rats, years of stink no shower would mitigate, a future of back pain, a wife who went fat, taxes, derelict kids who would only disappoint him.

What the fuck did I know? The truck disappeared. My phone buzzed. There was nothing from the landlord, only a text from Andrea asking me if I'd ordered the headphones. Fuck her. She deserved dog shit. That's what I wanted to send. A big styrofoam cooler of Great Dane shit, packed in dry ice to keep it fresh. Or from a Bull Mastiff. Any big dog would do.

I could leave it on her steps and set it aflame, like a suburban teenager.

Give Zero Fucks.

The house was still dark and the street had grown even quieter; the light breeze had ceased and the only sound was the crackle of the streetlights and the distant hush of the Gowanus Expressway.

I am a piece of shit, I thought to myself. I took out my phone and dialed, and tried to figure out where I'd get three hundred bucks.

"This is, like, the wrong energy," the girl said. Her accent somehow had grown thicker. She had just come out of the bathroom and was holding the envelope. The same Spanish script wove across her side. The air conditioning was turned up too high and was aimed straight at me, blasting my bare back. "There's not enough money here." A few limp twenties were fanned in her hand.

"I know. I'm sorry," I said, wishing I hadn't apologized. I lay on the table, a towel over my ass, and turned my head towards her.

She saw me looking and, suddenly self-conscious, threw an oversized t-shirt over her bra and thong. The shirt read *Now is the New Later*.

"What's with the shirt?"

She looked down and tented it out with her hands. "I don't know. I guess, like, now is a better time to do shit."

"No, I mean, why'd you put it on?"

"You didn't pay. "

"Come on," I said. "A hundred bucks is something."

She planted her hands on her hips, either defiant or just annoyed. "It's like you don't value this practice. It hurts my heart." The phrases came out with upspeak, like she was asking me a question, or my opinion.

I looked up at her, still hoping to change her mind. "I do value it." She was so nice the night before. Now she looked just mean. "I'm, like, a regular. Isn't there a discount? Like every tenth visit—"

"No."

"Like a punch card."

She let out a *pfft*. "This is tantra, not Dunkin' Donuts." She started to gather her things. "Go," she said. "You need to manifest abundance."

I sighed and sat up, draping the towel over my junk. There was nowhere to go and no more cash to be had. And I probably couldn't even get back the hundred I'd paid her already. "It won't take long," I said. "Maybe ten minutes."

She rolled her eyes and her voice softened. "I'm keeping this money and you get the fuck out of here." She stood by the door, her hand on the knob.

"Eight minutes," I said.

"Stop it! We aren't negotiating."

"I'll send it to you," I said.

"What, like in the mail?"

"Venmo!" I nearly shouted, excited.

"I don't want you Venmo-ing me," the girl said. "That's stupid. Get dressed." A hint of a smile appeared on her face.

"I'm sorry," I said. I knew I needed to try another route. "Where are you from?"

She sighed and flipped the overhead light on. A white fluorescent glow filled the room. Suddenly her makeup looked garish, her hair unwashed. A grating noise spat from the air conditioner. "Get dressed," she repeated.

I stood up and wrapped the towel around my waist. "Okay," I said. I shuffled over to the sofa and picked up my clothes. "It's been a hard day. My wife's moving to Whitney with a crossing guard." My voice cracked as the words spilled out. A desert landscape was tacked to the wall above the sofa in a cheap plastic frame and the smell of stale takeout flirted with whatever veil of essential oils she'd been diffusing before I arrived.

"What, like an old lady? Is that her girlfriend?"

"No, it's a guy."

"Oh. Weird. Where's Whitney?"

"Pennsylvania." I paused, looking down at the floor. "So that's why I'm here. For healing."

The table creaked as she sat down on it and lit a cigarette. "Healing costs money." She brushed the hair from her face. "A crossing guard," she said, shaking her head. "Is that, like, full-time?"

"I don't know."

"I mean, you only work in the morning and the afternoon, right?"

"I guess."

"It can't pay much." She took a drag on her cigarette. Her fingernails were bitten down to the skin. "I thought crossing guards were all old ladies."

"I probably deserve it," I said, hoping she'd disagree and take my side.

"You do come here a lot," she said.

"For healing," I said.

The girl blew a column of smoke. "Sure."

She wasn't that pretty, really. She was just normal. It didn't matter, though. My heart swelled with something—affection, maybe?

"I need to clear the space," she said. "Get dressed." She picked up a small chunk of wood and lit the end with a lighter. It trailed smoke as she swirled it in the air. It smelled cloying and harsh, like an air-freshener.

I waved it away with my boxer briefs.

"Stop," she said. "That's *palo santo*. It's sacred."

"Oh. Sorry." The smoke wafted away. "What's your name?" I asked.

"Mariana," she said. "But don't try to friend me or some shit like that."

"Mariana," I said under my breath. I put a tune to it. "*Mariana. ¿De donde eres, mi amor?*"

She laughed sharply. "Get the fuck outta here," she said.

I sang some more, trying to imitate the *bachata* I'd heard in my neighborhood. "*Mariana…. Por favor… toca mi polla…*"

"You're an asshole."

I kept singing and twirled around in the towel. "*Si, si, soy idiota, un gran idiota…*"

"*Huevón*," she laughed. "You're a fucking *huevón*."

"What's that?" I asked, still dancing.

"*No te preocupes.*" She put out her cigarette and looked at her phone. "Come on, move your ass. I have another client in like, twenty minutes."

"*No te* what?" I turned around and pointed my butt in her direction and shook it, still singing my tune."

"*No te preocupes*," she said. "Don't worry about it. What are you doing?"

"Moving my ass," I said.

She snorted. "*Huevón*," she repeated, smacking my ass.

"At least tell me if it's an insult," I said.

Mariana nodded and checked her phone again. "Yeah. But don't worry about it." She looked like a college kid in her silly t-shirt. I was suddenly embarrassed.

"You're cute," I said, covering.

"Don't flirt with me." Mariana pulled out another cigarette and lit it. Smoke floated in a dreamlike haze around her head. "Can I be straight with you?"

"Sure."

"No, really, *parcero*. Can I tell you the truth?" She took a long drag, and exhaled it dramatically. "You're fucked up, bro."

My gut tightened. She sensed it, apparently, touching my arm in sympathy.

"It's ok, honey. It's probably not your fault. But something's blocked. Your energy is way off."

The smoke tickled my throat and I swallowed. It felt familiar, that irritation, a reminder of countless back-seat car trips, long stretches of highway and eighties soft rock. *Your kiss is on my list.*

She stared at me for a second and her brow furrowed, like she was thinking hard. A hopeful buzz fluttered through my body; maybe she would reconsider. Maybe she liked me.

"I started meditating," I said, rolling to my side.

Mariana barely blinked "Do you have a shaman?" she asked.

A fucking shaman? I tried to think of what answer would get me a handjob. "No," I said, "but I'm open. I've been practicing mindfulness—"

Mariana shook her head. "This is a terrible idea," she said, waving her cigarette at me.

"No, no," I said, moving closer. My heart pounded.

She raised her hand to stop me. "No. Listen. Stop. It's not like that."

"Not like what?"

She grew quiet, and the air conditioner went silent at the same time, so that the only sound was the low hum of traffic on the nearby streets. "You need help."

"I do?"

She nodded, and took my hand in hers. An electric chill ran through my body as she brought the back of my hand to her cheek and closed her eyes. I shuddered and moved my body closer to hers, so that I could almost feel her warmth.

"*Parce,*" she said. Her voice vibrated through my hand and down my arm.

"*Si, mi amor.*"

She let go of my hand and placed her own hand on her chest. "No bullshit. Are you tired of all this?" Her eyes shone.

"Tired of what?"

"All this. The bullshit. The stress. The dark energy. Who you wound up being."

Wound up being? I had no fucking idea what she was talking about. "Yeah," I said. "I guess." I clenched my face, willing tears to appear.

Mariana took a sharp breath and wiped the glisten from my eyes with her bare hand. "Okay, then."

"What?" I asked, inching towards her.

She breathed out, a sweet rush of tobacco. "Do you have a passport?" she asked.

Chapter Five

I was sweating through my shirt, my legs chugging me away from that fucking place. Ram shouted at me on my headphones. *You want to know why you're fucking poor, you asshole? Just look at the fucking bums you hang around with.* He was right. I needed to find better people. I'd be a fucking idiot to take spiritual advice from a girl who gives handjobs for a living. She was obviously not winning at life. Dick after dick after dick.

Wasn't that the very definition of failing? Pulling on dicks for cash? What did she know? I came for a handjob, not spiritual advice. And besides, where was I going to get the money to go to Colombia?

Get the losers out of your life, Bucko. Fuck those sorry pieces of shit.

I plopped down on a stool and hunched over the diner counter. It was a grimy, old-school place in the same neighborhood where a few of the girls worked. They were open late, and I'd gotten used to going there afterwards, mostly to avoid Andrea. A sign written in pink Hi-Liter on a paper plate was stuck to the wall with a lone Band-Aid. *Restroom's for Customer's Only.*

I ordered my usual coffee and matzoh ball soup and got the bathroom code. I'd only be gone a minute.

On a trip to Whitney when Andrea and I first started dating, I'd seen a former high school bully behind the counter at a highway McDonald's. He was tall—I'd remembered how he had towered over me in hallways, how he'd back me into a locker and my face reached his chest—but in his Assistant Manager garb, he seemed to have shrunk. For years, my heart had fluttered in fear each time I'd seen his frame in the distance. But assembling orders and scooping fries, he'd lost the alpha status that had kept me on my heels.

Waiting in line, I'd Googled his pay—$25K, approximately—and made sure to greet him with a smirk. He barely registered who I was, if he did at all. Still, I'd won, hadn't I? I was the one with the cash in the transaction, I was the one free to come and go as I pleased. I wasn't trapped behind a counter in a polyester tie. *You suck!*

And he was working for McDonald's! It didn't even have a whiff of cool, a faint scent of ironic detachment that he could claim were he working in, say, Starbucks. Even a Starbucks barista could claim the dream of an empowered future—a visual artist, a screenwriter, a birth doula, a death doula. But a McDonald's Assistant Manager? Unlikely.

I'd won, even though he had no clue what I was doing with my life. Which, at that point, wasn't much. He knew that I knew that I'd won. In that scenario, *I* was the Hierro Acero. I was the Big Fucking Deal. Or at least I had the money for a Value Meal. What else is it to be a man, if not to lord some ephemeral sense of superiority over another poor schmuck?

The diner bathroom smelled like bleach. A harsh white tube flickered overhead, and a faded pine tree shaped air freshener hung from a dirty string. The walls were covered with a jumble of graffiti tags and Biggie stickers, and a wheeled mop bucket was pushed into a corner, still full of grey sludgy water. I shut the door behind me and locked it.

Mariana was a whole other level of failure. It might have said something about me that I was an occasional patron. But it was an hour here or there. It didn't define me. There are things that define you. Being a meth user, for example. Once or twice, fine, but the minute it becomes something you do regularly, then you're a meth user. A meth head, or whatever they call it.

Murder someone once, you're a murderer.

Jerk off a stranger for money, once or twice, well, that's just a phase. But beyond that! And she was giving me advice! Who was she to tell me I had spiritual blockages? It sounded like constipation, the way she was describing it. And her shaman— whatever the fuck that was—was the Ex-Lax my spirit needed.

It was probably a scam, anyway. I'd have to wire money somewhere, money I'd never see again. I didn't need a fucking *cleansing*. I needed to start working my ass off, twice as hard as everyone else.

I unzipped my pants and pictured her. I could replay a few moments from the prior night; when she'd unclasped her bra, when she took me in her hand, the surprised look on her face when I finished so soon. *What's the big surprise?* I'd thought.

Here in the diner bathroom, inhaling chemical fumes, I closed my eyes and remembered how it felt as she let her skin slide across mine, and I came into my hand. A dollop dripped through my fingers and onto my jeans. I washed up quickly and wiped my pants with wet paper towels, while cursing my- self for not having enough money to pay her. That was what drew the criticism, wasn't it? She'd never have had the guts to assess my chakras or whatever if I'd paid her in full. Fuck being broke. I was better than Mr. McDonalds.

An oblong damp streak trailed along my jeans from the top of my right thigh. I dabbed at it again, but it just needed to dry. I felt better, that was what mattered.

Give zero fucks. Quit being such a pussy. Ram was right. I just needed to stop it, stop half-assing my job, start making more money. Now that Andrea was gone, I'd go buck wild. Fuck mindfulness. I wouldn't need to pay for handjobs. I'd be the king of Tinder, the king of hook-ups. I'd spent too much time getting by. Forty was just around the corner—and then what? More days banging on phones hoping for some respite from this grind? I needed to do something bold. Cause my own fucking miracle. Gene had been chattering about opening an office in LA. I'd convince him to send me out there. I'd take the town by storm. I'd wear suits! I'd go to the gym! I'd find the next Hierro Acero and make him a star. I didn't need a shaman to tell me how to do that.

I marched back to the counter, past a few sleepy patrons. The hollow-eyed waitress ignored me as I slurped my soup. I dug into the matzoh ball and ate it in big, hot chunks. My mouth burned but I didn't care. It was time to suck it up and do what needed to be done, to stop being such a pussy.

I'd call Mom in the morning and ask her for help. She wouldn't leave me hanging. A little cash would help a lot.

I drank some piss-weak coffee and took out my wallet.

"The check, hon?" the waitress asked.

I nodded and pulled out the one card I thought would work.

"Fingers crossed," she said, sensing my hesitancy. We both held our breath as the machine paused, and exhaled as it printed out the little slip of paper that signified success.

I grinned from ear to ear and signed with a flourish, adding an extra dollar to the tip. "Have a great night," I said, and I marched out into the dark.

I fell asleep on the frayed love seat in the waiting area of our office. I'd taken my shoes off and rested my head on a balled-up windbreaker I'd left in the closet. I had five or six solid hours before anyone would come into work. I was wired, but exhausted, ready to start this new chapter of my life, to face the day without fear, or at least, with courage. I'd wash up in the morning, grab a coffee, and feign an early start on the phones. I was done with Mariana and women like her. I didn't need a shaman to tell me what I was doing wrong. It was time to stop acting like a pussy.

Flickers of colored light bounced through the windows and along the walls, glancing off a poster from a failed Broadway musical about a sexy vampire. I closed my eyes and the colors continued, though muted. I'd once had drinks with an acting coach, hoping for some tips for my clients. She was a fifty-something former actress in blowzy hippie garb, with her wrists wrapped in mala beads. Lorna sat next to me at a nearby bar sipping a straight up Manhattan. *Dreams*, she'd said, *that's how we access our creativity.* At the time I'd thought it ridiculous, pop-psych nonsense someone dreamed up after taking an undergrad course on Jung. I barely remembered my dreams, and I couldn't see how they related to my waking life.

Lorna had invited me to journal my dreams for a few days and see what came up. I was to keep a notebook by my bedside, and write down whatever I remembered as soon as I woke. Before I went to sleep, I could make a request to my unconscious: to reveal to me what I needed to learn.

I'd snickered as she gave the instructions and paid for our drinks, but for several nights that week I'd taken her counsel, and later each day pored over my scribbles trying to make sense of them. After the third night, I'd called her, confused. *Lorna*, I'd said, *what does any of this mean?* She laughed, a hearty laugh that made me think she was having another vermouth-soaked night. *I don't know, Alan*, she'd said, *what do you think it means?*

I'd practically hung up on her, furious that she couldn't give me the answers that I'd wanted. But here in the darkened office, surrounded by framed memories of others' failed creative leaps, I pored through all the advice I'd been hearing and had stepped over. I thought of Lorna and my illegible scribbles, and I made the same request: *Reveal to me what I need to learn.* And this time I added, *and make sure I can understand it.*

Engines moaned from the street, and tired horns bleated. Across the dark background of my eyelids, pinpricks of light sparkled and swirled, and waves of color floated across the field. I tilted my head back, and began to snore.

In the dream, I was in a house I knew wasn't mine. I'd rented it, and it was temporary, but I didn't know why. A rhythm started, like a pulsing rush of reeds in the wind, followed by a haunting whistling, a short, repetitive, foreign-sounding tune.

I was going through room after room looking for something but I didn't know what, and in the process, I discovered a door I hadn't known was there. Surprised, I entered, and descended some stairs into a dark passageway with a faint glow at its end. The rhythm grew louder, and the tune quieted. When I emerged from the corridor, I was in a warmly lit, clean bathroom, and immediately I knew what there was to do. I sat down to take a shit, and as I tightened my gut, a loud and profanely satisfying fart came from deep in my bowels. I felt it vibrate throughout my whole body, and grinned from ear to ear at having set it free.

Alan. Christ, Alan.

A disembodied voice—a man's voice—barked at me. The percussive rhythm grew louder. I squeezed again, and a high-pitched squeak popped out.

Jesus fucking Christ.

The voice was coming from upstairs, but it was coming closer and getting louder as the rhythm pulsed.

Wake the fuck up.

The music abruptly stopped. My eyes flickered and adjusted to the bright light. Blurry figures were corralled together into a grid of blues and greys. I blinked. Gene towered over me, his sweaty, unshaven face twisted into a scowl. He wasn't in his usual gym garb, but in a navy jacket and tie. Elizabeth stood just behind him, her face blank, and at the other end of the sofa was a blue-suited man with a halo of white hair that contrasted his tan skin. He stared into space as though his mind was elsewhere.

Gene leaned into me. I could smell the coffee on his breath. "Are you awake?"

I blinked again. "Yeah. Sorry." My head swirled. Elizabeth was wearing a striped dress I hadn't seen before. It emphasized her curves. I thought I could see her panty line. Nervous waves chattered through my gut. I stifled another fart. "I must have fallen asleep." I sat up carefully and rubbed my face where it had been pressing against the sofa's fabric. The office was not quite full, but the rest of the staff was carefully trying to avoid noticing the drama. Avi sat at his desk, purposefully staring at his computer screen.

"How long have you been here?" Gene asked.

"Just a little while," I said, standing up. My body creaked as I stretched. I tried to generate some of the attitude from the night before. *Give zero fucks.* "I got here early to do some work and fell asleep."

Gene looked me over from head to toe, assessing my lie. I quickly tucked in my shirt and smoothed my pants. The stain from the diner had dried into a whitish outline. I brushed it with my hand, hoping it would go away, but it remained. "Come into my office," Gene said.

Elizabeth wandered away. I watched her go. Gene and the guy in the suit went into Gene's office, waving me to join them. I muttered assent and followed, and the staff pretended to look away. Gene shut the door behind him and gestured to a worn chair. He sat down behind his desk while the other guy remained standing. Gene's face was grim. Dark bags hung under his eyes, accentuated by the stubble.

"This is Mike Schwartz," Gene said, gesturing. "He's our lawyer."

The guy in the suit extended his hand and I shook it even as my whole body trembled. He wore a thick gold watch and his skin was unusually smooth and taut. His tan looked even darker under the bright lights in Gene's office. "Mike," he said.

"Alan." I sat down.

"Right."

"Obviously," I said. "I mean, it's my name." Did I sound like a jerk? I tried to laugh it off and change the subject. "You're tan."

Mike's eyes fluttered. "I got burnt," he said.

"Ouch."

"Seriously," Mike said.

I looked over at Gene. "It's dangerous."

Mike shrugged, guilty. "I use, like, SPF—"

Gene interrupted. "Mike, do you want to explain?" He hitched up his pants in frustration.

Mike nodded and mouthed *sorry*. He took out a small spiral notebook and flipped through the pages. "We have a problem, really," he said, glancing at the paper. "Gene invited me in here."

My heart rattled. All the hubris that had bubbled up the previous night was gone. "What's the matter?" I said, like it was something minor, a parking ticket, a lost bathroom key. *No problem*, I tried to intone.

"You know about the investigation?" Mike said.

"Sort of. I mean, I don't know what—"

"Right, right," he said, waving his hand. "The thing is—"

Gene spoke sharply. "You haven't been doing great, Alan. I mean, if you'd been doing better."

"Hold on," Mike said. "Hold on. Gene, we talked about this."

Gene shrugged, admonished. "Sorry."

"Alan," Mike went on, "I told Gene he should have suspended you in the first place and he didn't want to do that."

"Out of respect," Gene said. "You've been here a while."

"Thanks," I mumbled.

"But if we're going to investigate—" Mike shook his head.

"It's expensive." Gene stood up behind his desk. He was wearing baggy jeans with his jacket and tie, as if he'd been on a video conference and didn't care how he looked from the waist down. "We have to talk to a lot of people."

"Gene, shhh," Mike said.

"Guys, I'm sorry, but I'm sure—"

Mike cut me off. "We think it'd be better for you to resign."

My heart crashed. I looked over at Gene but he was facing the window like he was admiring the view. "Gene?" I said. "I don't even know what happened."

"Never mind that." Mike stepped over to me and placed his hand on my shoulder. "If we investigate, it's going to be really uncomfortable."

"And expensive." Gene continued to look away.

"Guys—" I said, not finishing my sentence.

The digital clock on the wall glowed red with the time and date.

10:02:33 AM

8/8/17

The digits pulsed as each second passed. Mike's hand remained on my shoulder. I looked down at his fingers. Each nail was expertly trimmed, gleaming perfect haloes. The second hand on his fancy watch swept a smooth curve. I watched the red pin move in tiny, discernible increments.

"I'm sorry, Alan," Gene said.

"Gene," I said. I looked around the room. The whole thing felt dreamlike, reminding me of my descent a few minutes prior. What about the music, the hidden bathroom, the farts? I mulled the images I could remember as Gene and Mike stood by. What did any of it mean?

The clock approached the next minute and then advanced. August 8th. Several of my credit card minimums were due, and I hadn't paid any of them. I didn't have the money. How long could I ignore them for? I could take off. Maybe they'd come after Andrea. If I went to Colombia with Mariana, maybe she'd fuck me. I'd be showing real commitment. Balls. How could she say no?

Mike's hand pressed down. Tufts of coarse hair poked from his shirt; his arm looked like it belonged on a gorilla, offset by a chunky gold Rolex. "That's a nice watch," I said.

87

He tentatively held it up. His shirt cuff bore his initials: *MES*. "Check out what Gene's got," he said.

Gene held up his own wrist from across the room. It, too, bore a chunky gold case, the size of a small saucer.

Mike laughed. "That's nice."

"It is," I agreed.

Mike came closer to inspect it. "I don't even want to know how much—"

Gene snorted. "You don't, really."

"I do," I said. "Tell me how much your watch cost."

Gene opened his mouth to answer but Mike cut him off. "We can give you some severance."

"Two weeks pay," Gene said. He had taken his watch off and Mike was examining it while Gene beamed proudly. "And you can keep your health insurance for August."

"It is August," I said. "That's not exactly a gift." I shifted my weight on the seat and another small squeak popped out of my ass. Gene winced but I went on. "I've been doing okay. Not great, but okay."

"Look at you," he said, putting the watch back on. "You're a mess." He leaned in. "Tell me the truth, Alan." His heavy eyes glistened as he stared at me. "Did you sleep here?"

"I'm not a mess," I said. The crust on my jeans was flaking off. "I just came in early."

"I could check the cameras."

Mike nodded in agreement. "We could. Easily."

"There are no cameras," I said.

Mike looked over at Gene. "Is he right? I thought there were cameras."

Gene rolled his eyes. "What's the difference? Two weeks severance." He pointed at me. "This the last thing I want to deal with."

Andrea and Joe were probably just waking up for their morning fuck. Maybe she was eating his ass at that very moment. It seemed like the kind of thing to expect from the new Andrea. She was probably an ass eater. Maybe he watched football on his hands and knees while she did her work.

Mariana wouldn't have invited me to meet her shaman if she didn't like me. She wasn't just being nice. You don't invite someone to another continent just to be nice. I just needed some money.

"We don't have to give you anything," Gene said, caressing his watch.

"It's not enough," I said. "I need more."

Mike wore a thick wedding band. He looked like the kind of guy who'd cheat on his wife with his receptionist. He probably lived in New Jersey. "We don't have to give you shit."

Gene stood up and came around the desk to put his arm around my shoulder. He was bear-sized and sloppy, even playing dress-up. His meaty arm weighed across my back. "You were like a son to me."

His bulk sank me into the cushion. "I need more." My heart raced with the ask. I could buy a plane ticket and have enough to live for a while. Fuck the apartment, the credit cards. Fuck Andrea. "Give me three months. I'll go without a fuss. I'll tell everyone I'm leaving the business."

Gene and Mike looked at each other.

"I need it, Gene." I lifted his arm off of me. "I'm broke."

Mike put on his sympathetic face, but with the tan and the filler it made him look like a sad mannequin. "You'll find something."

"But I'm broke."

"No one cares," Gene said sharply.

Mike's eyes widened, surprised.

"You should go." Gene gestured toward the door. "Get your stuff. I'll write you a check."

"Two months," I said.

Gene shook his head.

"Fire me. I'll collect unemployment."

"No," Mike said, turning away.

I planted my feet on the ground and stood. Blood rushed through the veins in my head, and the room spun. Maybe I did need a shaman, or a saffron-robed Buddhist monk, or a kindly hippie plinking on a sarod or sitar or tabla. I needed something. I wanted to puke for the sake of drama. I wanted to run out and piss in a ficus, to overturn trash cans, to set something ablaze.

Instead, I gathered my things as everyone in the office watched in silence, took the check from Gene's hand, and left.

I packed my shit in a black garbage bag and tied the top in a fat knot. A cheap blazer I kept around for unexpected client visits, a pair of loafers, a photo of my grandparents, the chopping bowl—I'd left it there for safekeeping. I put my mug with the picture of Richard Nixon bowling on Avi's desk and told him to think of me. The check was folded up in my wallet. It wasn't much—less than fifteen hundred bucks—and it was all I had left. I'd cash it when I had the chance; there was no way I could deposit it into the account I shared with Andrea.

I got on the subway to Brooklyn. It was midday, so it wasn't too crowded, and I leaned against a window in a hard plastic seat to doze off. My classy Hefty luggage rested between my legs on the ground. The cars rattled down the track and I closed my eyes. Voices chattered and whispered.

A fetid scent wafted towards me and I waved it away. Fucking homeless people. It was like piss mixed with sweat mixed with puke. The smell got stronger and I opened my eyes, but there was no one around me. Midway down the car, a clean-cut mom looked away from me and clutched her toddler. I breathed in deep and reddened, embarrassed that it was me.

I put my headphones back in and closed my eyes again, breathing through my mouth to avoid my smell. *Imagine yourself at the top. That's where you belong,* Ram said. *Are you a lion or a piece of shit?* The subway rolled into a station. I could hear more people come on but kept my eyes shut, embarrassed. We were still in Manhattan; with my luck, I'd run into one of Andrea's friends who'd report my filth back to her. I wanted to see no one.

Spanish and Chinese voices murmured around me, and then faded as I fell asleep.

Are you Jewish? The voice in my head sounded familiar, a singsongy accent from the Old World, like a family friend. *Hey, chaver.*

I turned away, my eyes still closed, and the subway hit a bump and screeched around a corner. I looked up into the bright light. The train was above ground; water towers and power lines shaped the ratty Brooklyn skyline. Two young Hasidic men hovered over me. One was tall and thin with a patchy beard. His once-white shirt was mostly untucked, *tzitzit* hanging over a cracked leather belt. He carried a tattered prayer book in his hand. Hebrew letters were embossed in gold on the cover. There was a time I could have read them, but now they were just a jumble of shapes that could have been alien hieroglyphs. His hat was perched high on his head. It looked like it belonged to someone else.

The other man was reddish and round, his clothes pressed and clean. His beard glowed in the daylight, with streaks of blonde and silver.

I sat up straight and took out my headphones.

"Are you Jewish?" the neater one asked.

I blinked.

He reached out and handed me a business card with Hebrew writing and a photo of an elderly rabbi hunched over a prayer book. "Here," he said. "Take this."

I looked at the card and turned it over to reveal more Hebrew writing. "What am I supposed to do with this?" I asked.

"Are you Jewish?" the other one asked. He held out a leather-wrapped box trailing black straps. *Tefillin.* I'd seen Pop wear them once or twice during his bursts of faith. They came infrequently but predictably, like a comet. "Can we say a prayer?"

The train slowed as it rumbled into a station deep in Brooklyn. Maybe I needed a prayer. They could say some words in Hebrew and things would start to go right for me. Millions of people prayed daily. *50,000,000 Elvis Fans Can't Be Wrong.* "A prayer?"

The sloppy one looked at his partner and then back at me. "I'll help you."

I needed help.

He edged a little closer and reached out with a shiny strap. The red one smiled at me. His teeth were grimy and uneven, a jumble of decay. He smelled like onions.

I felt a sudden unease, a gut-punch of worry and mistrust. It seemed too easy, a scam. A slippery slope, the way Scientologists roped people in with their Free Personality Tests, or the Jehovas with their brochures. "What do you want from me?"

"It's a *mitzvah,*" Red said. He reached for my arm, but I pulled it away.

"I don't have any money," I said.

The men looked at each other, puzzled. "Just a short prayer."

I pressed back into my seat and eyed my crumpled Hefty bag.

The two men inched closer.

I slid sideways along the hard plastic seat and jumped to my feet. "No," I barked. I grabbed the bag and edged towards the door. "Leave me alone."

Space cleared around me as passengers stepped away.

"Sorry, mister," the slob said.

"Fuck off." The train halted abruptly and I turned away from them and pushed at the door. "Go bother someone else." I pushed again and the doors opened, and I fell onto the platform and landed on my hands and knees in front of a poster for Hierro Acero's latest movie, *A Gun and a Half.* Acero's muscled head was instantly familiar, even in silhouette. The bag caught on my foot and I pulled at it, hard, and looked back at the train.

The doors slammed shut. I watched the bewildered Hasids. They stared back at me, before turning to each other as the car rolled away. Fuck their prayers.

Passengers stepped around me and exited the platform. At the far end of the platform, a young cop spied me and gestured to his partner. I could make out the yellow Tasers hanging from their belts. They conferred before unhurriedly stepping in my direction. I stood quickly and dusted myself off. "I'm fine," I said out loud. My phone buzzed in my pocket. I pulled it out and pressed it to my ear.

"What are you doing?" It was Avi. I could hear loud voices and the steady thrum of house music in the background.

"I just got off the train," I said, panting. I looked up at the cops and forced a smile. The younger one said something to his partner, who laughed and pulled out his phone.

"Seven PM," he said. "You, me, Ram Hardy."

A wave of dizziness ran through my body. I looked down at myself, a borderline homeless wreck. "Seriously?"

"I got you into the Intensive, Alan. You should be thanking me."

"I don't have the money."

"Never mind that. You need this," he said. "They'll work something out with you."

"I can't, Avi." I thought about the fight with Andrea. "I'm not ready. Maybe later."

"Your life is *now*," he said.

"I'm a mess."

"No shit." He paused. In the background, someone shouted *asshole*. Avi shouted something back in Hebrew and laughed. "Alan, do what I say. You have a few hours. Get your shit together and meet me at seven. No, six forty-five. I'll text you the address."

"I don't have any money."

"Shut the fuck up," he said. He hung up.

I texted Sarah and told her I was locked out of my apartment, I had an important meeting and needed to shower, and Andrea was on the road. She sighed and said she'd have her doorman let me in and not to leave a mess. She was on her way home from Florida to start yoga teacher training. *My soul can't stand clutter, Alan.*

I hadn't been to her place since she and Jeff had invited us to Shabbat dinner in the Spring, during the brief period

Sarah was entertaining rabbinical school. It went badly; Jeff sat on the sofa and picked at his toenails. He called Andrea *bro* and talked about his stupid charity. He and his frat buddies raised money to get plastic surgery for ugly dogs to help them get adopted. He was really great at pitching it; the way he described the organization, it almost didn't sound stupid. He kept pulling out his phone and showing us videos of him and his drunk friends singing *Guantamera* dressed in oversized Mexican sombreros, which had something to do with their fundraising strategy. Sarah had insisted on wearing a dollar store veil while she lit the candles, and set it on fire in a matter of seconds, setting off smoke alarms and requiring a visit from the super. Even though Mom worked at the synagogue for all those years, Sarah was even less comfortable with Jewish protocols than I was; Mom had hardly fulfilled the traditional role, leaving Sarah to fumble her own way through.

She and Jeff had a nice apartment, a doorman high-rise on the UWS, above a Bed Bath and Beyond. The building was bland but luxurious, with a gym and yoga classes and elevators that worked. I stopped outside the building and looked at myself in a plate-glass window. I was a sweaty mess, unshaven and unwashed. In the dark reflection, holding my trash bag, I looked like I should be sleeping on a park bench.

I stood up straight and tucked in my dirty shirt into my cum-stained pants, smoothed out my hair, and went inside. The doorman let me up without a second look and had one of the building porters let me into the apartment.

The place was immaculate. The walls were high and white, decorated with store-bought art: photos of plants and beaches, a New York skyline similar to the one viewable out the window. Floor-to-ceiling windows looked out over the river and a small balcony. Granite countertops and stainless steel shelves kept the blandness intact. The glass coffee table was fanned with yoga magazines, their covers adorned with suitably fit white women, each with the same careful hairstyle.

Sarah kept her meditation area in the bedroom—a patterned South American tapestry draped over a table next to the window, stacked with crystals and brass singing bowls and candles. A dull metal Buddha in seated repose rested next to a silver-framed photo of Oprah laughing with the Dalai Lama. A maroon cushion and mat basked in a beam of light, squarely facing the altar. It looked like an ad for probiotic yogurt. I thought about chucking all of it off the balcony but instead stripped off my filthy clothes and got in the shower.

I turned the knob and let hot water rivet my face as I sampled Sarah's fancy body washes and shampoos. The chrome shower head was set to painful pinpricks. I stepped back and washed my junk with her bath pouf. My dick tingled.

None of the amenities belonged to Jeff, I guessed. He was a bar-of-soap kinda guy. He seemed like someone who went to a fancy barber shop for a straight razor shave and pretended he was friends with the Russian barber. I supposed Jeff had paid for all of Sarah's bath niceties. Maybe they'd fucked in this very stall.

People like Jeff didn't need Ram Hardy. He'd probably had a huge Bar Mitzvah, in a mirrored hall with oversized chandeliers, a deejay playing *Celebration,* and his Clearasil-dotted pals sneaking lipstick-ringed leftover glasses of Manischewitz. No expense spared. A professional videographer. A slideshow to the tune of *Sunrise, Sunset.* I bet it was the talk of Massapequa Park. Fuck him.

I dried off and dug through his closet for some clean clothes. He was a good six inches taller than me but his fancy underwear fit fine. It was made of some fabric that felt unnaturally soft against my skin. I looked through his t-shirts and jeans, but Ram was strictly a dress-up affair and I had no money to buy anything that fit.

A vape pen with a full cartridge sat on Sarah's nightstand. I took a long hit and coughed a few times before settling down and inhaling some more. The weed was strong—Jeff spent a lot of time in California for work and got the good stuff—and I was instantly buzzed.

Jeff's closet was packed with dark suits and white shirts. I stood there staring at them for a while and then picked one out that looked like it might fit. It didn't. The pants hung loose on my legs. I cuffed them as best I could and did the same with the jacket. Its tail hung mid-thigh. I took another hit and looked in the mirror. It was okay, given the alternatives. I had no other place to go than Ram's, and I couldn't show up without a suit. I put on a boring tie and and pair of loafers that were about four sizes too big, and sat on the bed to take another hit.

I fucking hated Jeff. He was the kind of guy who'd give a kidney to a stranger. He seemed incapable of stealing, or cheating, but he was so steeped in privilege he would never have to. Our family values were practical, borne of the Depression and the Holocaust; Pop always had a trunkful of Pepsi Light he'd stolen from a job and bricks of government cheese handed off by a friend. Mom had grown up in the Sheepshead Bay projects and Pop had worked under the table for forty years in order to keep their rent under a hundred bucks a month. His toolbox was a treasure chest of dead vacuum tubes and loose reels of solder he used to fix TVs and stereos for cash.

Grandma held court at the dining room table, selling an occasional sequined sweater Pop got off a truck in Chinatown. We bought lottery tickets and fell for scams, and we held ourselves out to be of high moral character, because any corners we cut were justified. *The pogroms!* I'd once heard Pop say, but he was born in Long Island City.

That manner of thinking was what sent Dad off to South America. Even these years later Mom held that the IRS had been *out to get him.* Corners had been cut, surely, but he'd been a *target*, owing to his Jewishness, or someone whose ass he'd refused to kiss, or some other righteous justification.

I'd read some of his missives, tucked away in Mom's dresser, and found myself agreeing with much of his logic. Taxes were unfair and skewed to fuck the poor—we counted ourselves among them, no matter our income—and there was a methodology to fighting back. His wallet was a forest of receipts—for Garden State tolls, for tunafish and coffee, for the gossip rags my mom called the *shit papers.* His sources of income were unclear, and he got paid in cash or in ladies' wear, bras and blouses and fuzzy slippers that Mom could sell to the neighbors like her mom had before her.

Dad had to know a reckoning would come; his passport and a stack of hundreds were always in the top drawer behind his boxers, until one day they weren't. Mom got stuck facing the IRS; she'd struck some kind of deal by saying he'd abandoned us, although I don't think she believed it herself.

Neither of them was interested in introspection. I wished they'd had Ram to kick their asses. I wished they'd had a guru, or a therapist. If they'd had a rabbi, he'd done a shit job.

I took another hit and smoothed out Jeff's jacket as I lay down on the duvet. Fuck the Jeffs of the world. I was glad for Sarah, but fuck him. Life *didn't* go that way for most of us. It reeked of unfairness.

The world swirled as I closed my eyes. Red geometric patterns were mottled by fine blue dots.

Those were the guys who got the plum jobs, the ones who could afford unpaid summer internships and minimum wage mailroom gigs. The Jeffs, who never worried about money, whose blissful stature was guaranteed. There would be a summer house, a boat, a BMW, lobster. There would always be rent, weed, rosé. They didn't need a Ram Hardy.

I felt myself falling asleep. *I should set an alarm*, I mumbled, and then everything went dark.

I dreamed that I was hungry, but it wasn't important. I was in a cinderblock room, the walls pocked and dusty. Hot white light streamed through fissures in the concrete. A curled yellow notice was fixed to the wall; dull grey tape held it in place. There were long benches made of scrap lumber, and long writing desks made of shiny, uneven boards. There was no door, just a rough opening in the wall.

I sat down. Sweat dripped down the center of my back and tickled my ass crack. The air was close and muggy, and as I opened my mouth to breathe it felt as if I'd been neglecting to do so, that I had to gasp for air, but no matter how deeply I inhaled, there was not enough oxygen, and I began to panic.

I clutched at my chest, helpless. *This is what I do,* I thought. I ballooned my lungs again and again, sucking in desperately and then despairingly.

Regardez, someone shouted, a man's voice. I looked up at the front of the room. A large blackboard covered the front wall, powdered in white chalk. I could make out French verb conjugations—*je vais, tu vas, il va*—and scattered about the board were fragments in other languages, alphabets and symbols, hieroglyphs and pictographs. Hebrew scribble formed among the markings. I somehow recognized my name. There was a code to decipher, but the lines of chalk began to rearrange and swirl into new shapes and nonsense words. *Regardez,* the voice shouted again, and I continued to gasp as I stared at the eddies of dust and begged them to settle into meaning.

Alan, someone shouted, but the squiggles were beginning to form into words, and so my eyes stayed riveted on the board.

Alan! Helpless, I turned and suddenly I was in my grandmother's bedroom as Bernice hovered over me. She giggled, waving her stark chiclet teeth, and then she wagged her preternaturally buoyant breasts, grazing my face. Bernice reached for my fly and leaned her head down towards my crotch. Then she gazed up at me, and with an expression of pure love, reached into her mouth and removed her dentures. They chattered as she tossed them over her shoulder.

I froze, still gasping, and Bernice clutched my belt and held me in place as she pulled at my pants. I pushed at her head and a coarse handful of hair came away, leaving a veiny bald spot. She ripped away my underwear and grabbed onto my dick with a gnarled, yellowed claw, shoving it between her gums. I thrashed but she held fast, grasping my ass with her talons.

Stop, I yelled, and I pushed on her shoulders and wriggled my body, but the more I fought, the more she sucked. She looked up at me with her jaundiced eyes and grinned, my dick between her lips, before she snorted and choked. *Alan,* she moaned, *Alan.*

Bernice! I shouted, and I watched her arm swing in a slow-motion curve, a glint of chrome clutched in her mottled fist that arced towards my head. Time advanced in increments, not a smooth sweep, but by a fraction of a degree with each breath. She was holding a socket wrench, the kind Pop had used to fix brakes or fan belts, and as it approached my temple

I thought about how heavy it must be and wondered if it was metric or standard. I turned to get a better view and in that instant, time cascaded, and the hard metal tool crashed into my ear with an undramatic thump. Stabbing pain rang squirreled through my skull.

Alan, she shouted again, my dick still in her mouth as she reared back for another swing. *Alan!* I craned my neck to move out of the way but time slowed again and I watched Bernice's claw tick through the still-hot air. As the wrench murmured toward me, inch by inch, Bernice's face began to glow.

I could feel the warmth on my belly, but somehow my dick was spared. Bernice's cheeks began to smolder. I pulled, but she dug her claws into my ass and pulled me into her mouth. The smoke crackled and flared, and flames crawled up her face and danced in her hair.

Sparks arced from her head and hot flares shot up in slowed-down tics of time. My skin burned but I was unharmed, until time cascaded once again, and the wrench flung through the air and crashed into my face.

I opened my eyes and rubbed my cheek. Sarah stood over me in her overpriced yoga gear, her arm reared back for another whack.

"Christ, Sarah," I shouted, rolling out of the way.

She swung playfully, grazing my head. "Wake the fuck up," she said. "You smell like weed." She grabbed the vape pen from where I'd left it on the bed and glowered at me for a moment before taking a hit. "Jeff's coming home soon."

"Great," I said.

"Is that his suit?" she asked. She sat down on the edge of the bed, next to me. "It doesn't fit."

I nodded and held my hand out for the pen. She handed it over and I took a hit. My head swirled. "Were you at yoga?"

She looked down at her *Namaste Y'all* t-shirt, printed with cartoon image of Ganesha. "I was in fucking Florida," she said. "Seriously, Alan. Is that your shit?" she asked, gesturing to the Hefty bag by the door. "You're like, borderline homeless guy."

I shrugged, still prone.

"Come on. Get your stuff and go." She grabbed the bag and went to hand it to me, but stopped. "Wait. What's in here?"

"Nothing," I said, waving her way. "Give it back."

Sarah tore at the knot holding the bag shut. "You have Mom's bowl, don't you? That's weird, Alan. She told me you took it."

"She gave it to me."

Sarah's face lit up with glee. "You can't take shit from Mom. She's not dead, Alan." She pulled the bag open and reached in.

"I thought death was just a social construct."

"Shut up. You're taking advantage of her like that fucking Crossfit coach," Sarah said.

"She offered it! I didn't even want it."

"She's like, senile."

"Maybe she's just wise, Sarah."

Sarah looked at me like I was a three year old, and then pulled a few papers and my ratty blazer from the bag. "What's this shit?" She held the jacket up in front of her. "Do you actually wear this?"

"It's from work," I said, sitting up.

"Work?" she said, digging around. "Did you get fired?"

I shrugged. "She's not senile."

Sarah raised an eyebrow at me and reached back into the bag. She pulled out the wooden bowl. "A-ha!"

I grabbed for the bowl but she held it away from me.

"Try practicing non-attachment," she said.

"What?"

"That's the source of your suffering," she said. "The Buddha said—"

"You're the one who's attached."

"No, you are," she said.

I tried a new tack. "It's for fucking tuna."

"So?" Sarah stepped back to keep the bowl out of my reach. "Mom's too trusting. You can't take her shit, Alan."

"I'm her son," I said. "I didn't steal anything."

"You can't even cook."

"I can make tuna."

"Really?" she said. "Why's she giving shit away, Alan?"

"Maybe she's practicing non-attachment," I said, self-assured.

Sarah sighed. "It's just a fucking bowl." She held the bowl against her chest and sang.

Ask any mermaid you happen to see.
What's the best tuna?
Chicken of the Sea!

I clapped. "You should be on Broadway."

Sarah bowed. "You think so?"

"No."

"Asshole."

"Whole ass," I said.

She snorted. "Hey, watch this." Sarah stood up straight, her face suddenly placid, as she held out her right hand at an angle against her waist. She swung her right leg up and caught it, before she leaned forward, her left leg locked in place. Her left hand pointed toward the ceiling and then swung forward in an arc, towards the altar. She stared straight ahead, her foot wiggling to maintain balance, her lips pursed with effort.

"You forgot your skates, Tonya Harding." I reached for the sole of her raised foot. "Tickle tickle," I said, wiggling my fingers.

"Dick," she said, dropping her foot to the floor. "It's yoga. You should try it."

"I'd rather die."

"Pfft," she said. "You're so fucking stressed, Alan. You'll have a heart attack."

I'd have welcomed a heart attack. Sick people always got slack. Maybe someone would start a GoFundMe to pay off my debts. "I'm fine," I sighed.

"You should at least try it." She grinned and held her right hand out at her side. "Right hand," she said.

I shook my head.

"Right fucking hand, Alan."

I didn't move.

"I'll call Mom," she said, chewing her lip. "I'm trying to help you."

"You'll call Mom? Seriously?"

"If you died, I'd never forgive myself."

"Sarah—"

"Alan," she said, cupping the back of my head with her cold palm. "Trust me."

"You're the one who needs help."

"At least sit with me," she said, pulling her hand away. She reached under the bed and pulled out a meditation cushion that matched the one in front of the altar. "Meditate." Sarah arranged the two cushions next to each other and sat down, gesturing to me.

"I should go."

"After you sit," she said. She lit an expensive-looking candle.

I stared at her for a moment.

"Trust me," she said.

"This is stupid," I replied, but I sat down on the cushion next to her. I could still feel the weed in my head, and as I crossed my legs, a buzz settled into my body. I took a breath and looked up at the altar. Oprah and the Dalai Lama looked so happy. I wondered if they were faking it, or if they were high.

Sarah had settled into lotus position, her feet tucked in neatly against her thighs.

"I can't stay long," I said.

She nodded. "Just follow your breath." Sarah picked up a thick wooden striker and rested it against a brass bowl before tapping it lightly. A bright, sweet tone filled the room, resonating as it faded.

I closed my eyes and inhaled. Air flowed into my nostrils and filled my lungs. My belly expanded and then contracted. I opened my eyes a crack. Translucent crystals covered the cloth that surrounded the bowl. Sarah thought they were imbued with healing powers, attributed to *energy* that did something to her *chakras*. She was always doing a cleanse, studying reiki or ionizing some particles.

"May I be happy," she said.

"Sure."

"Now you say it."

I looked around the room. The digital clock on her nightstand read 6:25. "I need to go soon."

"So say it."

"Who am I talking to?" I asked.

"Doesn't matter. Just say it."

"Fine," I grumbled. "May I be happy."

"May I be safe," she said.

I rolled my eyes. "May I be safe."

"May I be healthy."

"May I be healthy."

"May I be peaceful and at ease."

I looked up at Oprah and the Dalai Lama. They looked peaceful and at ease. I'd heard Oprah was worth billions. No wonder. "Sure," I said. "May I be peaceful and at ease."

"Now just follow your breath," she said.

I closed my eyes again. *May I give zero fucks.* My belly rose as I breathed, a gasping pile of dough. Flab never mattered with Andrea—I'd long given up on looking decent—but now that I was single I needed to work on my abs. Crunches and zero carbs. That would be my mantra. *May I have a six pack.*

Sarah's breath rushed loudly from her throat and out her nose, just shy of a snore.

May I stop being such a pussy. Fuck New York. I could move to LA. I could dress like I gave a shit. I could get a job with a future and stop hanging around with fucking losers. I could hike and do yoga and ride a bicycle. I could get a dog. Mom would be proud, for once. I had a few bucks. I could ask her for help, until I got my shit together.

It was all a wake up call—Andrea, work, all of it—and it was time to start kicking ass.

I jumped to my feet.

"Where are you going?" Sarah asked.

"Love you," I said. I shoved everything back into my bag, including the bowl, and split.

Chapter Six

Avi was waiting for me when I came out of the bathroom, looking better than I'd ever seen him. His stubble was no longer sloppy, his forehead shine was gone, and the too-big suit he'd worn at the Javits Center had been replaced by something that fit and probably cost more than he could afford. He looked like a Mossad agent from a spy movie.

He clapped me on the shoulder and then stepped back to take a look. "Nice suit," he said, adjusting my lapels. Avi eyed my trash bag luggage. "We'll find a place for that."

I'd mopped my forehead and tucked everything back into place in the hotel restroom. Coming off the high, I felt relaxed, if not confident. "I can't afford this, Avi," I said.

Avi pretended he hadn't heard me and took me by the arm. We rode the escalator up to the hotel meeting room. I made sure my dangling cuffs didn't get caught in the steps. Avi held my arm at the top and led me to a table with rows of name tags in sans-serif font, on thick white cardstock, four columns of five. Avi grabbed my Hefty bag and tossed it in a coat closet. The tag with my name on it had a round red sticker in one corner. It was the only one marked like that.

Avi caught me looking. "Don't worry about that," he said. "We'll handle it later."

A dark-suited young man with a sharply trimmed beard checked my name off a list. He was smiling like he couldn't stop. His name tag said *Claude.* He handed me a light blue lanyard that read *Ram Hardy / GZF* over and over. Claude's upper body was disproportionately large, like he'd skipped leg days at the gym for his entire life.

I attached the tag to the lanyard and stuck it in my pocket. Claude stepped between me and the door.

"Sorry," he said.

Avi eyed me and hung the tag around his neck. I shrugged and did the same. Claude gave a thin smile and stepped aside. Avi gestured towards the meeting room.

"Can we get a coffee?" I asked.

"Shut up," Avi said.

We walked through double doors into the room. The tables were arranged in a "U" and skirted with fabric. Each chair faced a perfect place setting: a yellow legal pad with the same *Ram Hardy / GZF* logo embossed on the top, three freshly sharpened pencils to the left, a place card for each participant, a carafe of water and a clean, empty glass.

Stackable hotel chairs surrounded the table, with an elevated director's chair in the dead center of the room. Video cameras were perched on tripods in each corner, the usual tangle of wires hidden by black fabric sleeves.

Harsh lights flickered. Most of the seats were still empty; we were a few minutes early. Three paunchy banker-types, all veiny noses and bloat, sat at the end closest to the front, looking like they had majored in keggers in the eighties.

One of the bankers fucked around with his ThinkPad, showing the other douchebags something that had them all laughing.

Avi rested his hand on my shoulder. "Morons," he whispered.

The bankers' place cards laid askew in front of them, their legal pads pushed to the table's edge. My heart pounded. I remembered Ram at the Javits Center. *Impeccability, you fucks!* I could hear it in his voice, every consonant over-pronounced for emphasis. *How the fuck can you expect anyone to trust you when you can't even fucking tie your shoes right!*

Who the fuck uses a ThinkPad anyway?

My stomach fluttered. I had no money, just a severance check and a bunch of credit cards that were already at their limits. I was the opposite of impeccable. My pants dragged on the floor, I'd just been fired, and I was still a little high. I knew what Ram would say. *You're a fucking loser. Go home.*

On my other side, a buzzcut with fresh acne sat down in a chair, thumbs-upping me. I thumbs-upped him back.

We were all there for the same thing, weren't we? We were tired of being losers, tired of being fired, cheated on, swept aside. Tired of being told to get lost, fuck off, *buy me a new set of headphones.*

I was the kind of person you can say *fuck off* to.

No one would say that to Ram. He'd tear their heads off.

The room filled up, men buzzing with anticipation and low-grade anxiety.

"This is it, Alan," Avi said. "This is where your life turns a corner." The way he said it, in his Israeli accent, made me feel like it was possible. The kid next to me picked at his teeth with a straw.

The crowd was a microcosm of the Javits Center, mostly white, mostly paunchy. It helped me feel better, like when I used to visit Andrea in Whitney. I had felt like an eight there, instead of a five in New York. That sense helped with my nerves; I could be slightly smug and judgy. I imagined the powdered donut sugar on their fat little fingers, their fire-extinguisher-sized cups with remnants of mocha-pumpkin-chip-Dunkaccinos, their syrupy protein bars marketed for health and fitness. I hoped Ram would call them out on their bullshit habits that kept them failing at life.

The chatter stopped. I swiveled my head to catch Claude striding up to the front of the room, his hands on his hips like a superhero, his posture accentuated by his giant chest and shoulders. The chatter quieted. Claude lowered his hands before buttoning his suit jacket and tugging it flat.

"Ram will be here in just a few minutes. Settle down. Get focused." He spoke in a low monotone, as though imparting a secret. "Organize." He glanced over at the still-open ThinkPad. "Put that away."

The banker with the laptop startled, and slammed the lid shut before slipping it into his rolling salesy briefcase.

"Most of you were at the big event at the Javits Center." He paused for emphasis and took stock of the room. "This is not that. This is not *casual*. Put everything away that wasn't here when you walked in. When Ram enters," Claude said, looking at each of us, one after the other, "you should applaud like you mean it. And don't turn to watch him come in." The kid next to me folded the straw he was using to pick his teeth and stuck it in his pocket. Claude glanced at the people on the sides of the room. His voice lowered to a whisper. "If you can see him, fine, but don't turn. He hates that."

How do you get to be Claude? Was he one of Ram's success stories? Where was his Patek Philippe, his Blancpain? *Hang around me*, Ram had told us, and *you'll get what you want.*

Claude's eyes darted about. He pointed to an oversized Starbucks cup. A suited staff person pulled it away before its owner could protest. And then on some unknown cue, Claude's eyes began to sparkle and a crazy big smile crossed his face. "Here he is!" he shouted, like he was announcing a rock concert or a costumed wrestling match. AC/DC's *Back in Black* leapt from the sound system, a gut punch of bass. At once, the guitar started, a buzzsaw of rhythm. Claude clapped, a beat at a time, flicking his gaze around the room to let us know to join in. And then we did, one by one, and the applause sped up and overlapped, gaining momentum. I wanted to turn and catch a glimpse of Ram but I was afraid to disobey. Others were pretending not to look, glancing, barely turning. Then I noticed those on the sides of the room, their faces lit up with glee, four-year-olds opening birthday presents. They were clapping so hard I worried for their hands, and it continued, an elation that filled the room and made my heart swell.

The kid next to me pounded on the table. Each time his pasty fists hit the tablecloth my pencils bounced closer to the edge. Claude clapped even louder, giving me permission to start pounding my fists along too. The vibrations ran up my forearms.

The room bristled with grit and energy, a dizzying swirl of excitement that kept going the other participants quickly began to still. As they slowed, I kept going, and then halted as I realized that everyone in the room was looking at me.

My heart leapt and a wash of chemicals spilled into my bloodstream. My breath quickened, and then with a jolt, two heavy hands clamped down on my shoulders. By instinct I looked down. They were gnarled and hard, like aged grapevines.

I caught myself looking and stared straight ahead. Every last person in the room gaped at me, or at whatever creature stood behind me.

The music stopped. Some fidgeting and breathing filled the room, and then silence.

He pressed down harder on my shoulders. I felt myself sinking into my seat. I straightened up to fight back.

Ram growled like an old-school Marine drill sergeant. "Good fucking job," he said. He rasped right into my ear, leaning over so close I could smell the coffee he drank. I dared not inhale. "Good job, kiddo." He stood up and released my shoulders. My spine decompressed. "Most of you would fucking cave. You'd slink down in your seats until you were a puddle under the table." He patted me on the back. If it were anyone else I'd feel patronized but instead I felt like a proud toddler and held back my grin. "Lesson number one. *Don't back down.* Backing down is for losers. If you want to be a loser living your dumb happy life, fine, but then get the fuck out and go back to Tempe. Go back to Salt Lake City or wherever the fuck you came from and argue with your fat wife about the credit card bill, if that's what you want."

Ram walked around the left side of the tables and strode to the front of the room. He lumbered, like his ropy muscles got in the way of his gait. On stage at Javits, next to Hierro Acero's huge frame, he had looked like a semi-normal human being; his power had seemed to emanate from his voice. But here, close up, Ram was physically intimidating, like a wiry pitbull who was barely held back from clamping his jaws on any of our throats. His crimson tie was pulled tight around his neck, tucked into an old-fashioned pinstripe vest. A matching pocket square wagged from his jacket pocket.

With each step, the building rumbled. Ram's white hair was buzzed nearly to the scalp. He looked like he could grab me and throw me against the wall, even at seventy or whatever.

Claude perched with the other staff, hands flat on the table, back straight. His skin had grown pallid, and his eye were squinted like he was trying not to shit himself.

Ram pushed his chair out of the way, examining all of us. His eyes rested on each participant for a few seconds, their breath halting as though his gaze was a pause button. One of the doughy bankers gasped for air when Ram moved past him. He looked away from the rest of us, embarrassed.

"Don't check out," Ram barked. "Stay with us." The banker snapped his head forward, his jaw clenched. "This is what you motherfuckers do," he said. "You check out. You check out from life. The minute things get real or something fucks with your fragile little ego, you check out." Ram paced towards the bottom of the "U," past Avi. A lanky blond jock with perfect teeth stared at him with a generic smile. "That's what you do, Golden Boy. You smile and look pretty and no one bothers you. You're still getting by on the same shit you used in high school. What are you, forty?"

The jock nodded. "Forty-two," he said.

"Forty-two? Then why'd you fucking nod? Is forty-two the same as forty?" Ram stood right up against the table, uncomfortably close to the jock. I looked past Avi, who was staring blankly like he'd been paralyzed by some neurotoxin.

Golden Boy's pretty head craned to meet Ram's gaze. "No."

"Then why'd you nod?"

His teeth gleamed. "I was just agreeing with you."

Ram turned and studied the room. "Was he agreeing with me?"

I tried not to breathe too loudly. We were still and funereal, but Ram was in a different reality. He spun back around to his victim and slammed his paw on the table. The pencils jumped and rolled off onto the carpet. "This is what you do, motherfuckers. I am talking to all of you. You fucking tolerate the intolerable. Someone says forty and you say *yeah, forty-two,* same fucking thing. This is why you don't get what you want.

This is why the most important thing you have to do with your time is to push a fucking cart around Wal-Mart looking for your favorite flavor of Doritos." He wrenched his face into a cry. "*Poor me, they ran out of chipotle ranch. I'll have to buy jalapeño cheddar. Wah wah.*"

"This is how you live your fucking pathetic lives. You are so scared to go after what you really want that you numb yourself to the absolute fucking unworkability and resignation of your lives. You shop. You watch fucking Netflix." He filled his lungs, starving the rest of us for oxygen. "How many of you drink? Smoke a little weed now and then?" He looked around the room. A few hands lifted. The bankers stifled a chuckle on the *weed* line. Ram reared up on his hind legs and flailed his arms. I cringed, afraid he would smack me with a claw.

Ram caught my withdrawal from the corner of his eye. He turned his head to face me but then stopped and cocked his head in the air like a dog hearing a whistle. His body stiffened and he pivoted to survey the room. One of the bankers squashed a snicker and stared straight ahead. Ram clocked him like a prison guard.

"What's that?"

The banker ignored him, staring ahead as if Ram was speaking with someone else. His friends were frozen in place. The three of them looked like a diorama of eighties greed.

"One warning. For all of you," Ram said. His voice grew a little louder. "I do *not* fuck around and you should know that." He look around at all of us and points, emphasizing every word. "This is not the fucking Javits Center with a thousand people where you can scream and cheer and get away with bullshit. I'll send you the fuck home and keep your fucking money."

He paced back to his chair. "You know my story," he said, lowering his voice to deliver the spiel we'd heard before.

It was the video that welcomed you to his website, and he'd rattled through it at the Javits. I didn't care. I wanted to hear it again.

"I bitched and moaned until I was thirty-five about how unfair life was. I was broke and alone. Every opportunity that came up, I found a way to kill it off. I was afraid of my own fucking shadow." He paused, shifted his weight. "I had man tits. I wanted to fucking kill myself. It was them—not me—they were the problem. My fucking boss, he should have given me better accounts. *What the fuck am I supposed to do with these dead accounts?* My mom—she left me hanging to figure out life on my own. Never mind she was working sixty hours a week and taking care of four kids. *Fuck you Mom!* The government—*it's a fucking consipiracy.* Or the Jews."

The air tingled.

"I couldn't get a date. Can you believe that?"

I looked down at the table.

"Always someone's fault. The world's unfair and people suck." He addressed the fattest banker. "Sound familiar?" The man nodded. Ram paused, searching for the right word. "You numb little boys." He shakes his head. "Children. Fucking children. How do I know you're children?"

The room remained completely quiet.

Ram's face turned red. "That was not a fucking rhetorical question? How do I fucking know you're children."

Twenty sets of eyes darted around the room looking to see who would answer. My hand shot up before I knew what I was doing. Across the room, a banker lifted his hand halfway, and then the kid next to me lifted his hand barely to his chin. Avi stayed frozen.

"I should send all of you home," Ram said. "It wouldn't be the first time, right Claudia?"

Claude nodded like a wind-up toy, ignoring Ram's feminization.

I started to lower my hand. Claude glowered at me until I straightened my arm. He nodded.

"I could send all of you home and keep your fucking money," he reminded us. He grinned at the thought, and made a fist. "You'd go home, pissed off. Post some nasty Yelp reviews. *Wah wah, Ram stole my money.* But this is what you signed up for, children."

My bowels rumbled and my arm started to tire. I took a breath and swept the room, not daring to move my head. We looked like a museum display of the wishful.

Sweat beaded on Ram's forehead, rolling down his pink skin. "If I sent you home you might just finally take a look at yourself in the mirror and think, *how did I get to be such a vile piece of shit that Ram was unwilling to work with me?* Each of you idiots paid me five grand to be here so you must think I know what the fuck I'm talking about." He wiped his buzzed head with a clean handkerchief and spied my hand. "What?"

My belly quivered. I lowered my hand a little, and then a little more. "I—you asked a question—I, uh—"

He pivoted, leaning over me across the table. "What?"

Ram filled my field of vision, his torso at my eyeline. My pulse pounded in my ears. I forced the words out. "Children. You asked us. How you know." I gulped some air.

"Smart man," Ram growls. "So what's the answer?"

I stiffened in my chair and eyed the other men without moving a millimeter. No one met my gaze; the bankers stared straight ahead in military formation. A breath. "Well, we came to you for help."

Ram slammed his palm on the table in front of me, sending pencils rolling to the carpet. I clenched my asshole shut just in time.

"Asking me for help's the first fucking responsible thing you've done in your fucking life." He pointed at my name tag. "Except you don't even have the balls to commit."

I looked down at where his finger was pointing. The red sticker stood out like a wound.

"You can't even commit to a fucking course that could potentially change your life. You know what red means, right? *No dinero, señor.*"

"I told Avi—"

"This is why you're fucking poor, Alan. This is why your life is a fucking train wreck." He pointed a claw at Avi, who froze in place. "You're lucky this guy gives a shit. If it wasn't for him dragging you here, you'd be fucked."

Avi looked away. Maybe he was embarrassed.

"I don't have any money, Avi," I said. "I'm sorry—"

"Yes, you do," Avi mumbled. A rumble swept through the room and then silenced at Ram's glare. Avi's voice grew stronger as the syllables formed in his mouth. He pushed his chair back to look at me. "You *do*."

The check was still in my wallet, folded into quarters. I shook my head.

"Gene gave you some money. I saw him."

"That's all I have, Avi." I turned to Ram. "It's all I have. It's not enough."

"That's a shame," Ram said. His eyes swept the room. "It's a shame, isn't it, fellas?"

The kid next to me nodded aimlessly.

"Poor baby," Ram said. "He's broke. Poor Alan." He moved over to Avi and clutched his shoulder. Avi looked stricken. "This man here, he's *standing* for you, Alan."

"I am," Avi said, his voice low and hoarse.

"What for?" Ram asked. "Why would you help another human being like that? Why wouldn't you just leave him to wander around fucking Costco looking for his fucking habanero flavored Doritos?"

Avi looked at me. His face was flush. He looked down at the table. Ram's hand tightened on Avi's frame, and Avi sat bolt upright. His eyes locked with mine. "I'll lend you the rest," he said. "You can pay me back."

"What for?" Ram asked again. "Do you have money coming out of your asshole," he said, laughing. "Do you?" A few men chuckled. "That would be great, if you could do that. Spray hundreds out of your butt. That would be something to see." Ram cackled at his own joke.

Avi shook his head. "I feel bad."

"Cut the shit, Avi. Act like a fucking Israeli soldier." Ram said.

"I feel sorry for you. You're such a—" Avi paused. "Loser." He spat the words out. "I can't stand to see you keep doing this shit." His words sped up as he talked, and his accent thickened. "I just wish you would stop being such a pussy," he said, sighing. Avi's eyes gleamed and his voice cracked. "I don't even know why I'm doing this. I can't afford it either."

The already-quiet room hushed further.

"That felt good, didn't it?" Ram said. Avi let out a rush of air and smiled faintly. "You're being *responsible,*" Ram bellowed. "Unlike this asshole." He gestured in my direction, dismissing me. "Life begins when you start taking responsibility. For yourself and for other human beings. That's when the results start to come. The miracles."

The bankers looked at each other.

"I—" I said, surprised to hear it coming out of my mouth. The room stayed quiet. "I *am* responsible," I blurted. The sound of my voice rang in my head, behind my face, and down into my throat.

Ram laughed. It seemed to come out of nowhere, like I'd told him an unexpected joke. "You're responsible for *nothing*," he said, shaking his head and crossing the room to his high director's chair. He sat down, still laughing, looking at each of us like we were toddlers on a playdate. "I can tell by just looking at you. All of you. You've got the money in your pockets and nothing else." He paused and looked around. "Unless your fucking daddy's paying the bills. And then you're even more pathetic." Ram swung back to Avi. "What's he do for a living?"

"Nothing. I mean, he got fired," Avi said.

"Of course you got fired," Ram said to me. He repeated himself. "You're responsible for *nothing*. Who the hell would want you working for them?"

I pushed my chair back. Its legs dragged along the industrial carpet.

"You're not going anywhere," he said, and I froze. It was as if he was in charge of my body; moving of my own volition seemed inconceivable. "That's the same shit. Being responsible would look like thanking this dumb motherfucker who's willing to give you the money for this goddamn seminar that would change your life so you don't have to keep walking around like a piece of shit loser in a suit that doesn't fit." He took a sharp breath and pointed at Avi. "There's your miracle, bucko. He's sitting right there. Thank him like a fucking *man*."

I stared at him from across the room. I wanted this. I wanted to be one of his success stories. I wanted to come back in a year and bound across the stage and yell at fat people and introduce Ram to a huge crowd. I wanted to be jacked.

"How many of you think you're responsible?" Ram leaned back in his chair. His words hung in the air. "You're thinking about it too much, Alan. You're trying to find the right answer. Makes you weak. Just listen for once. Avi and I are not going to relate to you as a tiny complaining piece of shit, Alan. You've forgotten who you really are."

Avi nodded.

Who I really am? Ram had no idea. I was the living dead. I'd lost almost everything. No handjob would make that feel any better. There was no safe harbor anymore; I couldn't ask Sarah for help. It was too humiliating. And Mom was already so disappointed.

I just wanted to go home. I wanted to eat American cheese slices out of the refrigerator. I want to sort my loose change into neat piles and clip my toenails. I wanted to crawl into bed.

"This is your shot, Alan," he said. "You gonna grow a pair?"

The chair was hard under my thighs, its sharp front edge pressed into my skin. The air conditioning hissed and a metal vent rattled. A damp and pungent waft of sweat ghosted through my nostrils, and my nose twitched.

"Alan," he said, startling me.

I looked up at Ram. I knew he meant well, but I was hopeless. I pressed my feet against the floor and felt them begin to bear my weight. I pushed the chair back and stood up, wobbling for a moment in Jeff's too-big shoes. "Thanks, Avi," I said, steadying myself. "Sorry."

Ram stepped forward as if to grab me, but the table was in the way. "I'm your last chance, Alan."

Avi jumped to his feet. "Listen to him, Alan," he said. "It's Ram, Alan. He can fix this. He can fix you." He reached for my shoulder but I batted his hand away before he could touch me. He looked down at his own arm, surprised.

I turned towards the door. Claude scrambled toward me, but I held my hand up like it had magic powers, and I was surprised when he stopped. "Thanks for trying," I said, and I walked out.

I bolted through the dark, over to Ninth Avenue, where I'd seen a check cashing storefront behind scratched plate glass. The heavy air smelled like a grungy steam room. Layers of vinegary sweat, car drippings, and hot garbage assaulted me as I walked. My trash bag luggage hung over my shoulder. A boarded-up construction site had been plastered with posters for *A Gun and a Half.* Acero's chiseled head followed me down the block, a grid of menacing silhouettes. I crossed the street.

The shop was sandwiched between a cluttered bodega and a fogged-up liquor store. I walked out with a sheaf of hundreds and twenties stuffed into my breast pocket. I ducked into the bodega to call Mariana's service. A fat gray cat slunk past me and dashed behind the counter. Red and green pixels blasted *Sandwich's $5.99 Now! Now! Now! Free Soda!* from a screen hung on the wall.

The same European-sounding woman told me Mariana was booked for the rest of the night. She had other girls available, she said. She rattled a few fake names: *Crystal, Amber, Nikki.* I'd asked for Autumn, the name Mariana had used.

I told the woman I'd think about it and hung up. I grabbed a bottle of Diet Coke from the fridge and flicked through the girls' pictures on the website. I'd seen a few of them before and they'd been fine, the way cheap street pizza was fine when I was high. They were all in vaguely spiritual poses, but naked.

I clicked on Mariana's photo. She was balanced on one foot, her hands in prayer position. Mariana's face was blurred, her eyes reduced to deepset shadows. The tattoo on her side faded into penumbra. I could just make out the words *¡bendita ilusión!* I'd been pissed off when I left her the last time, over her intimation that I needed fixing, as much as I knew she was right. Plus, she was unwilling to cut me a break. But I could tell she cared, at least a little.

An old man sat on a wooden stool behind the counter. Worn duct tape fringed from the seat. The man wore thick black glasses. His white beard was a crescent around his hardened face. I set down my Hefty bag, dropped a twenty on the counter, and pointed at the plastic cubes on the shelves behind him where scratch-offs were accordioned in neat rows.

The man handed me four tickets and then pointed to the soda. I paid for it and scratched the cards madly with a coin. The first three were duds but I won four bucks on the last one and waved it with glee. The old man smiled, showing his last few amber and gray-flecked teeth.

I cashed in the ticket and bought another twenty dollars' worth. They were all letdowns and I was down thirty-six bucks. The old man rocked quietly on his stool. I reached into my pocket for another twenty but stopped myself. Ram's voice rang in my head. *Dumb motherfucker. Loser.* I swigged the soda. It burned in my chest.

"Good night," I said to the clerk.

He nodded gently in response.

I stood outside and thought about going back to the seminar. It hadn't been that long. Ram would take the fanned bills from my hand with a smile. But then what? I would be no less broke, no less unemployed, no less fucked.

I slipped into the liquor store and bought a small bottle of Jack. The tattooed guy behind the counter stared at his phone as he took my money. Outside, I poured half of it into the Diet Coke. I swirled it around and took a swig, and then another.

The bourbon felt warm in my belly and put to rest any fantasy of going back. I started walking east, past trash bins and broken glass, wheelless bicycle frames chained to street signs and the feathery remains of a pigeon ingloriously mashed into the curb.

The air was still hot and Jeff's wool suit was steeped in sweat. The pant cuffs had started to unravel and dragged behind me like spurs. I stopped and stuffed them into the boaty shoes and then drank some more. There was no saving me. There was nothing more than hard work and struggle ahead. I didn't need to spend five grand to know that. I stuck my earbuds in and clicked on Ram's app.

You have pissed your entire fucking life down the toilet. You're a fucking moron if you think otherwise. I huffed down the block and finished the drink, then tossed the soda bottle in a trash bin. My legs pumped with purpose. *You have to come to the realization that you have pissed your entire life away. That's the truth.* I drank straight from the Jack bottle. The booze burned in my throat and landed heavy in my gut. *If you want to be a fucking stupid loser who coaches little league in Utica, be my fucking guest. Keep pissing your life away.*

Was this supposed to help? Ram was like a drill sergeant, breaking us down by showing us the bankruptcy of our lives. But where was the upside? I didn't need anyone else to tell me I was a piece of shit; of that fact, I was certain.

I crossed avenues, race-walking east. The booze had given me some small measure of confidence. Tonight, at least, I knew what to do.

I shoved aside an oversized trash bin spray-painted with the building's address and pressed my head against the iron bars outside Mariana's window. A stooped-over old lady in a flowery housedress walked her little grey dog a few houses down. The dog struggled to shit, like it was on its last legs. The woman stared in my direction before deciding to look away. Her dress reminded me of what Sarah had been wearing in Florida, something from a thrift store sale rack.

A faint vibration came through the metal, a weak musical pulse. Behind the iron bars, glass glowed under the streetlights. Familiar curtains blocked any view inside. I stood up straight and held onto the bars to steady myself.

The old lady was gone. I shifted and pressed my head harder into the metal. The alcohol was still warm in my chest and the rhythmic buzz resolved into a familiar-sounding melody. It was Mariana's music: she was in there with a client. The only other sounds came from outside, from taxi tires on the avenues and the electrical streetlight hum. I wished I had more to drink.

I rattled the front door. It opened with a pop, but the second door was locked and unmoving. A grid of wire mesh reinforced its glass. Mariana's grey metal door was just inside. The first time I saw her, I had walked in on her eating lo mein. I could picture her in her cheap push-up bra, the Spanish script along her ribs. Tonight I could lie next to her and trace the lines on her glowing skin and she could tell me what the words meant. Maybe she had some weed.

The vestibule was littered with filmy bags and drugstore circulars. Battered grey mailboxes lined the wall like wounded soldiers, their name-badges blank or blurred or scratched-out. I leaned against them and waited with my trash bag.

Ram was probably screaming the same old shit at someone at that very moment, about how pathetic they were, how their future was bankrupt. But whether or not he was right didn't change the future. I'd long been ashamed and it hadn't made any difference. It hadn't made me care less about what people thought. It hadn't made me less of a pussy.

A dull click came from inside. I looked up. Mariana's door was ajar, and then it swung open. I pressed myself into the vestibule's corner as a doughy man with drooping eyes shuffled out into the hallway. He wore a cheap navy suit, like he'd long worked on high gray floor full of cubicles and took his lunch from a halal cart. *Hot sauce white sauce?* The little hair he still had was ashen and grim. He looked at the door as if he was about to say something, but it shut firmly in his face. The man visibly sighed and turned to leave, for Westchester, or Stamford, or someplace worse.

I waited for him to open the door and slipped in. He startled, and dashed to the street without looking back. I stood in front of Mariana's stickered entrance and knocked.

The door opened a crack and then quickly shut. It reopened, a security chain stretched across the gap. Mariana looked out, a worn terrycloth robe wrapped around her body. "*¿Que necesitas?*" She spoke abruptly, like she'd never seen me before.

"Mariana," I said.

She blinked. "You need an appointment, *parcero*." She paused, like she was thinking of what to say next. "Call the number. You can't just come by here."

I rested my head against the door frame. "I have money," I said.

Mariana shook her head. "I have another client soon," she said.

"I won't take long."

She let out a *pfft*. "Go, *parce*. You need some fucking help, bro." Mariana pushed on the door and it closed with a click. I fished in my pocket and pulled out a hundred dollar bill. Then I got down on my knees and slid the money most of the way under the door, holding down the end with two fingers.

"Mariana," I said, tapping on the metal door with my knuckles. I heard a shuffle inside, and then felt a tug as the bill disappeared from my hand. I grinned. "Open the door," I said.

The hallway was quiet. I pressed my ear against the door but couldn't hear anything. I knocked again. "Fuck," I said. "Mariana!"

The harsh white lights overhead buzzed, and a truck rumbled past the building. I could wait. Her next customer would be there soon. But then what?

I rapped my knuckles against the door once more. "Mariana," I said, but the door stayed shut. I knocked again, barely making a sound. "At least give me my money back," I mumbled, but I'd given up already, and I left.

Chapter Seven

The apartment looked familiar, but there were a few things out of place. The big TV was missing; instead, there were rough holes in the drywall where it had been attached. I winced, thinking about my security deposit. Cardboard boxes were stacked unevenly against the wall at the foot of the bed, forming a lopsided pyramid. Andrea's closet door was open. A flock of plastic hangers straggled from a metal bar; all her clothes were gone. Bright daylight streamed through the lone window.

My head throbbed as I propped myself up against the headboard. I was still in Jeff's suit and shoes. Dark streaks soiled my knees, and a fetid scent hung in the air. I tried to piece together how I'd gotten there.

I'd slept on the same sheets Joe had used to wipe his dick, the same place they'd been fucking. I leaned over and pressed my face into the bed. It smelled like a teenager's gym locker. Something in my stomach wanted to come up and out.

Down the hall, more boxes were scattered throughout the place, some stacked in twos and threes. I let the bathroom faucet run and looked in the mirror. An unrecognizable face looked back at me, unshaven, heavy-lidded, greasy-skinned. *You've pissed your life away*, Ram had said. I needed to delete that fucking app.

The sink was flecked with toothpaste and hair. Andrea's hair, maybe, and whiskers that could have been Joe's or could have been mine. My head throbbed some more. I slurped water from my cupped hands and threw Jeff's suit on the floor. I found my toothbrush and some toothpaste in an open box on the back of the toilet and brushed. Then I stood under the shower and let hot water run over me until it started to run cold.

The living room was in worse shape than the bedroom, scattered with boxes and trash bags. A trail of water dripped behind me as I scavenged for a towel and some clothes. My own precious Hefty bag slumped near the front door, its top tied in an oversized knot. The big window was open, apparently how'd I'd entered. There was a puddle of dried vomit on the floor nearby, probably mine. It was chunkier than I would have expected.

Boxes were half-packed with things to which Andrea had laid claim: the cheap flatware we'd bought at Ikea, my over-stuffed meditation cushions, a scented candle I'd been gifted by a client, the WaterPik she'd never used. Maybe if she had, we could have saved two grand on root canals.

Another carton held a collection of mismatched plastic containers, mostly absent lids, a tangle of unusable chargers, a can of corn. I imagined Andrea's tantrum, tossing anything of value into a crate, if only to keep it out of my hands. I scrabbled through the boxes, leaving glossy puddles around me until I found what I needed.

I dried off and got dressed. My phone was a powerless brick, and I found a charger in a kitchen drawer and plugged it in. As the phone lit up, I saw that it was after ten. A rush of worry passed over me quickly—had I overslept? But I had no place to be. I gripped the counter and breathed until the feeling settled.

And, suddenly, another wave of panic hit. I rushed into the bathroom and rifled through the suit pockets. My heart pounded again. There was not enough air. I was sure the money was gone; I was fucked. The feeling swelled until I put my hands on the sheaf of cash. I counted it quickly; there was still over a thousand bucks. Breath slowly filled my chest. I'd spent some, but it was mostly intact. Whatever I'd done after leaving Mariana's place hadn't cost much.

The phone rang and I dashed to grab it. It was Sarah calling; I hit the red *decline* button. What could I say? I'd sprinted out the door in her boyfriend's suit. I knew her next step: she'd call Mom, which would set off a whole chain of upset, especially after the Bernice incident. Mom hadn't called me since I'd been home, so I knew she was still mad, and I didn't want to make it worse.

The phone rang again and I answered it without looking at the screen. "Sarah," I said.

"Who's Sarah?"

I instantly recognized Mariana's accent and stood up straight, as if she could see me. "She's my sister," I said. "I thought it was her."

"I got jealous," she said, laughing.

"Really?"

"No."

"Oh. How did you get my number?"

"I was just making sure you're alive, *parce*. You were a mess last night." She shouted to someone in Spanish and giggled at whatever they said back. I couldn't understand any of it. "Listen, bro. You need some help."

My head swirled. I leaned against the kitchen counter. "I'm fine."

She yelled something else in Spanish. *Ya voy,* maybe, followed by something I couldn't put together. "Sorry, honey," she said to me.

My gut roiled, and I swallowed to keep its contents down. "Can I come see you?"

"I'm leaving, honey," she said. "I'm flying to Colombia."

"When?"

"I told you, today. You should come, *parcero.* I don't invite everyone to see Taita."

"Who?"

"My shaman," she said. "He'll straighten out your energy. You're all twisted around, honey. You come down for a few days and you'll be a new man."

On the fridge, a Graceland magnet held up a Polaroid of my grandparents, a faded and curled square from before I was born. Pop wore a blonde wig and woman's pajamas. One hand carried a plastic Jack-o-Lantern candy basket. Grandma had a lit cigarette stuck between a set of plastic buck teeth. She wore thick black glasses, but I couldn't tell whether they were part of the costume. I could almost smell the stale smoke that clung to their walls.

"I can't," I said. I took the photo down and looked at it closely. They were smiling, in on the joke.

"You have a passport, right?"

"Yeah, but—"

"Alan."

"I need a job," I said. "I can't go flying off to South America to see a fucking shaman. I need to clean shit up. I need to get my life together." I stopped, realizing I'd raised my voice. "I'm sorry."

"*No importa, mi amor,*" she said. "Listen, sunshine. This is a one-time offer. I've never done this before, not with a client."

"Mariana—"

"Alan," she said, forcefully enough that I shut up. "Aren't you tired of living this way?"

I scrambled to gather my things. Mariana was already on her way to JFK and I hadn't even bought a ticket. We were flying to Bogotá. From there, we'd catch another flight to the south, near the border with Ecuador.

The whole thing was crazy. I was chasing a sex worker to South America to see her shaman. I'd been fired, I watched my wife get fucked by a small-town crossing guard, I got caught jerking off outside an old lady's window in a retirement home. My mom might be fucking her Crossfit coach.

Divorce, bankruptcy—there were options. There were other jobs.

I did not have to run away.

Maybe I did give too many fucks. There was an oversized duffel bag in the closet, a huge camouflage sack I'd bought in a Pennsylvania Wal-Mart. What would I need to wear in Colombia? It had to be hot there. I grabbed my cargo shorts, the ones that Andrea had said made me look like a lesbian, and a few t-shirts that I wore on my occasional gym visits.

I took one last look around the room. The wooden bowl sat on the floor next to my Hefty bag. Andrea would probably throw it out. I grabbed it and walked out, the duffel bag strap hung over my shoulder. The door shut behind me with a quiet thunk. Fuck this place.

We rolled down Eastern Parkway in a space-gray Altima, past streams of Hasidim. The men grouped in twos and threes in their heavy coats and hats, under the still-screaming sun, while their wigged wives followed in larger swarms, ankles covered, strollers in formation. My baby-faced driver Iqbal shouted into his headphone in some rhythmic, elegant language, as he'd been doing since I got in the car. I'd read his name off the license affixed to the dashboard. The wispy beginnings of a beard were budding along his jaw. House music pulsed over the air conditioner, which was howling to keep up with the heat.

I punched the debit card number into my phone for the third time. The airline website kept freezing, and when I'd tried to call, the recording told me the wait time was fifteen minutes.

Gray dots lit up on the screen, one after the other, indicating progress. I gripped the phone until my hand hurt. The car slowed at Utica Ave., where any semblance of gentrification had given way to storefront medical clinics and janky fast food joints.

"Look at these cunts," Iqbal said as we ground to a halt. He pointed to the road ahead. A line of delivery trucks were making their way around an arc of traffic cones, which blocked off a Con Ed van and an open manhole. Neon vested workers stood by, bewildered. "Look at this shit." His words slurred together in an accented stream. *Lookadisshit.*

We were in the middle lane, with no egress on either side. Cars and trucks fought for available space, hands laid on horns, hoping to squeeze into the single open lane. The Nissan jerked ahead a yard at a time. The screen on my phone showed a little over an hour before takeoff, and the gray dots had given way to an error message. "Fuck." I opened the window and craned my neck to see how far ahead the traffic was blocked, but I couldn't see past the row of trucks. My hand squeezed the door handle, as if it had a mind of its own—ready to fling me into traffic, where I would bound over cars and leap onto a passing A train, the duffel strapped to my back.

"You are late?" He asked. He pointed to his phone on the dash. "Will be in traffic for twelve minutes. What time is your flight?"

I told him and he laughed. "Well, maybe you will get lucky," he said. He held up a finger and shouted something unintelligible into his phone, then snorted. I closed my eyes and began to follow my breath.

"I told my wife you might miss your flight, she says she is sorry to hear that and she wants to know where you are going."

"Colombia," I said. I sat back in my seat and closed my eyes, hoping to end the conversation.

"Motherfucking Escobar!" he said, excited. "I saw the show. Are you a drug lord?" He turned around in his seat with a smile. "Don't worry, I won't tell anyone."

I shook my head and pointed to the road. He looked back and kept driving, a few inches at a time.

"Then why?"

I shrugged. A sea of red lights stretched ahead.

"I don't know!" he said into the phone, in English. He laughed. "She is nosy."

The car lurched ahead. The horns that surrounded us began to bleat and cry until they formed a sea of noise. *Ruido*, I remembered. I said it to myself. *Ruido, ruido, ruido.* The few Spanish words I had would have to be enough. Mariana could translate for me if I ever made it there, but I barely knew her.

The phone buzzed. *Are you close?*

No, I replied.

Each foot, slamming onto a trunk, a roof, a hood, too-late fists waved at me in the distance, a superhuman leap onto the back of a train as I hurtle through space against sticky-hot wind.

"I am usually an optimistic person, by nature," Iqbal said. Our eyes met in the mirror.

I shook my head. "Keep going." This was it. Me and Mariana, snuggled up under a blanket from here to Bogotá. I willed the car forward and it nudged along.

"You speak Spanish?" Iqbal asked, not waiting for an answer. "*Estoy tan emocionado de hablar contigo en Español.*"

"*Si, un poquito,*" I said. "I am learning."

He laughed and said something to his wife on the phone. "She said you need to learn quick." He rammed the horn and swerved around another truck. A gap emerged and he floored the gas to make the light at the next corner. The Nissan hurtled down the road, gathering speed and pressing me back into the seat, until Iqbal jammed on the brake behind a duct-taped minivan.

My phone rang and I grinned; for a brief moment I was sure it was Mariana, sure she was excited that I was coming with her, that I had trusted her. We had formed a bond, she and I, and Mariana was beginning to feel it.

"Do you like Linda Ronstadt?" Mom's voice graveled across the miles.

"Who?"

"The singer."

Iqbal whipped the cab around a double-parked delivery truck, pressing me against the door. "Linda Ronstadt?" I asked.

Iqbal eyed me in the rear view mirror. I mouthed *it's my mom* to him. He whispered back. *Linda Ronstadt?* I nodded.

"Everyone from the box is going."

"To see Linda Ronstadt?"

"It's a tribute. Gwo can get us tickets. He loves Linda Ron-stadt."

"He does? That seems weird—"

"Stop being such a bigot, Alan. Haitians can like Linda Ronstadt."

"I guess."

Iqbal held up a finger and smiled at me in the mirror, before he reached for the volume knob and turned it to the right.

I've been cheated

Been mistreated

When will I be loved?

Linda's voice blasted through the car stereo as Iqbal pounced on the gas, squishing me into the cheap upholstery as he rocketed around the van. The Altima sped down Atlantic with the guitar and drums, past outdated billboards and red-bricked old age homes.

Iqbal was singing along as we turned onto South Conduit, past truckyards and junkyards, miming the drum fills with his empty hands.

"I have to work, Mom. I can't come down for a Linda Ronstadt concert." It came out a little more sharply than I'd wanted it to.

Mom was quiet for a moment. "I told you it's a tribute," she said. "Not the real Linda Ronstadt. She's retired."

"Oh."

The cab's wheels clicked along the road joints.

"I'm sure it's very good," I said.

"Well, maybe you should ask Andrea," Mom said. "Maybe she wants to go."

It stung a little.

I've been made blue
I've been lied to
When will I be loved?

I looked at my phone. Fifty-two minutes until the flight. I didn't even have a ticket. "Maybe," I said.

This was my future, if I kept working hard. A Delray Beach condo, two-packs a day, and Eddie Mekka singing *Rags to Riches*. I could live the dream.

"How's Carol?" I asked, my go-to whenever I couldn't think of what to say.

"Still with the bronchitis."

"Has she seen a doctor?"

"I gave her a nebulizer," she said.

"You what?" I said.

"A nebulizer. What's the big deal? You put the medicine in and breathe in like a cigarette. Only it's medicine. Hold on." She shouted past the phone. "Carol, where's my lighter?"

I could hear Carol shout back from the next room. *How the fuck should I know?*

"Hold on, Alan." The phone clunked. I knew she'd put it down on the Formica table while she rummaged through her Hefty-sized purse for a light. She muttered to herself as she searched. *I buy ten fucking lighters. God forbid I should have one when I need it.*

Fifty minutes. We were zooming past the long term parking lot. "Mom, I have to go," I said. "I have to catch a flight."

"A flight?"

"For work," I said. "I'll call you when I can."

"Where are you going?"

"I'll call you," I said. "I love you." I hung up the phone.

Iqbal shook his head and clicked his phone. House music resumed and he accelerated hard into the exit for JFK. "You might make it," he said.

Ahead, massive cargo planes lined up outside aging warehouses, while while trucks and lifts sped between them. A new-looking passenger jet rested in a cavernous hangar. I wondered where it would go first. It looked big enough to go anywhere. Shanghai, Sydney, Cleveland.

Not long after we first met, Andrea and I got drunk on Mezcal and watched the late flights land at Latrobe. *These planes ain't goin' nowhere*, she'd said, wiping away tears. I'd pretended not to notice.

We're boarding, Mariana texted. The Altima pulled up to the terminal and triple parked while neon vest-wearing traffic cops shouted and waved.

"Thank you," I said, but he was already out of the cab hoisting my duffel from the trunk. I shook his hand and dashed into the building.

"Buddy," he shouted.

I looked back. Iqbal stared at me through the open window.

"You know what Escobar said, right?"

I shook my head and glanced at the terminal.

"*La vida está llena de sorpresas*," he said, in a beautiful accent.

I stared at him, not understanding.

"Life is full of suprises," he shouted to me, and with a wave, he drove off.

The last fucking place I wanted to be was Fort Lauderdale, but there I was, at the Jack Nicklaus Golden Bear Grill in the airport, repeating Spanish verbs to myself and waiting for my quesadilla. *Comí, comiste, comió.*

I'd missed Mariana at JFK; once I'd walked into the comically vast terminal and seen the long lines, I'd known there was no shot of making it. The only flight I could get had a long layover in Florida. I texted Mariana the info, and she replied that she'd meet me at the Bogotá airport and from there, we'd fly to the jungle.

Now the restaurant was full of Jews in transit. Men in pleated slacks and golf shirts jingled change in their pockets while their wives one-upped each other about their children. *He calls me every day.* Always *he.* The girls were incidental.

I looked at one of the men at the table next to me. He was with his wife—his hand rested on the woman's next to him—and another couple. Food spread out in front of them in heaps and piles. He was jowly and shnozzy, loose skin hanging around his neck in pockets and folds, his cheeks glowing rose. Clouds of white hair rose above his ears, set off by the black frame of his heavy glasses.

Was that my predictable future? What would Ram say? I still had his app on my phone but I'd been avoiding it. I was beyond repair, at least by conventional means. The old Jews near me looked like they'd never had a moment of existential despair; maybe it had been drowned out by a litany of practicalities. My grandparents didn't worry about *purpose.* They cared about what was on sale.

The old man saw me looking in his direction and squinted his eyes in a warm smile.

I looked back at my phone. Google said it was thirty-nine minutes to Mom's. In theory, I could hop in a cab and spend an hour and still be back in time for my flight. I'd be the best son ever, for a few minutes. I imagined my triumphant entry—trumpets ablaze, *hear ye, hear ye*—and my woeful retreat. How would I cover my lie? I wasn't dressed for a business trip, hadn't packed for one. Mom's internal bullshit detector was pretty sharp; she'd been lied to plenty. The rode hard waitress flew by with a tray of drinks, avoiding eye contact. "Excuse me," I called after her.

I could find a quiet corner and sit cross-legged, listening to my brain chatter tell me what a piece of shit I was.

One of the old men shouted to me from across the table. "When's your flight?"

"I have time," I said, looking away.

"He's just hungry," his wife said, raising her hand. She was wearing a gold lamé bib over her shiny blouse. "Honey!" she shouted—nearly a shriek—and the waitress whipped her head in our direction like she'd heard a fart. The woman pointed at me. "He needs something."

The waitress held up a finger and disappeared.

The old man laughed. "Martha's the boss," he said.

The other couple nodded grimly; they'd learned *that* lesson.

The waitress brought my quesadilla and Martha grinned at me. *See?* she mouthed.

I nodded and started to eat.

"You could say thank you," she said.

"Sorry," I said, chewing. "Thank you." The quesadilla was a big congealed lump in my mouth. I swallowed hard to get it down.

She shrugged and went back to arguing with her husband.

Fuck her. Fuck all of them. I was not going to live my life that way. Was this how Andrea and I would have ended up? My grandparents were the same, full of argument, full of complaint, full of drama. They were judgmental and too nice at the same time.

But the drama was probably what had killed them. After my grandmother had been diagnosed with congestive heart disease, she'd ignored Dr. Kapoor's advice. They needed a Jew's opinion. A week later, Dr. Shapiro confirmed the diagnosis and her grim prospects, and my grandfather dropped dead in the examination room.

The doctor had just left the room when Pop clutched his chest and fell to the floor like he'd been shot. Grandma had been struggling to beat a level on Candy Crush and missed the whole thing until she heard the thud of his head against the cabinet. She let out a scream. In the excitement, her own heart gave out and she collapsed by his side, her velour tracksuit draped over his prone body on the tile floor. I pictured them, a prone pile of Jew, arms and legs twisted, Pop gripping his *chai*, an unlit Parliament in Grandma's puffy, manicured hand. They'd lived their whole lives to end up a grim sculpture on a tile floor.

I had dodged a bullet. That was our future. Me and Andrea. A couple of waxy corpses in tracksuits on a doctor's linoleum floor, a walletful of Denny's coupons and a trunk full of sale-priced tunafish. Our bodies contorted. *Retorcido. En jarras.* My Spanish vocabulary was useless; I knew words like *anchor* and *yeast,* but I could never remember how to order a meal. I wished I'd studied more. I wished a lot of things.

I chewed on my quesadilla. It was like a giant microwaved gummy bear of cheese. A gluey mess. I gave up on chewing and swallowed a big chunk. It stuck in my throat, a solid plug of tortilla and Jack. I tried to swallow again but nothing moved. For a moment, it was nothing. In a flash, thoughts flew by: how far is the walk to the gate? Do I want a coffee? I remembered a line from a poem we'd read in high school: *Do I dare to eat a peach?*

The room got silent. The Jews' mouths contorted with laughter but no sound came out. Food flew from Martha's mouth onto her bib in a slow-motion spray. Her husband wiped the flecks from his glasses with a soft white handkerchief he pulled from his pocket in a dramatic flourish.

A roar began. At first in my ears, a low rumble that grew in volume and speed as it spread. To the sides of my head and then to its crown, a whoosh of blood that overtook everything else. I stood and tried to force a cough. My legs wobbled beneath me. *Is this it? Am I going to die in the Fort Lauderdale Airport?* I clawed at my throat, worried that my mother would find out I'd been a half-hour away and hadn't visited.

The Jews laughed and chewed and spat. I stumbled back before Martha's eyes caught mine and her face went from glee to terror. She spat some more, hailstones of gristle. I watched them arc through the air and land on her bib and in her water glass.

And then: *it's really not that bad.* A sense of peace washed over me, the way an antelope succumbs to a big cat's claws. The room haloed as Martha slung her hand in my direction, pointed at me like a comic book villain would shoot a venomous beam, and her mouth opened in scream. But there was no sound from her, only the continued roar of blood in my ears and a spray of food from her face. Heads turned toward me and I sat back down in my chair, relaxed, like I was taking a nap. Above me, the ceiling swirled with color and my hands dropped to my sides.

And then I rose up from my chair without any effort like I was floating, as my feet came off the ground. Gravity was reversed. My body shook. I looked down to see trunk-thick arms wrapped around me from behind. They were dark and mottled and seemed too big to be human, or maybe I had shrunk to miniature, thick woody vines pulling me into the air, meaty mitts sunk into my chest that lifted me like a newborn, knotted and striated, waves of muscle and skin.

As easily as my thumbs would pop a sheet of bubble wrap, fists pressed into my gut and forced out a small surge of air. Something moved. A guttural cough wracked from deep in my lungs as a chunk flew from my mouth. I watched the oblong felon crescent and peak in a perfect arc. *Arco. La roca vuela.* Spanish words scurried through my brain as the wad of cheese and tortilla tumbled end-over-end like a tiny little football, and I willed it to its target like I'd have willed a football through the uprights for the extra point, and it did, it stayed true on its path, coming down in a whistling plunge to the cheers of eighty thousand fans, right into Martha's wide-open mouth.

"You eat too fast," he said. He hadn't quite put me down yet. Even while I spat cheese remnants and after I'd wiped my mouth, the giant kept one arm around my waist, as if I belonged to him and he had to protect me from choking again. He handed me a glass. "Drink some water." He pronounced it *dwink* and I wanted to crack a joke. He waited and watched me drink the water.

A crowd had formed around Martha, nursing her back from panic. *He might have a disease*, someone said. *My cousin got hepatitis from a toilet seat.* I sat and looked up at the immense man. He had a toddler's pudgy face and gritty stubble on his chestnut head, and he wore a drab uniform with the airport's logo. He smiled, a bulwark against his size. "You okay?"

"Yeah." I looked around. The other diners were gradually going back to their own business. The haggard waitress skirted past me and dropped the check like it was a turd she wanted to get rid of. Over the loudspeaker, a man's voice announced a flight delay.

The big guy just stood there. His ID badge hung from a lanyard at my eye level. It was embossed with a picture of him, unsmiling, his hair a little longer, the same uniform shirt. Next to the photo, his name: *Peterson*, and another name that was obscured by smudges on the plastic badge holder.

"Mr. Peterson," I said. "Thank you."

He smiled. "Just Peterson," he said. "Or *Gwo*. It means big."

"*Gwo*," I said. Another fucking Gwo. Who knew there were two? I reached out to shake his hand. He reciprocated for the briefest moment and then pulled his hand away. My fingers had felt like a child's in his grip, like he might suddenly crush them inadvertently. I searched for what to say. "You're lucky," I said.

He went blank. "What?"

"Being so big," I stammered, embarrassed at my directness, and tried to cover. "It must be great."

Gwo looked at me, puzzled. He must have been being modest. He had to know that being so big was an unfair advantage. He couldn't deny it: people treated you differently. They had to be nicer to you. There was an unsaid privilege, like being in the presence of a billionaire. Doors opened.

A pencil-thick ridged scar ran down one of his arms, from the elbow to just above his wrist. It looked worn, like it had faded with time. He'd probably been in some natural disaster, or maybe a fight or a wreck.

I still had a scar on my left shin, from when I'd gotten drunk in college and banged my leg into metal fire escape steps. It had hurt for days.

"Do you need anything?" Gwo asked. "I have to get back to work."

He was just waiting there like I was supposed to tip him. "I only have twenties."

"Sorry?"

I shook my head. "I mean, thank you. Anyway."

"It's okay." He nodded and clapped me on the back. "Chew better."

"I chew fine," I snapped.

He said, "OK," and then turned and started to leave. He looked back at me once more, as if to make sure I was still breathing.

"I'm good," I said.

He nodded at me and left. I watched him ease through the terminal in his hugeness, greeting other workers as he passed with hand slaps and hugs. Anybody could have saved me. It didn't make him special. He was born big. I could Heimlich someone, too. Fuck him, coasting through life, laughing and joking, unthreatened, valued. He'll ride on this story for days. He'll tell everyone how he saved the dumb Jew's life. Dumb fuck probably goes to church. I imagined him standing on a pulpit—is that what they call it?—testifying about how the Lord commanded him to save me, the heathen Jew. *Praise Jesus! He saved a poor sinner!* Probably mocking me right now to his airport buddies. *Dumb white fuck.*

Life was simpler for people like that. It wasn't just this giant. It was everybody. What did Mariana have to offer the world? And yet she skated by, laughing, while a jerk like me chased her across the globe. What would she do when she was no longer hot? *There is only now*, Sarah would say. *The future is a conversation.*

Ram yelled at people for a living. That was his unique value proposition. I remember learning that phrase in a marketing class in college. *Unique value proposition.* What do you do? *I yell at people.*

Joe, a life of low expectations, filled with football and nachos, happy to be fucking my wife. Even Avi had traveled the world. It was easy for them.

I could have been a rabbi. People look up to rabbis. You go to school, learn some Hebrew, and then for the rest of your life, people come to you for advice. They look up to you. I could have done crunches and posed shirtless for the synagogue calendar, pumped my biceps and gotten a Magen David tattoo. The cool rabbi.

Why did it have to be so hard? I grimaced as I picked up the check and paid it with my dwindling stack of cash.

Martha's husband slid into a chair across from me with surprising ease. "You okay?"

I nodded. "Was I supposed to tip him?"

He rolled his eyes like I was joking. "I think he saved your life."

"I only had twenties."

He chuckled.

"I mean, he works here, right? He's getting paid," I said.

"Probably." He started to get up to leave.

"Sorry. About your wife."

He shrugged a whole body shrug, a contortion where his head and neck sunk into his torso and his face twisted into a question mark, then settled back into the chair.

"I mean, she's not dead," I said.

"She's just upset."

"Sorry," I said.

"It's just cheese."

"And tortilla," I said.

He looked away from me as if thinking about what to say.

"I'm not sick or anything."

"You're sure?"

"I don't think so," I said. *I have gonorrhea*, I wanted to say.

He adjusted his thick black frames and looked over at Martha. She was on the phone recounting her drama. "What's your name?"

I looked at the time on my phone. Still over two hours until my flight. "Maurice," I mumbled, before realizing how stupid that sounded. "Sorry. No. Alan," I said.

"You're sure?"

I nodded.

"Alan." He said my name like he was assessing it. "You live here in Florida?"

"God, no," I said. "Brooklyn."

"Brooklyn!" he shouted. "We're from Brooklyn." He gestured to gather his wife's attention, but she was caught up in her story. He yelled her name. "Martha!"

Martha held up a finger and kept talking. He waved her off, annoyed. "Sheepshead Bay," he said to me.

"Park Slope."

"Oh." He seemed disappointed. "That's where you were born?"

"No."

"You moved *to* Brooklyn?"

"Yeah."

"Nobody moves *to* Brooklyn," he said.

"Now they do." I started to get to my feet.

"No shit," he said. "Martha won't believe it. Who the hell moves to Brooklyn?" He took out a toothpick and fished around in a gap in his gumline. "I'm Marty." He pulled out the splinter of wood and examined the debris that had been stuck in place, before wiping it off on a napkin, satisfied.

"Marty," I said. "Marty and Marsha." I pushed in my chair.

"Martha."

"Martha, sorry," I said.

Marty tapped the fingers of one hand on the table, while he crinkled a Sweet 'n Low packet with the other. "You really moved to Brooklyn?"

"Yeah." I stood there. "I have to get going," I said.

Marty was quiet for a second, like he didn't know what else to say, but he knew I didn't really have to go anywhere. "You have family down here?"

"Yeah," I said. "Mom's in Delray."

He mouthed *Delray*, like he was processing the word. "There's a bagel place I like there. Bagel King."

Martha stopped her conversation to yell at him. "Bagel Twin!" she said.

"No, in Delray," he yelled back.

She shook her head and held up a finger so she could finish her call. Marty leaned closer to me and whispered. "It's Bagel King. She's thinking of Twin Bagel."

"Okay."

"In Boca. Not in Delray." He paused. "Delray's nice."

"I guess."

"You're a good kid, coming to visit her." The old man fiddled with his cheap watch, uncomfortable. It was like he'd seen this scene in a movie somewhere, and had to play his role. *Better go check on the guy, have a moment.* He'd seen me choke, felt some responsibility, wanted to pat me on the back and reassure himself so he had a nice story to tell his friends. I wanted to upend his fantasy, his bland, jowly life. *No, Marty. I didn't come here to visit Mom. I'm chasing a sex worker to Colombia to meet her shaman. Maybe if I do what she wants, she'll fuck me.* I was a good Jewish boy who'd come to visit his mom, not a jobless fuckup. Fuck him and his false teeth.

"I gotta run, Marty," I said, edging towards the exit.

He waved at me, and then Martha noticed I was leaving and she waved, too. And the other old Jews at their table started waving and shouting *goodbye Alan* and blowing air kisses. Around them, tables of ruddy-faced old people, all speckles and spots, caught on, like they didn't want to miss out on the action. They waved in unison, a like tethered seaweed moving with the current, broad smiles and rickety teeth. *Goodbye!* they yelled.

I scanned the lot of them, this wolfpack of shiny skin and lost collagen, Aqua-Netted hair and unnatural sequins. They waved to me, their chai necklaces swaying, from their chairs, their motorized scooters, their collapsible walkers. Heat rose in my cheeks, and blood pounded hard in my head.

I left.

Chapter Eight

I sat on a ledge in the airport near El Cafetalito, my back against the window. I'd landed to a text from Mariana telling me where to wait. The signs she had said would be there were there. *Bandas. Salidas. Chanel.*

A short line of tired travelers queued for coffee. I counted my pesos, a fat wad of colorful notes with meaningless numbers I'd traded for some of my dollars. Mysterious men stared back at me from the crisp papers, mustaches and beards, hair slicked with pomade. *Veinte mil pesos. Cinco mil pesos.* A woman graced the 10,000 peso note. Her hair was parted down the center in a sharp line along her scalp, shadows covering her right side that added to the mystery. She was my reference point, the sole woman in the stack. She represented a little over three dollars. My common denominator. *Diez mil.* I would try to get more of these bills as change.

I readied myself for my first Spanish interaction; earlier, the immigration officer had greeted me in English, dashing my attempt. I leaned against the window and hid my mouth with an open hand, practicing the words. *Un cafe Americano, por favor. Si, con leche. Un cafe Americano, por favor. Con leche.*

I took a deep breath and stood up, pulling my duffel behind me. No one paid any attention. The line moved, and a teenaged girl smiled at me from behind the counter. Her mouth glittered with braces, and the sides of her face were pocked with acne scars. She seemed sweet, working for shit wages serving coffee. I bet her parents were proud of her.

"*Hola,*" I said.

She nodded.

"*Un café, por favor.*"

"*¿Con leche?*" she asked. I nodded and handed her one of the bills I'd counted. She took it and quickly returned my change in coins, which I dropped all over the floor. I scrambled to pick them up and muttered a quick *gracias*. I scowled and took my coffee over to the ledge where I waited for Mariana.

My back pressed against the cold glass. I sipped the sharp-tasting coffee and took a breath. Through the window, mist formed into puddles where taxis and vans skimmed the curb. Glowing red brake lights formed bright halos in the grey, like a living Impressionist painting. Where was fucking Mariana? I checked my phone again, but there was nothing new since I'd landed. I clicked on the Ram app. *Stop being such a pussy.* Ram's growl bounced around my head. I wasn't being a pussy. I just didn't like not knowing. *Start taking some fucking responsibility*, he said. I shut it off.

People were happy to see each other. In this part of the airport, flights were coming in from around the world. Signs announced Panama City, Madrid, Miami. Amsterdam, Quito, Sao Paolo. Los Angeles, Dallas. Leather-jacketed men maneuvered baggage carts filled to teetering with duct-taped boxes and fraying luggage. Pigtailed girls dragged their candy-colored My Little Pony rollerboards, enveloped in tearful family reunions. I tried to guess where they came from, tried to steal a peek at their airline tags. MIA. GRU. BAQ.

It made me nervous, watching all these people, so happy to meet their families. It meant something, picking someone up. I had never picked up Andrea at LaGuardia, and she hadn't done the same for me. Neither of us had ever offered. It made no logical sense to make the trip, to wait at baggage claim holding a sign, or flowers. She didn't need that, nor did I.

Why would anyone do that?

My grandparents had always picked Sarah and me up at the airport. They'd meet us at the gate, back when that was allowed. Sarah and I would run down the jet bridge into their arms. We were alone, hurtling through space at six hundred miles an hour and suddenly a door opened and we were loved.

Around me, tearful reunions were happening. People hugged and wiped their eyes. Was that what heartfelt was like? Or was it all an act, people playing roles they'd learned from a script, a living soap opera with stage directions: *cry here.*

Andrea and I had lived along a different gradient. It was black and white: fighting/not fighting. Seething/not seething. Resigned/oblivious, drunk, or numb.

Along the window, travelers lingered and children scrawled their names on the foggy panes. My phone remained quiet. There had to be a flight home soon.

I didn't even know where we were going, just that we were catching another plane to somewhere near Ecuador and Peru. *South,* she'd said. Bogotá was somewhere in the middle of the country, a few hundred miles from any border.

Earlier, I had looked at Google Maps and tried to figure out our destination, but the area she'd described was a wash of green with small dots indicating tiny towns. They were connected by rivers, but it seemed, few roads. I wished I'd gotten the details from her, but what difference would it have made? Would I fly, alone, to a small Colombian village, with my twenty words of Spanish, and wander the streets until I found this shaman she was talking about?

Besides, I gave zero fucks about this shaman. This trip was my *fuck it*. I was chasing a beautiful young woman with tattooed ribs. Maybe I'd trip balls on some jungle mushrooms. But one day soon, we'd laugh about how we met and the chase that had ensued, lying in post-coital torpor.

She would have to show up first. I sipped my coffee and scanned the terminal. Each dark-haired woman brought a swell of hope to my throat, and an equal swell of disappointment as they proved not to be her. I reached for my phone to call her again, and a text popped up.

I'm late, she wrote. Then two more texts appeared. *I'm on my way back to the airport. I'll meet you at the plane.* She followed with the details, for a domestic flight that was due to leave in an hour on an airline I'd never heard of. I could go to the ticket counter on my way; she'd called ahead and made a reservation for me. All I had to do was pay.

Puerto Leguizamo. I looked on the map on my phone. It was a small speck on the hairline river that marked the frontier between Colombia and Peru, deep in a mossy green field that spanned borders. Ecuador was maybe fifty kilometers to the west. None of the village names that showed up on the map looked at all familiar.

Give zero fucks, I said to myself.

I tossed the rest of my coffee in the trash, hoisted my bag, and headed for the plane.

There was no Mariana at the gate, but I boarded the creaky turboprop, confident that she'd emerge from the halo of light at the entranceway. As the seats filled, my eyes darted to each passenger and to the few faces I could see outside the window. Perhaps I'd missed her; she might be behind me, or on the steps and just outside my view.

But the door shut, and no one else was coming. I stayed in my seat, teetering between fear and *fuck it*. There were no more texts. The plane rattled through the clouds and I stared out and rehearsed my Spanish phrases under the engines' drone. *Necesito un hotel. Necesito un taxi.* I would find a place to stay for the night and hope that Mariana showed, or got in touch. I stared at the seat in front of me and tried to ignore its worn edges. The plane was probably older than me.

The plane grazed the clouds. Through patches, swaths of green gave way to snaking rivers which gave way to more trees. We began to descend, and the trees parted, revealing small shacks and a tiny road. We shook with a gust and rose with an updraft before the plane bounced and ground to a halt on the fractured runway.

As the plane taxied, we approached something that looked like a shed. It was constructed of paint-flaked two-by-fours and concrete, corrugated metal and unreadable ads for scary hotels. This was not an airport. It should have had a different name. An airstrip, maybe. I glanced down at my phone but it showed no service.

¿Donde están los taxis?

Descending down the metal stairs I pushed the air aside like a warm velvet curtain. My step lagged; I was instantly tired and soaked in sweat. Charcoal perfumed the air, along with fumes from the plane, and some foreign earthy smell that I guessed might be the nearby river. I wiped my forehead with the fringe of my t-shirt, leaving behind a dark spot.

On the cracked tarmac, a young porter pulled a cart that looked meant for a donkey using his gloved hands, creaking it up to the plane to unload our luggage. He looked cheerful enough. He had the requisite fluorescent yellow vest although there was no traffic of which to speak. He dragged the cart with a teenager's overly confident gait.

The porter tugged at the door until it opened. He dumped the bags on the donkey cart until they were ready to spill over. My duffel bounced along, streaked with dirt and grease. It landed somewhere in the middle of the pile and I hoped the wooden bowl was safe. I tried to keep it in my sightline until the queue moved and I marched along the vaguely demarcated pathway to the exit. Just a track through the covered areas of the structure, it followed out onto a small walk where three wheeled moto-taxis idled.

I passed through, bewildered. The air was filled with Spanish chatter. I tried to catch a word or two.

Si. Gracias. Por supuesto.

None of my vocabulary mattered. *Galletas. Mochila. Dedo.*

My phone dinged. A picture was coming in from Mariana; it was taking a moment to load, and my heart thumped with excitement. I had done it. I was here. She had to be impressed. Maybe she was sending me a naked selfie. I pictured her in the massage room, about to unclasp her bra. Even in the unease, the heat and the crowd, I felt a familiar tingle.

The picture finished loading. It must have been a mistake. It was as if I was looking at an illustration, a painted depiction of something unreal. Leather, feathers, folds. An impressionist blur of shine and color, the borders between hues indistinct and shifting.

I blinked, and after a moment my eyes adjusted. The haze faded, like smoke dissipating into the sky, and the image began to resolve before snapping into focus. The screen showed an older man dressed in some ceremonial costume. His face was framed in dark hair, giving his brown skin an unnatural glow. A warm smile left creases around his eyes and mouth, and a crown of feathers sat atop his head, in bright yellows and reds. A necklace adorned with small bones hung from his neck. He was surrounded by broad green leaves, against a harsh blue sky. He was looking off, uninterested in the observer, or possibly unaware.

The tingle in my groin was gone.

A short text came in. *Taita Alberto*, it said.

I wrote her back. *Where are you?*

Spanish murmurs flowed through the crowd, rising to chatter as we filed into a metal-topped shed that looked like it was meant to contain livestock. It was cooler in the shade. I leaned against a crumbling concrete wall watching more passengers fall into the arms of their loved ones. I looked at my phone. Nothing else was coming through.

A throng buzzed around a concrete pen with a wooden half-door. The same neon-jacketed porter was tossing our bags over the walls. They landed on the pen's dirt floor and bounced before settling. Men scurried and grabbed and dragged the bags away as quickly as they had appeared.

My bag flew through the air, the hazy light catching the fabric at the peak of its arc, illuminating a streak of shiny black grease.

Lined-up bodies blocked my way. I stuck my arms through and snatched the duffel out of the crowd. It was filthy, like it had been tied to the plane and dragged along the runway. The crowd started to thin as people gather their things and jump into moto-taxis. I unzipped the bag and quickly check to make sure the wooden bowl was intact.

Nothing from Mariana. I was having trouble maintaining the *fuck it*. Was she that callous? That uncaring? She had to know I'd be helpless in Puerto Leguizamo. It seemed deliberately cruel and horrible. Still, I knew that the minute I saw her, I'd forget all of it.

A cluster of drivers waited by the muddy exit. Each one was disheveled in a different way; unlaced sneakers, paint-spattered jeans, a shirt not quite fastened over a hanging belly. They buzzed at each other like they'd had this conversation before.

One of them laughed out loud. He looked different from the others. His jeans were torn in a careful pattern, like they'd been designed that way. He wore a crisp pink dress shirt and a gold chain around his neck, and silver chains hung from his belt, leading to his wallet. His hair was gelled into a sharp peak. Most of the men had thick, unruly mustaches but his was short and plastered to his skin like he was a teenager with a grease problem.

I clutched my bag. A plaid-shirted driver, belly hanging over his cinched belt scurried over, a little bit of a waddle. *¿Puedo ayudarte?* I shook my head, staring at my phone and willing it to ring. He didn't seem to hear me, and grabbed at my bag. *Ven conmigo*, he said, and dragging my duffel along the ground.

I reached for the strap. It escaped my grip. The bag slipped through the thinning throng. There were still enough people to make it confusing. The driver disappeared from my view, and I began to panic—my breath, short, my heart pounding—until I glimpsed him throwing it into the back of a moto taxi.

"Hey," I shouted. I rifled through my limited vocabulary. "*¡Ayúdeme!*"

A space cleared around me. The driver looked at me, confused, and then took my bag from the back of his moto taxi and placed it on the ground. He mumbled a stream of Spanish and a few of the drivers near him laughed and everyone went back to what they were doing.

I marched over like I won and grabbed my bag, hoisting it onto my back. It was a heavy, awkward load, and I was already clammy with sweat. The drivers turned their backs to me like I was being shunned.

Fuck them. Give zero fucks. My lizard brain screamed *go home*. Instead, I scanned up and down the road. In one direction, it turned into dirt and ended at a copse up a small hill. To the left, moto taxis buzzed and women trudged pushing carts. What would Ram do? Hierro Acero would have had his own jet, his own tinted-window SUV.

I popped in my headphones and clicked the Ram app. Then I started to walk.

This is it, pal. Are you fucking happy?

The drivers ignored me. Street noise overtook the airport hum. With each step heat rose from the pavement. Every ray that fell from the sky beat into my head. I needed sunblock.

You're a quitter. That's why you're a fucking loser. Zero fucking balls. Scared of your own shadow.

I picked up my pace with my heavy duffel in tow but the women ahead of me disappeared into the distance at twice my speed. A moto taxi appeared, heading up the hill toward me. The driver squinted as he approached, trying to explain this strange creature to himself.

I was out of place, a pale white guy huffing a duffel bag, like a llama walking down Flatbush Avenue.

You worry too much about what other people think. You give way too many fucks. You back down. You're a fucking pussy, that's why your life looks the way it looks.

Cement block buildings peppered the landscape, dotted with unfamiliar foliage. A toddler girl in a faded Minnie Mouse tank top poked her head out from a doorway. She held a bent plastic bat in her hand, like a wiffle ball game went awry. She stared at me as I walked by, her other hand in her mouth.

Grow a fucking pair.

A teenage boy slipped past me on a bicycle. Our eyes locked as he moved by, his legs straining against the pedals as if being chased. He looked away and veered from a broken cinder block left in the road, almost tumbling into a drainage ditch before righting himself and speeding off.

I watched him grow smaller in the distance as Ram shouted his insults. *You're a whiny baby. Wah wah.*

Hey, mister.

Another voice filtered through Ram's shouts. I took out my headphones. Someone was saying something to me, in accented English. It was getting louder.

Hey, mister. Hey. Hey, mister. Hey.

I turned my head. Another moto-taxi rolled along the road. It was one of the drivers from the airport. I'd noticed him among the throng. Meticulous. Gold chains, the crisp pink shirt, the hair gel, flawless in the thick heat. The bike halted just ahead of me. The driver craned his head around and looked back at me through the canopy. The motor puttered, barely audible.

"¿*Como estas?*" He grinned, showing a gap behind his front teeth.

"Ummmm… *bueno,*" I said. "*Muy bueno.*"

He shut off the engine. "You are Mariana friend?" he said. "Mariana," he repeated.

I bristled, adjusting my bag. "Who are you?"

He mumbled an answer.

"*Coño?*" I asked.

He held my gaze. "No, *amigo.* Toño." He gestured to the back seat. "*Ven aquí. Por favor.* Come."

I looked back up the road toward the airport. I hadn't heard the plane leave. I wanted to go back, wave my passport, beg for a seat back to Bogotà. I wanted to find a nice airport hotel in Bogotà, a shower, a friendly shuttle ride back and forth, airport food, airport coffee. I could be back in the US in a day, day and a half.

"Come," he said. "I take you to see *Taita*." His voice carried no urgency in his voice, no pressure.

"¿Donde está Mariana?" I asked.

"*No sé. Ella está viniendo, supongo.*"

I understood the gist of what he said—some of the words, his body language. She was coming, more or less. I needed to chill. *Stop being such a pussy.*

I stopped in my tracks. Is that what they do? An American shows up. Why else would one be in this little armpit village? Easy mark. *Ven conmigo. Por favor.* Next thing I know I'm spitting blood at an ATM with a gun in my ribs.

I'd read a little bit about the town on my phone while in line the Bogotá airport. Puerto Leguizamo used to be rebel territory. Even now, guidebooks said to steer clear. But Mariana hadn't even told me to *ten cuidado*.

A loud burp rose from my belly. Toño laughed and I cracked a smile. "Ok," I said. "*Vamos.*"

It wasn't clear whether we were in a store, or a warehouse, or someone's garage. Some of the elements were familiar: Metal shelves. A babyfaced, big-titted cashier. Refrigerators with glass doors, but dark and mostly empty: a few bottles of Poker beer, a can of *kola champagne*. Pillow-sized bags of rice stacked on a pallet, wrapped in ribbons of plastic. Giant doors on rails had been rolled open, letting enough light in to see the front sections. The back of the store was lit by a single flickering fluorescent tube.

Toño followed me around with a wobbling toddler-sized cart. It made him look like an uncostumed clown. He grabbed items and tossed them into the basket, mumbling at me in mixed English and Spanish. Toño sang a tune to himself, something I'd heard, but couldn't place. He looked relaxed, like he'd done this before, but several times he halted mid-aisle and U-turned to grab something we forgot. "You need *arroz*," he said.

He loaded heavy plastic sacks of drinking water into the cart. *Agua.* As far as I could understand, we would go see Taita afterwards. My lizard brain tried to process the scam. He was going to make me buy tons of groceries and then ditch me. Why he would do that rather than just rob me of my pesos is unclear.

We stacked cans of tuna, dried beans, bunches of green plantains, peanut butter, coffee.

Our way out, Toño turned around and led me to the back. Stacks of rubber boots in plastic bags were pyramided on metal shelves. He gestured to them. "You buy," he said, straightening his still-crisp shirt.

I picked up a bag. The sizes were unfamiliar. The boots were all utility, and sludge-colored. I sat down on an over-turned bucket, sliped off my sandals and tried them on until I found a pair that fit my sweaty feet. I put the rest back in their bags and on the shelf for the next poor sucker.

I looked to Toño. "*Terminado?*"

Toño tossed a brown brick of *panela* into the cart and then gestured to the cashier.

She was on the phone and we were an interruption. She was cute and young—sparkly braces, a little extra flesh hanging over her tight jeans—and she could have been anywhere, but she was here.

We waited for a moment but she turned away to continue her call. I smiled at Toño, my *what can you do?* smile. He shook his head and barked something at her in rapid-fire Spanish—I made out *muévelo*—and she jerked to attention, and dropped her phone next to the register before grabbing our items and punching keys.

Toño placed each item into a waxy plantain carton as she rang it up, the water sacks all gathered into a mesh bag that held onions. The cashier finished, and gave me a blank stare.

"*Nada mas,*" I said. "That's all."

Toño pointed to the green numbers on the register. "Pay," he said.

Of course. That was the price. But there were too many digits. My heart leapt: a scam. A ripoff. Danger. I held my scream and did the quick math. Pesos, not dollars. More like fifty bucks, including the boots.

I let out my breath.

My grandparents had kept cartons of Pepsi Light in their hall closet. He'd worked for some company that had a contract with PepsiCo, and he was at their plant every month or two. Each time, he came home with the trunk of his brown Buick LeSabre filled with Pepsi Light. *They had extra.* I had accepted this without question until I was twelve. I was visiting them and Pop was unloading the car using a metal granny cart. The cardboard cases painted the car's enormous trunk.

"That's a lot of soda," I said. I reached into the trunk to help him but he shooed me away. It was an unspoken rule: he was in charge of all lifting and carrying in the family. "Why do you get so much?"

He grunted as he placed two cases into the cart.

We went inside and I watched him put away the soda. He moved the older cases out, placed the new ones in and replaced the originals top.

"You've gotta take what you can get, Alan. Be on the lookout," he said.

I looked at the tower of cans, my grandfather hunched over managing his spoils. I was at once embarrassed and resigned. That was our lot: scam or be scammed.

With Toño's help, I loaded the groceries into the back of his moto-taxi. The onion sack felt like lifting a small adult; it flopped, dead weight. The sun crawled a little lower but it was still hot. I hopped in and looked at my phone, not expecting anything, and then my heart skipped to see a missed call from Mariana. Fuck.

I dialed her right back but it went straight to voicemail. I didn't bother leaving a message.

Toño drove the moto-taxi down a bumpy road that ended by the river. A rusted-out house-sized boat with a flat bottom sat halfway in the water, angled on a concrete landing. I couldn't tell if it was in use or had been abandoned. Battered canoes sat tied in the muck.

Toño pulled up next to a once-white two story building and shut off the motor. A toddler sat on the steps in a grimy tank top and no pants. He was eating something out of a ceramic bowl with his hands. I tried not to look at his dick.

Across the street, a chipped blue storefront was framed by white plastic chairs. A paper sign advertising *Cerveza Poker* was tacked to the door: three young men carrying a giant, ice-coated bottle, taller than any of them. A bad Photoshop job, not meant to look real. *Para plan ahorro, La Grande.* The men were laughing and looked determined.

Toño hoisted the box of groceries onto his belt buckle. He gestured toward the steps. I lifted the onion sack of water onto my shoulder and staggered behind him. The toddler ignored me as I passed.

Toño bumped against the door at the top and it opened. I followed him past a dark living room cluttered with boxes and mismatched furniture. Muffled singing came from behind a closed door. It was a high-pitched man's voice, but I couldn't make out the words.

Past that was a small kitchen. Toño put the box on top of a low cabinet and gestured to the corner. I dropped the bag of water and followed him back into the living room where he sank into the white leather sofa. He patted the cushion next to him. "*Espera.*"

I sat and scanned the room. A toddler's telephone—a rolling toy with eyes and a face—poked out from under the couch. Paint-scarred wooden building blocks formed a pile that looked like it had been stacked and then demolished, like a castle after a pitched battle. Next to that were a pile of tattered books. A mouse held a chocolate chip cookie on the cover of one. *Si le das una galleta a un ratón,* it said. *Galleta* was cookie, I remembered.

There was a chunky crystal ashtray piled with yellowed, unfiltered butts, detritus washed up on an ashen beach. As we quieted, the voice behind the door got clearer. A low rhythm underlined the flowing melody. It sounded like rough sanding, like someone smoothing out an uneven plank by hand. I wish I knew the word for sandpaper. *Papel de* something.

The voice behind the door sang in short cadences. It quavered at the upper register. The few words that came through had an unfamiliar sound. It didn't sound like Spanish.

"What is that?" I asked.

Toño shrugged, noncommittal.

I stared at the door. The rhythm continued, unwavering, the high voice floating over the pattern. Bright light flowed through the front door, airborne dust illuminated in its path.

Dust was always there but only seen when conditions are right. I followed a fleck in the air, floating on some unseen current until it went invisible.

The voice slowed and the shaking followed. Then the rhythm stopped but the voice went on, singing short phrases. Without the pulsing background, the voice became clearer and got lower.

There was something comforting in the singing, like a lullaby I'd heard before.

What the fuck was I doing here, on a shitty leather sofa in a shitty apartment in a shitty town far from anything I knew. I couldn't even go home if I wanted to. I wanted to go back to where it had all started. When had I first fucked up? That first lap dance in a dark back room that smelled like drugstore perfume? A tattooed stripper rubbing against my dick to some clichéd stripper song? *Don't you wish your girlfriend was hot like me?*

Or was it before that?

It wasn't Andrea's fault. It couldn't have gone any other way. We were a perfect match, pawns to our past, playing out predetermined patterns. A fucking cliché from a Springsteen song.

I could have banged my head against a wall for being so stupid. Joe had been naked and helpless. I could have mashed his fat face into the bigscreen TV. I could have puked right in Gene's office and then walked the fuck out. And fuck Mariana. It was cruel, sending me to a foreign country, knowing I didn't know the language.

I felt the anger rise in my chest; it was familiar, and normally, it fed upon itself and grew and snowballed. I was used to that. It would build and take shape. A life of its own. Listening to Ram fed it, too. The grinding music, the constant assault, the *fucks* and *shits*. Psyching us up to *kick ass*.

But here, as I listened to the rough percussion, my expectation gave way; the feelings that usually became more and more real as my story turned into the truth, started to evade my grasp and evaporate. I couldn't keep them going. All I had left was the rhythmic hum, the stagnant air on my skin, and the town's faint, fecund scent of charcoal and must.

The voice behind the door slowed to a few, drawn out syllables. There a was grunt, like a deep exhalation, and then silence, except for a low electrical murmur. And then the door swung open. Toño jumped to his feet in anticipation. I creaked to my feet, nervous.

A man stepped out, slate hair peeking out from underneath a camouflage trucker cap. His short-sleeved white dress shirt was pressed, and a lit cigarette dangled from one hand. He was older, maybe in his fifties, but his skin was smooth and his face looked rested.

The man mumbled something to Toño. I couldn't hear him. Toño darted into the next room and came out with a wiry middle-aged woman on his arm. She was dabbing at her eyes with a tissue, a wide grin on her face. As she passed the man in the cap she touched his arm and whispered *gracias, Taita.* The man in the cap nodded to her as she left.

"*De nada,*" he said, like he'd just made her a sandwich.

I'd been told I make people nervous. Andrea had said it to me more than once. I couldn't argue that it was impossible; I saw people like that every day in New York, surrounded by a field of agitation, like the waves of magnetism that surrounded the earth. I wondered if animals could detect those vibrations, like the coming of an earthquake.

But if those people existed, then it could be true that there were people around whom there was a field of peace. I'd experienced moments like that; coming into my grandmother's home, the rush of perfume and stale cigarette smoke. Even in the chaos, there was comfort.

The man in the cap stood, unmoving, watching the woman depart, and in his presence my usual chatter melted away.

Toño escorted her down the stairs.

"*Taita*," I said quietly. I stood still, suddenly self-conscious, not sure what to do, what to look at. I tried to remember the image Mariana had sent me on the phone but it was a blur of feathers and beads. The low thrum stopped. Birds chirped and buzzed, uninterested.

I stammered out some words in my halting Spanish. "*Hola, Taita. Soy Alan. Vengo de Nueva York.*"

The older man stood back a step and looked at me coldly. The creases on his face seemed to deepen, as if he was worried about something he saw on my face. But a smile crept across his mouth, breaking into a wide grin. "David Silver," he said, laughing. He extended his hand. I grasped it with relief and shook.

"No," I said. "*Soy* Alan."

He shook his head and laughed. Toño came back inside and Taita shouted to him like he was announcing a jackpot. "*Se parece a David Silver, ¿no?*"

Toño grabbed my shoulder and turned me to face him. "*Sí,* David Silver," Toño laughed. "*Beverly Hills, 90210. Nos encanta mucho.*" He looked at the cheap watch on his wrist and excitedly pointed at the boxy television. "*Vamos a mirar, ahorita.*"

"*Mierda.*" Taita picked up a remote from the sofa and clicked and the screen glowed with a commercial.

I was in the middle of nowhere with a shaman who thought I looked like a character from a 90's TV show. We were about to watch *Beverly Hills, 90210* together. I came to South America for this.

I forced some words out. "*¿Habló con Mariana?*"

Taita sat on the sofa. "*Siéntate,* David Silver." He patted a spot next to him. "*No te preocupes.*"

I sat down on the cracked leather as Taita lit another cigarette. Toño sat down, too, and glanced over to me.

"*Calmate,*" Toño said.

The room had filled with a haze, a warm glow as the sun streamed through the doorway. Taita's face was placid as he smoked, and the show's guitar-driven theme music began. He clicked the remote and turned the volume up until it distorted.

I took out my phone and stared at its screen. There were texts I hadn't read, from Mom and Sarah, and one from Andrea asking about her headphones. But still nothing from Mariana. I started to send her a new message, but Taita plucked my phone from my hand and slipped it into his breast pocket, behind his cigarettes. "*Calmate,*" he shouted, over the TV.

The screen flickered with the fuzzy satellite signal. Toño pointed to the TV, to gather my attention. Unlike the flat screens we had at home, it was comically large plastic box with cables coming out the back, atop a cheap glass-fronted pressboard frame. The screen was smudged with greasy streaks, possibly from whatever kids inhabited the place.

I listened to the dialogue in Spanish, dubbed voices that sounded nothing like the original actors. Their lips moved with no regard for the sounds.

Taita sat next to me, chuckling softly. "*Ya he visto este,*" he yelled.

Toño nodded. "*Yo también.*" He pointed at the screen as an actor appeared. "David Silver," he said, grinning. He repeated himself. "David Silver!"

"*¿Donde está Mariana?*" I asked, but my words were muffled by the TV and the men's laughter.

Chapter Nine

My flip-flops sank into the muddy bank, and muck slid between my toes. I hoped there was a hot shower where we were going, or at least a garden hose. I wasn't good with grime or sweat. I belonged in air conditioning, like the rest of my family.

The river water glowed in the dense heat. Taita unraveled a length of grimy rope holding a worn canoe in place on the marshy shore. He gestured to the mesh bags containing our food and other supplies. They rested on a dry section of earth. I lifted one, a cinderblock of meat-red beans poking from its opening. An angry ache blossomed in my lower back. I adjusted, the pain backed off, and I wobbled the bag toward the boat's lip. I glanced around to see who was watching.

"Where are we going?" I asked, in English; I couldn't find the words in Spanish, or maybe I'd just given up. *You give up too easy*, Ram had said. *You hit a speed bump and you act like it's a fucking mountain.* His words bounced around inside my head, whether I wanted to hear them or not.

Taita grabbed the bag with no effort and set it in place in the middle of the boat. The boat barely quivered. Another canoe putted by, a long shaft extending from its motor that skimmed the water at an angle. Above the treeline, the sky began to grey, but the air was still heavy with heat.

I tried again. "¿Mariana? *¿Ella está viniendo?*"

Taita grunted something in response.

Toño marched down the hill with another bag in one hand and a boat motor balanced on his shoulder, its bulbous red head resting against his own. The shaft was like a spindly tree, absurdly long, its tiny propellor nearly scraping the ground. Toño handled it with ease, like he'd probably done a million times before. I'd have dumped it in the mud in record time, snapped the shaft or banged the metal frame into my own skull.

He set the bag down on a dry spot and climbed into the boat. Instead of rocking, it stood as still as if he were a ghost floating in the hull. I imagined myself climbing in and falling straight into the muck, along with all our supplies.

"*No puedo nadar,*" I said, but no one was listening.

Toño locked the motor in place, the shaft tilted above the water. He connected the gas line, which was in turn connected to a fuel tank Taita had carried with him from the house. I had been curious about this when I saw it. Why was the fuel in the house? Was he worried about crime? I wish I knew enough Spanish to ask. *Preoccupes? Preoccupado? Crimen?* I knew that whatever I said would sound stupid. I filed the question away for Mariana's arrival. She would either know the answer or interpret the question for me.

I hated asking stupid questions. Sarah had a knack for mocking my mistakes. *It's not a "blessing in the skies," Alan.* My question wasn't important, anyway.

Toño grabbed the rest of the supplies and waved me into the boat. He bounced in and out like he was walking on solid ground. I stepped in carefully, panicked with wobble until Toño clamped his hand on my wrist. I lowered myself onto a splintery wooden seat and craned my neck around to see Taita tug the motor to life. It gasped and then chugged along. Taita dipped the tarnished shaft into the water and we slipped out into the river like a crocodile. The sun spotlit the clouds, its aura barely visible just a few degrees above the treetops.

A few hundred yards out and the canoe traffic faded as we buzzed along. Our boat passed a few larger vessels—slow-moving freight barges, a multilevel passenger ship the size of a school bus with ratty clotheslines tied across the deck, a healthy-looking mutt barking at every boat that went by. A mop-haired man in cutoff jeans shorts smoked a cigarette on the bow. He was shirtless and bore a collection of blurry tattoos, greenish like trails of oxidized copper. The man flicked his butt into the water. The way he looked at me as he flicked it implied disrespect, or dismissal. I cringed but said nothing.

I took it personally, but I took everything that way. The slate sky started to hiss and then tiny bullets of spray popped onto the river's brown surface. It was directed at me; the sky had been clear all day.

Toño sat on the bow, his face contorted in thought. I looked back at Taita, his eyes squinting against the rain. His black hair whipped in the wind and the spray pinged my skin. It was hard to tell whether it was from the sky or from our wake.

The canoe rocked on the water. We bounced along the approaching placid surface, our clear path. Birds lit on the flora around us, dipped down to grab an insect. I held myself steady on the canoe's frame.

The water rippled, and I suddenly remembered something. I shouted at Toño. ¿Hay delfines? He ignored me. I had heard there were pink dolphins in the rivers around here, but it was hard to imagine.

I grabbed the seat to steady myself and as I did, a vision overtook me: my throat filled with brown river water, gagging, my flailing form sucked into the current with a gurgle. An outstretched hand the last bit above the surface, spinning. Critters chattering in celebration at the coming bounty. I saw it from the riverbank, as though separate from my body, an observer watching the cycle of life play itself out.

No one would know for a while. Who would Taita call? If my passport went under with me, he wouldn't even find out my name. Mariana certainly didn't know much.

Mom would panic when I didn't return her calls. Sarah would leave increasingly desperate messages. *Call me, you fucking fuck.* Even considering it made me feel loved. I wondered if Andrea would be upset?

Mom would find out, eventually. She found out everything. My name would turn up in a computer; I'd left the country, like her ex-husband. She would make it about her. A South Florida news anchor, dark suit, blue tie, coiffed hair, somber tone. *A tragic death.* You should never leave the country. Cut to Mom, stoic, veiled. *He knew better.*

I hoped she never found out I'd had a layover in Fort Lauderdale and didn't come to see her.

What, are you crazy? she would have asked if I'd even mentioned Colombia, much less a remote river village. I'd have had to listen to stories about parasites and meningitis, about murders and rebels and organ theft. But I was safe, according to Wikipedia. There was a truce, or a treaty, or something.

I would leave that part out if I ever had the opportunity to recount the story, to Ram, or Avi, or Andrea.

The motor whined as Taita zipped down the waterway. In Bogotá, I had looked up what kinds of dangers lurked in the river. I translated keywords and searched for them in the articles. *Pelligro, cocodrilo.* I had hoped for a response like *no search results found*, but instead there were page after page of news stories and photos. *Caimán, piraña.*

I stopped reading.

Hurtling past the mudbank, I scanned for crocs sunning themselves in the dirt. Instead, I found scrappy-looking birds picking at feathered carrion, twisted driftwood and muddy reeds. The rain stung my eyes and I wiped it away with my fist. The sky's grey deepened as the weak sun threatened to hide behind the treeline.

Bouncing down the river, I sucked in the air, exhilarated. How long had it been? An hour? More? Each patch of brush, each shack filled me with *deja vu.*

Ahead, the clouds ended like they'd been cut with a table saw and the grey sky gave way to a sudden hazy blue. The rain slowed, an occasional drop stinging my skin or pinging the river's surface.

I stared at the green and brown riverbank as it rushed by. I was mesmerized by the scenery, the muck and fronds and the occasional shack or canoe. The engine's whine subsided to a low hum and the propeller burbled in the shallow water. I looked up with a start. Ahead and to our right was a steep, sludge-covered hill. Unsound stairs made of bowed scrap wood rose from the water, a rope drawn tight on each side as a handhold.

A young man in frayed cutoff shorts and a once-white tank top stood halfway up the steps. Black rubber boots reached to his knees. He waved at the boat and walked down to meet us. I watched him swagger, a swarthy stubble patch on his chin, arms veined with muscle. My heart sank.

Taita cut the engine and we coasted up onto the mud. He jumped out with a small splash. Taita grabbed a rope tied to the canoe and wrapped it around a broken-off stake.

Toño was already out, hoisting our gear onto the steps. The guy in the cutoffs glanced at me with no expression. I was irrelevant. He grabbed some bags and bounded up the hill. I looked away.

Taita's hands were full, too, so I wobbled my way to the front of the boat and stepped onto the mudbank. My sandals made sucking sounds as I lifted my feet. I hoisted my bag onto my back, an unbalanced load, and the wooden tuna bowl inside dug into my shoulder blade. The young man was already heading back down and brushed past me. Fuck him. I grabbed the nearest bag—the onion sack of water—and threw it over my shoulder along with my duffel and grunted up the steps. My back twinged. It was almost more than I could handle. I huffed and struggled to put one foot in front of the other to reach where he was standing. He shuffled aside, just enough for me to pass.

I caught my breath. *Fine.* I forced a smile. *"Me llamo Alan."*

He nodded and let me go by. "Miguel," he said, and then he walked down to the boat and grabbed another bag. He strode up the steps at full speed, practically skipping.

A few more gasps and I made it to the top. A narrow, gravel pathway lead past a woodpile to a large wooden shack high on stilts. A skinny chicken and her babies pecked around the edge of the path. On the flat ground, the weight on my back was more manageable.

Some of our bags were on the ground by rickety wooden steps that lead to the doorway. But there was no door; a curtain was pulled aside revealing a spare, dark interior. I dropped my duffel and the water sack and looked at where we were.

The shack was one of four in a row, each almost identical. I wondered why they were on stilts; after climbing all those steps I couldn't imagine the river rising this high. Across from the houses was a basketball half-court, a faded backboard and cracked cement. A freshly-painted arc marked the three-point zone.

I turned back to the steps. Taita carried two overstuffed bags. He stopped in front of the woodpile for a moment before continuing. Toño came up behind him, a bag in one hand and the motor over his shoulder. He spied the woodpile, too. He eyed Taita, smiling. Both men dropped their loads by the shack as Miguel came up the stairs. He grinned at Toño and waved for me to join them. I stood next to Miguel and waited. Toño nodded at me.

Taita kicked aside some branches and already-split wood to reveal a thick tree bough. It was gnarled and crooked, hacked at each end like it had been cut with a pocket knife. He picked up an axe from the ground that seemed to come from nowhere.

Taita examined the axe blade, running his thumb along the edge. He wiped it on his pant leg, and apparently satisfied, swung it at the bough. The limb bounced in the dirt as tiny chips flew into the air. Taita pulled the axe for another swing, leaving a small gouge in the wood. He swung again, and the blade landed right in the groove, spraying dust.

Toño stood, riveted, like he was watching a fucking magic show.

The wood settled on the ground before Taita whacked it again and again. He stopped and wiped his forehead with his calloused hand. A deep "V" was carved into the branch.

Miguel nudged me. I looked over at him, startled. He was grinning with excitement. He pointed at the wood, giving a thumbs-up. Toño raised his thumb in response.

Taita swung and chopped it once more, and then he stepped on one side of the wood and pulled the other toward him, snapping it in half.

Miguel raised his fist and let out a whoop. Toño clapped his hands together and patted Taita on the back. Taita nodded, satisfied, and dropped the axe on the ground next to the split halves. The men retreated to the house in an air of celebration.

I looked around. The sky was passing into dusk and the clouds had disappeared. I was helpless, mostly. I could not even shit without a guide. I wanted to ask a hundred questions—*where are we sleeping? What kind of weird shaman shit are we doing? Have you heard from Mariana?*—but who would I ask? My Spanish was useless. And what did it matter? Most of my questions were useless, too, except for those that addressed my immediate needs: *Can I have some food? Where is the bathroom?*

I stared at the open doorway to the shack. The curtain hung across the entrance and then Miguel pushed it aside and hopped down. He whistled at me, sharp and shrill. "*Ponte las botas,*" he shouted.

It sounded like an order. "*¿Cómo?*"

He pointed at one of the bags on the ground. "*Botas, tonto.*" *Botas.* Boots. He dug through the supplies, looking for something.

My boots were there, the new ones wrapped in plastic. I took off my flip-flops. My feet were caked with dirt, but I slipped them in. My skin began to sweat, and the rough inside of the boots rubbed against my toes.

Miguel shoved a bundle of raggedy clothes into an oversized backpack and waved me along. "*Vamos,*" he said, and he started walking down the path, towards a thicket of trees. I clipped my sandals onto my duffel and lifted it onto my shoulders, jogging to follow him. He looks back and points. "*¿El agua?*"

The onion sack of water sat where I had left it. "You're kidding?" I said, shaking my head. But he was gone already, marching down the path.

Fuck. I doubled back to the water and grunted to get it onto my shoulder, the duffel across my back. The boots immediately dug into my feet; I'd barely taken a step and I could feel the blisters starting to rise. Mom had always told me to save my receipts, but I didn't have one for the boots. Nordstrom's would take anything back, receipt or not, another fact long-hammered into my skull. Maybe they'd take the boots.

Miguel was a hundred yards ahead of me and had begun to disappear into the treeline. I hustled. Each bounce in my step stabbed into my heels and ankle, and the top edge of the boots scraped just behind my knee. My feet slipped, slick with sweat, stinging the broken skin.

There was no movement from the shack. I turned and shouted to Miguel. "*¿Cuando ellos van?*" but he either didn't hear me or he was ignoring me, or maybe my Spanish was so piss-poor that he was offended.

I kept walking.

I rocked side to side in a frayed, woven hammock tied to the rafters of a large wooden shack. There were shaky chest-high walls and a corrugated roof, and the empty space between them left a five foot gap around most of the room. T-shirts drooped from sagging clotheslines like tired old men. There was still dimming light, enough to gaze out on the livestock pen on one side. The corral looked like it had been made of scrap wood, with gaps and knots and warped sections that seemed unsafe or at least, insufficient to keep the animals penned in. A small, patchy horse squished manure and mud underfoot. On the other side, rolling, tree-spotted hills meandered to the horizon. A wide thicket of deep-green treetops floated a few hundred yards in the distance.

The main space was filled with a half-dozen hammocks like mine, covered in thick netting that bunched on the ropes like caterpillar tents. There were two small rooms jigsawed from scrap wood at the shack's center. Off to one side was an open kitchen, with a smoking iron stove filled with ashen remnants. A low glow warmed the room.

A young woman with a braided plait swept the floor with a tattered broom, its handle secured with silvery tape. The kids played nearby. A gap-toothed boy who looked about five was wearing a mustard colored mock turtleneck that came to his thighs. His colorful superhero briefs poked out from underneath. The girl—maybe his sister—was a couple of years younger. She wore pink pajamas with a cotton candy number "2" on the chest. I thought they belonged to Miguel; he seemed familiar with them, although he didn't pay them much attention. He had patted them on the head as he passed but was otherwise all workhorse business.

Mismatched plates and cups were stacked on a wooden shelf, and an open package of crumbling *panela* sat forgotten on top of a plastic chair. A drum of rainwater was perched on a wooden frame above a makeshift sink, the furrowed roof positioned to run off into the container.

We'd walked an hour, at least, to find this place, through thick vegetation and thigh-high mud that had found its way into my boots and had squished against my raw heels. I had fallen more than once, dumped my duffel into puddles and scraped my shins against rotting logs. I trailed Miguel the whole way, but he was far enough ahead to avoid small talk.

I'd hiked a couple of times at Camp Beth Elohim, but those paths were well-worn and I'd only had to carry my military-style canteen. It was natural, but contained, which was the way I preferred it. That was what I thought of as nature: the manicured loop around Prospect Park, a canopy of flowering trees along 9th Street, near the F train, a supervised jaunt along a manmade pond.

I rocked in my hammock, enveloped in mosquito netting. Miguel had seen my Deep Woods Off and laughed. He'd handed me a water bottle full of brown liquid. He mimed spreading it on my skin, and so I did. In the dusklight the dark potion left broad streaks across my arms and legs. It smelled like tobacco and alcohol and something chemical, and it stung where my skin was raw. The repellant did the opposite; each time I stepped outside the cocoon, mosquitoes feasted on my exposed flesh. I slapped at the back of my neck, my calves, my forearms, and scratched at the welts. I longed for my aerosol can of chemical poison, but was ashamed to take it out.

Around the room the other hammocks were still and empty. I heard Miguel and the woman talking in the kitchen area but couldn't make out anything they said. She'd been looking after the kids; I assumed she was Miguel's wife.

We hadn't eaten, and there was no sign of food being prepared. The kids seemed to have disappeared. My phone showed no bars. I breathed, willing myself to remain motionless. The hammock swayed and the shadows extended until the room was nearly dark.

How had everything had fallen apart so quickly? I had been doing okay. I was making a living—not a great living, but enough. When had we crossed the line? It was before the strip clubs, before the counseling, before the handjobs. What accounted for the downturn? What led to this, shack in the middle of fucking nowhere, a hundred word Spanish vocabulary, and a mosquito bloodletting?

Still, I had to take responsibility. I was the one rubbing my face between silicone tits night after night. I was the one getting jerked off by strangers. Ram was right about that.

Maybe Mom had been right, too. She'd told me the truth, once, when things started getting serious with Andrea. I'd made a mistake, Mom had said, Andrea was a *shiksa*, and we were doomed. *Why can't you just go on J-Date?* She had started reading to me from their website. *Its mission is about strengthening the Jewish community. What could be bad about that, sustaining Jewish traditions? They're good traditions!* I was a catch, she'd said. A nice Jewish boy like me. Not like my father, the tax evader, on the run from the IRS. He was an anomaly.

If I'd just gone on J-Date I wouldn't have been clawing at my itchy legs in a hammock in fucking rebel territory under a mosquito net waiting for a girl who would probably never show up and if she did she might never fuck me anyway and it certainly wouldn't be here in this hammock.

Mom would be upset. Worried, more than anything.

What would Ram say? Maybe I'd get a pat on the back for having the balls to come. I wished I could text him, or even Avi. But my phone might as well have been a brick in my pocket. I'd turned it off to save battery; there were no outlets to be seen, and no generator.

The night grew darker, until the sky's purplish glow turned to black. Clicks and murmurs began to arise from the grass and trees, from insects and frogs—things that belonged here. I fumbled my way to the outhouse for a pee, teetering on warped boards laid across swaths of mud and swatting away the bugs. As my eyes adjusted to the starlight and crescent moon, I noticed the makeshift horse fence I'd seen when I arrived. In the daylight, the horses were drawn and skittish; they'd retreated to the far edges of their trampled enclosure.

But in the dark, they were emboldened. Maybe they couldn't sense my presence, or maybe they chose to ignore it. Under the cover of night, their hubris emerged and they wandered closer to me and to the fence. From the scrappy outhouse's falling-down doorway, I could see their enormous shadows ghost through the vegetation. They were harmless, I knew, but their size implied threat, their near-silence intimidating among the chirps and croaks that emerged from the dirt.

An acrid fog wafted through the shack. I held my breath, stood at the wooden hole and let loose. The urine sizzled at the bottom of a deep hole. The hut was a respite from the bugs; they probably couldn't stand the rank air.

I looked around for a place to wash my hands, but there was no sink. Mom would have *plotzed*. She had taught me well: wash your hands, don't run with a knife or scissors, never put them in my mouth. I knew not to swim for half an hour after eating, and to reapply sunscreen. I carried my wallet in my front pocket, and when strangers on the street in Brooklyn asked for directions, I stepped back and shouted my advice to avoid getting robbed.

I should have known better. I could have brought Wet Wipes, or Purell.

In her pre-Crossfit days, those were Mom's priorities. Be careful.

I sniffled. An ammonia-scented draft caught my nose. I snorted and sucked in a deep lungful of outhouse air. The smell landed with a flutter, and then a punch. My guts heaved, spewing spit and hack into the hole. I reeled out of the shed before taking another breath. I banged the door open and planted my feet in the muck.

Outside, the air was fetid and close, but breathable. Divebombed by a mosquito wolfpack, I stepped back again before taking another gulp. It was fresher. I gazed into the dark and waved away the bugs. Shifting silhouettes could have been inanimate shadows, or equine forms, or ghosts from my imagination. The outhouse was already veiled in the weak starlight, a hazy outline against the black night.

A whisper began, a rhythmic rush. It floated above me like it was caught on the wind, before its direction took shape. The sound came from the house above, like a quiet crunch of dry leaves on an autumnal day, golden and red-hued foliage fallen into neatly humped piles, marched upon in a perfect and escalating pattern.

I looked up at the shack, a few yards away. A faint candle flicker glowed through the gap between the wall and the roof, and as the whisper grew louder, the light grew brighter.

I stepped out of the mud and onto the boards. They squirmed beneath my feet, and I extended my arms in the classic tightrope walker's pose, heightening the drama, until I reached the bottom of the creaky steps. The bugs were gone, except those swarming in the house's glow. I teetered up the steps, and onto the deck.

The room hung with shadows and light, the hammocks moving like fan blades among candles' glow. Two figures, obscured by netting and darkness, sat in cheap plastic chairs against the far wall. At their feet on the wooden floor were two people sitting crosslegged: an adult man and a child. Their faces were hidden, but as I came closer I saw the boy's yellowish shirt. Miguel was next to him; he heard me come in and turned briefly, gesturing to the floor at his side.

The rhythm was louder, like a rush of reeds in the wind, but it had no source. Instead, it seemed to fill the room from every direction. I stepped closer.

Taita was in one of the chairs, his head wrapped in a tall crown whose feathers glowed in primary colors in the low light. An embroidered shirt in bold green and gold, bright yellow and deep blue echoed the crown. It was draped over his shoulders, over a grey long-sleeved shirt. A necklace of olive-sized wooden beads hung from his throat, held by worn thread. He looked ahead, but didn't acknowledge my approach.

At his side was an even older man. He was mostly toothless, with only a flash of yellow nub on either side of his lower jaw, and a hanging kernel from the top. He squinted into the light of the lone candle in between the two of them. He was dressed like Taita, only more ornately, with ropes of different colored wooden beads and an even taller crown. His skin was unwrinkled except around his eyes, where deep creases channeled along the temples. The rhythm quieted, like the wind had lost its force.

Miguel gestured at me again, and his face was open and friendly. I sat down next to him, with the boy on his other side. He peered around and smiled at me. He was gap toothed, too.

Taita reached for something on the ground and pulled it onto his lap. In that wild setting, it was impossible to fathom what he'd grabbed. It looked unreal; we were in a place where almost everything was from the earth—trees and grass and cattle and fire and thatched roofs and mud—and I expected consistency—plants, feathers, a primitive drum or even a modern tambourine—any of these would have made sense. As I squinted into the candlelight, the shape on Taita's lap looked more foreign to me than the crown on his head. It was a strange, uniform shade of brown, a blur that crinkled with his movement, standing straight in his lap as if of its own accord.

Taita's rough hands slid along its sides, and the brown wrapping crumpled; it was only a plastic bag, the flimsy kind you'd get in a bodega. Inside was a soda bottle, oversized and bullet-shaped. Its label was torn off, and it was filled nearly to the top with a light brown liquid. It was like an alien totem, the unveiling of an artifact so ancient, it appeared modern. But it was just a soda bottle.

Taita turned it over and then back upright, and then did so again. Whatever was inside moved with the consistency of grainy syrup.

My heart fluttered. I turned to Miguel. "*¿Qué estamos haciendo?*" I said in a whisper. What are we doing? "*¿Qué es eso?*" What is that?

Miguel ignored me and leaned away very slightly. A moth fluttered frantically between us and curved around the candles before retreating into the shadows. I scratched at my calves by instinct, but the mosquitoes had stopped biting.

Taita turned the bottle over again.

I repeated myself, a little louder. "*Taita,*" I said, "*¿qué estamos haciendo?*" The flutter turned into a thump. Who could I call? I was trapped, at least for the night. In the morning, I could hike back to the river and find someone to take me somewhere. I could flag a passing boat, wave my pesos and shout *por favor*. At home, I was poor, but here my dwindling stack of pesos meant something. If I could get back to Puerto Leguizamo, or anyplace with a bus, or even cellphone reception, I'd be okay.

Taita looked up at me and placed the bottle on his lap. His eyes wrinkled like he was trying to figure something out. The old man leaned towards him and murmured something I couldn't make out. Taita laughed out loud, and then nodded at me, as if he were about to address my question. "*Todo está perfecto,*" he said. "*Relajarte, parce.*"

"*Rela—*"

"*Relajarte,*" he said. Taita reached over and patted my knee like I was a kindergartner. "Relax." He laughed and muttered something to the old man, who grinned. His gums shone in the candlelight and his squinting eyes flickered and caught mine.

I froze, and then spoke. "*Taita*," I said, looking at both of them. "This was a mistake. *Un error.*" But as the words came out of my mouth, they lost steam; the nervous energy melted, and the tension I'd been holding in my chest released with an exhalation. My shoulders dropped away from my ears. Both men kept smiling. "*Hice un error, amigos,*" I mumbled.

"*Entiendo,*" he said, and he motioned to me to sit back. On command, I fell back onto the floor and watched the candle flicker. A whisper of resistance rose and faded before I could generate any fight. Shadows jumped across the men's faces, and the brown-clouded plastic bottle on Taita's lap. The worry stirred again and then dissipated. Taita leaned over the container and removed the lid, which he placed on the floor next to his chair.

He held the bottle with one hand and looked down its the opening. His face was ancient, carved from centuries-old hardwood. The shaman pursed his lips and blew without effort. A delicate melody floated into the air, suffusing the space with its quiet vibration. Taita kept whistling, directly into the bottle, as though he was calling someone or something to come out. The sound was joyful, a call to play, a familiar cry for reunion. I watched, jittering, waiting for something to happen. But there was nothing but the sound filling the room.

He stopped whistling, and murmured something to the old man, who laughed, and handed Taita a metal cup. Taita held the cup in one hand and gestured to the little boy, who crawled over and sat in front of Taita's feet. The shaman tilted the bottle and poured just a touch of the brown mixture into the cup. He placed the bottle between his feet and held the cup in both hands.

The little boy sat crosslegged and looked up at Taita. He hugged his own elbows and shivered, before sitting up straight.

The shaman looked down at the boy and smiled warmly. He looked into the cup and resumed his whistle, the same quiet melody. My thoughts began to wander. *This* was her shaman? I flew three thousand miles to watch a guy with a feathered hat whistle into a two-liter Coke bottle. I was a fucking moron.

My head spun as I looked around the room. The floor was spread with dust; mold and rot was sure to flow deep into my lungs and decay into tumors and rot. I had to get home. I could make a deal with Ram. *Jew him down.* Maybe that was just what I needed to get back on my feet. A drill sergeant, someone to hold me to account, yell at me, tell me what to do. A few months of that and I'd be shipshape.

I would not end up like this, a broke Jew on the run in South America. It was a family joke I never expected to repeat. I wished Ram could have gotten his hands on my father and wrestled some sense into him. Dad was a whirlwind of trainwreck, in unbuttoned untucked dress shirts, one hand grappling a spent whisky glass, the other clutching an ashy Marlboro. He had a sloppy slickness that passed for cool in photos from the seventies. By the time my memories began, his paunch had grown and his hairline had receded, like our hope for normalcy. I had wanted a father who wore clean polo shirts and woke up before I did, one whose rants ended before saying something he couldn't take back.

Ram could have shaped him up. Maybe. But I was wrong to run away; I needed someone like that, to shape me up. A burst of energy ran through my spine and tensed my legs. I couldn't stay there. It was as if I was in the middle of a row in a movie theater and I was desperate to pee; I just needed a break in the action to fumble past the obstacle course on either side, legs, popcorn, soda bottles—at least one of which I would overturn. *Sorry.* I was ready to leave at the next opportunity.

Taita was calm. Not New York City post-yoga, pre-brunch calm. There was a real ease on his face. He looked like a stone monument that had weathered endless seasons, or one of those Easter Island statues. It was as if he knew something the rest of us didn't; he'd watched the movie and he knew how it ended.

He finished his whistling and blew a puff of air into the cup with a flourish. He handed it to the little boy with a nod. The child took the metal cup in both hands like he knew what he was doing. He squinched his nose and grinned, and then tipped back the cup as he drank. The boy swallowed and handed the cup back to Taita. The old man next to Taita smiled. "*Buen trabajo,*" he said. The boy made a face and stuck out his tongue, the universal sign for disgust.

Everyone seemed happy. No one looked afraid. My legs tensed again.

Taita looked at me. His eyes were soft. My churning waned and then melted away, like a curl of smoke dissipating into nothingness.

I had never been afraid on planes, even when bourbons were sloshing out of their plastic cups, and rollaboards were rattling in the overhead compartments. It didn't matter if the businessman next to me had wet his Dockers and was saying Hail Marys. I was cool.

Pray for us sinners.

Now and at the hour of our death.

I paid none of it any mind, and remembered Mom in her floppy hat, Florida-bound. *If the stewardess isn't scared, why should you be, tateleh?*

This was a different kind of turbulence. These *shamans* were giving drugs to a little boy. I *was* scared.

Stop being such a pussy.

The boy looked unharmed. He was grinning, probably proud of himself that he'd drunk whatever foul potion they'd fed him. He sat back down and grinned at me before sticking out his tongue, but this time it was a friendly jab. His eyes were clear.

Or they would drug me and take a kidney.

This was what I'd paid Ram for, wasn't it? Balls? *You don't have the balls to commit*, he'd said.

I sat straight and looked at the older men. "*¿Puedo ir?*" I turned to Miguel. "Is that ok? Can I go? *Quiero ir.*"

He shrugged and I nodded my thanks. I kneeled in front of Taita. My knees throbbed as they pressed into the rough wood. He looked down at the cup. "*¿Cuál es tu nombre?*" he asked.

"*Mi—*"

"*Tu nombre.*" He coughed. "Your name."

I opened my mouth, about to tell a lie. It was automatic, but I caught myself. "Alan," I said.

"Alan," he repeated. Taita picked up the bottle and poured into the metal cup in his lap. I watched the brown syrup flow from the bottle in the low light, expecting him to stop pouring, but he went on, raising the bottle's angle until the cup was nearly full. The dark surface shone in the candlelight. Tiny bubbles rose to its surface in a complex pattern, a rose, or star, or shapes that suggested a fractal, but they fizzed and popped and were gone before my inferior temporal cortex caught up. I'd read about this process somewhere—a clickbait article, likely, that led to an oversimplified distortion of something from a medical journal.

Images were just patterns of light on the retina, until they were carried through the optic nerve as signals and found their interpreted home in the brain. I could get this. What I saw was not necessarily given by what was actually there—*this* particular shadow, *that* gradiation. It was simply a match for my expectations, constrained by the limits of my understanding.

Taita repeated my name and then lifted the cup out in front of him, at chin height. He closed his eyes and pulled the cup towards him, whistling into the liquid. It was the same tune as he'd used with the boy. The dark surface rippled, tiny rubber waves that escalated with his breath.

I watched him whistle, and the tension in my body first broke apart, and then sublimed into nothingness. In the near darkness, a column of air was almost visible as it emerged from his lips. It must have been turbulence, a tumble of dust particles that gave the stream its hint of opacity, as if light was bending around its edges. Or maybe his whistle warped the air with imbued energy.

It was the same simple melody. In the way my eyes caught light and passed it along to my brain to interpret, the raw vibrations entering my ear canal transformed. What at first seemed playful altered, even as the notes remained constant. The same whistling, the same loving sweetness became a calling forth. It was as if Taita was marching for the woods and had reached their edge. Now that he was there, he was shouting for his playmates.

My knees were pressed into the floor. Rough wood pinched a thin layer of flesh and pushed against bone. I leaned back to relieve the strain and rested my palms, facing down on the smooth surface above my knees. Taita's whistle continued, a hopeful dirge, if there ever was such a thing. He was calling something or someone, a familiar beckoning.

"*Listo,*" he said, handing me the cup.

I took it in both hands. The metal was warm from his grasp. My heart pounded in my ears. "*Gracias, Taita,*" I said. I held it in front of my lips and looked down. The surface was a rich brown, like melted chocolate. I lowered my face to the cup.

"*No lo hueles.*" The little boy's voice perked up from behind me. I had no idea what he was saying.

Taita shook his head. "*Toma,*" he said, gesturing. He squinted his eyes and watched me as I brought the cup to my lips. I tasted the metal as I tipped my head back to drink.

The sludge hit the back of my throat almost instantly, a caustic, earthy, rotten taste. Its thickness meant it took its time coating my tongue, so that even as I swallowed, the horrid taste remained. I gulped, and scraped my taste buds with my front teeth, but it made no difference.

The two old men smiled at me and at each other.

"*Agua,*" I asked. I swallowed again, hoping to push down the taste. The sludge inched its way down my throat.

Taita shook his head, grinning, and gestured at me to sit back down.

I stepped back and sat on the floor. I could feel the drink making its way into my stomach; as soon as it hit, my gut started to churn and I felt a gag coming on. I gulped to keep the junk down, even as I felt it climbing back up my esophagus. The taste lingered in my mouth, clung to my cheeks and the back of my throat. I kept swallowing, hoping to get rid of the bitterness and keep from vomiting.

The shamans continued the ceremony. Miguel shuffled forward and drank as I did, although he made a show of it being no big deal. Then Taita poured for the older shaman and then himself, whistling the same joyful, mournful tune. The two leatherfaced men in their feathered crowns drank the potion like they were drinking water; its foul flavor meant nothing to them. I thought about making a joke that it was an acquired taste, but couldn't begin to put the words together in Spanish.

After the shamans finished drinking, the little boy stood up and stretched as if he had just finished a long nap. He looked around the dark room for a moment before recognizing his hammock and climbing in, pulling the net all around him. Miguel followed him, checking to see that the net touched the ground on all sides, and then climbed into his own hammock next to the boy.

I looked up at the shamans, who had both lit fat brown cigarettes. They sat and smoked, their focus soft. After a moment, Taita gestured to me. "*Acuéstate un rato,*" he said. The old man next to him nodded in agreement.

I didn't know what the words meant, but figured he wanted me to do what Miguel and the boy were doing. I went back to my hammock, pulled the net around myself, and closed my eyes. The fabric whispered along the wood floor and I could once again hear the chirp of frogs and insects in the nearby trees. It was already quite dark; through my closed eyelids there were glimmers of reds and yellows. With a flicker, they disappeared and I knew the candlelight had gone. All there was in my field of vision was a field of black, the only pinlights those of memory, or of latent neural stimulation: blobs of white and red and orange that faded as my nerves settled into rest.

As the colors disappeared I wondered whether that was true—whether my senses remained aroused long after a stimulus was gone. Surely, pain worked that way; there was the initial throb or piercing jolt when, say, a toe is stubbed. But the agony continued for at least a few moments after the bump.

It was no different with sound. My ears continued to ring in the wake of a loud noise, filling my head with high-pitched ringing.

I watched the lights disappear into the blackness, but new pinpricks arose, tiny purple dots in the deep distance, a rotating Lite-Brite that expanded and expanded, before the lights disappeared leaving the background a rich, faraway black.

Chapter Ten

My body rocked in space, swaying in the hammock, back and forth and I rode the waves and basked in the swirling visuals. I was a pendulum, oscillating by dint of inertia, and I relaxed into the waves.

My attention locked onto one image at a time: the *Wheel of Fortune*-style boards in miniature, gridded panels whirling, snapping from white blanks into black letters that never fully formed words. They floated in my periphery, unafraid, and then whizzed away when I attempted focus.

Then there were gears that rotated a click at a time, each cog fully awake and aware of my presence. Trapezoids and hexagons connected and congealed and divided like single-celled life, then broke open to reveal wormholes into vivid three-dimensional hyperreality, crystal worlds and impossible living landscapes.

The visuals came and went, broken by periods of blackness or simple geometrics suspended in space. Throughout, there was the rhythmic swish of the leaf rattles and there were the high voices of the shamans' songs that connected me to a sense of place, however unfamiliar. There were words I could recognize, even in my altered state: *limpia, pura medicina,* and words that were unfamiliar, strands of syllables that didn't even sound Spanish, strung together in melody.

The hammock launched me into space, a rollercoaster in the dark. Instinctively I knew to release my breath, to relax, and with that ease I accelerated and shot into the sky.

This is nice. I floated in blackness among pinpricks of color and geometry. It was a magic carpet ride, a relaxing spectacle of light and motion. I raced through an unmappable world, a visitor, at once alone and surrounded by some greater aware-ness, some*thing* guiding the journey.

Is that what you came for? The question arose without any sound.

Who, me? I said these words aloud, surprised to hear my voice in the air. No response came. *Yo no sé.* I don't know. I spoke loudly, unembarrassed. *Yo quiero más.* I want more.

Okay, then, came the response, and in the blackness my momentum reached a peak, and then, like I had creaked to the top of a rollercoaster, I fell, helpless, accelerating, flailing, grabbing for something, anything, and spun into the void.

The wooden wall dug into my chest as I leaned over it and hurled into the darkness. Vomit sprayed from my mouth in technicolor, neon streams that landed in the dirt and slith-ered away like panicked worms. I felt the churning of another round and puked again. The colors were more muted this time, like I was seeing them through gauze. Suddenly I noticed that I was sobbing. I spat out the remaining gritty foulness from my mouth as I choked on my tears. I felt a moment of relief, but I knew I wasn't finished.

My gut rumbled. I stepped back from the wall and breathed in the fetid air. Shadows danced around the room, given by the single candle flickering at Taita's feet. He and the older shaman chanted and sang. Their leaf rattles swished in perfect rhythm, like jungle metronomes.

Across from me, another figure retched over the wall, his sobs interrupted by vomity coughs and fragments of language. *Yo puedo solo*, Miguel cried, drawing out the last word into a child's moan. *Yo puedo soloooo*. He repeated himself and held onto the wall with the tips of his fingers. *Yo puedo solo*. His voice trailed into soft whimpers, and his knees buckled, leaving him resting his face against a rough wooden stud. His arms hung from the ledge, barely keeping him upright.

I turned back and stared out into the black, readying myself for another purge. Faint shadows cast by the dim candlelight and the yellow crescent moon played along the fencing, and across the muddy pathway to the outhouse. I leaned over the wall and pressed into my gut, hoping to let go of whatever sickness I carried, but nothing came.

I wobbled back to my hammock and pulled the mosquito netting around me, holding the ropes above my head until the swaying stopped. In the darkness, digital displays careened through my perception, green dot-matrix patterns, more letters that formed into the threat of words.

This is what you came for, I heard, but there was no one speaking, just the continued swish of the leaf rattles and the unintelligible songs from the shamans. I hadn't come for this; I had come for Mariana. I had come to get away, to run from the mess I'd made. I was chasing a woman who wasn't even there.

Mariana's tattooed words slid across the blackness, barely visible, like a snake in the jungle or a grasshopper in a hedge. ¡bendita ilusión! I strained to see her, but there was no body, no curve of her ribs, no hint of her breast, only words: *que una fontana fluía dentro de mi corazón.* I understood none of it.

The sentence flowed and faded into the darkness, and dazzling geometrics spun in a coordinated dance as the hammock began again to sway and float. The digital zipper spun by, too, but its letters had been replaced by symbols, Sanskrit or Hindi, maybe. Where had I left the card I'd bought at the Javits Center? It said *Stop Being Such a Pussy* in Hindi; I'd kept it on my desk at work, but it hadn't done its trick.

Another rumble bubbled in my gut, but lower. I blinked and there was a familiar beige Samsonite suitcase by a familiar door. My hand outstretched as if of its own volition, grasping for the luggage, but my fingertips only grazed the handle. The bag seemed to move farther away. I grunted and sobbed, but it was out of my reach.

Quit your whining! The blackness turned a deep brick red. Ram's voice echoed throughout the cabin, drowning out the rhythm and the shamans voices. My stomach gurgled and I opened my eyes. He was there, at the foot of my hammock, a muted Ram in his three-piece suit, blurred as if he was behind fogged glass. He reached for me and I froze before scrambling my feet toward the floor, catching them in the netting and tripping to my knees.

Ram hovered over me, his face murky, threatening but unmoving. I turned and crawled toward the wall, the rough floor digging into my skin, and I reached my fingertips and lifted my body to crane over the edge. A wave of energy rode up from below my ribs. Vomit shot into the darkness like bursts from a Roman candle.

And with that, the rumble that had been percolating in my lower innards gained momentum. I jumped to my feet and raced for the steps, wobbling down then as quickly as I could and catching myself before I fell.

The mud sucked at my feet. I teetered onto the boards and shuffled toward the outhouse. The pressure was building and I clenched my asshole shut as dazzling red skyrockets burst from the periphery. I shoved the door aside and squatted over the boards, letting loose a violent, hot purge. My breath came in short, panting bursts. Grids of moving geometry filled the darkness as my bowels churned and emptied. The tiny room reeked of harsh, aged shit. I cleaned myself up with a few torn squares of toilet paper and burst outside.

The shamans' voices carried urgently from the house. Bile crawled up my throat, and I leaned over the fence to spit it out before doubling over and puking up whatever remnants were still in my body. They dripped into the mud like they belonged there.

I coughed, and my cough turned into a paroxysm of sobs, a hard weeping that found its way through my whole body until I convulsed and spasmed. My arms ached with the effort. I cried some more and shouted into the darkness. "I can't do this." Snot and tears streamed off my face. I wiped them with a filthy sleeve, leaving a wet trail. "Make it stop. I can't do this."

It was the scent at first that stopped me, a familiar cloy of drugstore perfume and tobacco that came out of nowhere against the lush notes of shit and horses and mud and jungle. My cries caught in my throat and I blinked back my tears.

You are doing it. A gravelly voice sounded from beyond the fence. It was at once ordinary and long-lost, unique and ubiquitous, a familiar memory that instantly warmed and relaxed me. Beyond the fence, an orange coal floated in the air, surrounded by a curl of smoke. *Relax, honey.* The scent brightened, and I inhaled as if it were pure oxygen.

The coal brightened as my grandmother took a deep drag. The broad outline of her housedress and the silhouette of her coiffed hair waxed in the glow, and the sour hint of her Parliament 100 tingled my nose.

Grandma coughed and hacked, a melody I'd been hearing since birth.

"Help me," I cried. "What do I do?"

Her cough settled into throat-clearing as she spoke. *What should you do?*

I nodded. "I need help."

You really want to know?

"Yes," I moaned.

She paused, and then waved her cigarette at me like a magic wand. *Take a fucking shower, Alan,* she said.

I sniffed at the acrid air. "It's not that bad."

The hot ash lifted to her face. She took another drag. *It's bad,* she said. *You smell terrible.* The outline of her hairdo moved as if she was thinking. *Did you shit yourself?* she asked.

"No," I said. My face broke into a smile, and then the glow subsided and the perfume smell faded, and the lumbering shadow of a horse appeared where Grandma had been standing.

I woke up to birdsong and bug chatter, the hum of a million diaphanous wings and the rustle of leaves. Daylight filtered through the mosquito netting, and with it came the low murmur of conversation and the clatter of pots.

"*Buenos días, señor.*" A tiny voice startled me, squeaky and cartoonish. It was right next to my head. The little girl stood there, in her pink pajamas, covered in a tattered and striped apron. She was clutching a plastic toy frying pan. "*Despierta,*" she said, waving at me sternly and shaking her frying pan. "*Vamos a comer.*"

I shook myself out of the hammock. "*Gracias,*" I said. I watched her bound away, a tiny sprite.

The other hammocks had been thrown over the ceiling beams to clear space. I tossed mine over and got it to stay put after a few tries. The room looked like it had been swept while I slept.

In the kitchen, the stove was jammed with sticks and coals, roaring and sputtering with flame. Pots threatened to boil over. Coffee's rich notes floated over the smell of burning wood. The young braided woman ignored the fire while she wiped the little boy's grimy face with a washcloth, leaving shiny streaks on his skin. The little girl played on the floor with her plastic pan and some wooden utensils.

"*Hola,*" the boy said.

"*Hola.*"

The woman looked up at me with a smile. She was tiny, as if she belonged in a museum diorama. "*Hola,*" she said.

I smiled back. "*Café,*" I said, fumbling the words. "*Yo quiero.*"

She laughed and shook her head. "*Lavarte. Cepillarte los dientes.*" She motioned to me as if she was brushing her teeth. She took a chipped coffee mug down from a hook and filled it with water from a bag that hung on the wall. "*Afuera. Puedes lavarte.*" She handed me the water and gestured toward the door. "*Por el camino.*"

I winced, desperate for coffee, but didn't argue. I didn't need a mirror to know I looked like a guy who spent the night spraying the dirt with vomit. I pulled a towel and fresh clothes from my bag, along with soap and a toothbrush and toothpaste, and stepped out into the bright sun. Its warmth coursed through my body, and I basked for a moment before my own foul scent shook me out of my reverie. Grandma had been right.

Up the hill from the house, a pair of thin horses meandered along the wooden fence. I followed a worn footpath the opposite way, across the clearing, through an opening and past a copse of out-of-place young trees, geysered from the earth. Beneath my feet, the ground wobbled, as if threatening to open; whatever I had drunk last night wasn't entirely out of my system. I stopped until the shaking settled, and then kept on.

The trail cut through tall brush and into the forest. At the edge, I peered in, afraid to step into the woody shadow. The trees teemed with sound, and the ground was carpeted with life, with decaying flora finding its way back into the earth, and vibrant greens and reds bursting from the forest's fecund floor. Ahead, a hundred yards or so, I could barely make out a wooden platform and an artificial blue basin. I made my way into the thicket and the path grew mucky and narrow and the air cooled. The canopy thickened, but light found its way through in beams, setting broad leaves to shimmer and keeping the path visible.

The basin was an oversized plastic drum, filled nearly to the rim with rainwater. A metal gutter hung over it, leading from a corrugated panel that was fixed to a high tree. A child's beach bucket floated along the drum's blue edge. I set down my things and stepped onto the wooden grid of pallets to undress. From where I stood, the path was nearly invisible, as though it had been subsumed by the thick growth.

I poured a bucket of water over my head and stood, startled, in a beam of sunlight, and then soaped my torso and then my limbs. My skin bristled. I stuck my nose into a freshly washed armpit and inhaled. It smelled of rainwater, earthy and cold. The forest was alive around me, as I washed and brushed my teeth and rinsed my body. In the distance, birds whistled their unfamiliar whistles, calling to each other, and leaves rushed and rustled as a breeze passed, chilling my naked skin.

I grinned and scratched my balls with joy. I was alive, unburdened; everything that had weighed me down was gone, or irrelevant, or absurd. That I'd even had such fears seemed silly; I had no animosity toward Andrea, or Joe, or Gene, no worries about money, no interest in getting anywhere or achieving anything.

Even Ram's presence felt different to me, the love in his heart and his deeply hidden kindness, and the suffering that led him to be the way he was, the suffering that led so many men to look to him for direction. It made sense.

I scratched my balls one more time because it felt good, and then dried off and got dressed. Birds sang directly to me, and I whistled back, carrying my dirty clothes as I trotted up the path and out into the sun.

Up the hill, the horses greeted me with whinnies, pawing at the ground. "*Hola, caballos,*" I yelled, excited. They turned their heads and looked behind them, and then back at me. Backlit by the sun, a figure appeared as it crested the hill. My heart pounded and my pace quickened as I recognized a woman's outline, and as I drew closer I broke into a run, sure of who it was.

"Mariana," I yelled, dropping my things along the pathway and sprinting towards her. As the distance closed, her face broke into a wide smile, and she held her arms out to welcome me. I pulled her into an embrace. "You made it," I said.

"*Si,*" she said, still hugging me. "I'm sorry, Alan. I missed the plane—"

"It's fine," I said, laughing. I stepped back to look at her. Her dark hair was pulled back into a tight ponytail. Her clothes were mud-spattered from the hike, and she wore no makeup, but she was radiant. I wanted to kiss her.

She looked at me, into my eyes. "You had a ceremony last night," she said.

"Yes. Wow."

"Crazy, right?"

"*Si*," I said, "*en verdad.*"

She touched my arm and stepped toward me. I steadied myself, ready for her lips to press against mine, but her gaze went far-off and she screamed. "*Mis niños*," she shouted, laughing as she sprinted towards the house and the kids scrambled to meet her.

Mariana relaxed against Miguel's chest as he finished his breakfast, her chair against his. She stroked his scraggly beard, watching their kids bounce along the rough wooden floor. He leaned into her hand like a rescue dog. Her tattoo peeked from the bottom of her tank top; I could make out *mi corazón* near her waist, and then she shifted, and the words disappeared.

"I missed my babies."

I sipped my coffee. "I didn't know."

"I'm a fucking asshole," she said, nuzzling closer to him. Her eyes closed. "*Perdoname, mi Amor.*"

Miguel shook his head. "*Basta.*"

"I should have been here yesterday," she said. Despite her regret, she looked happy, and softer than when I'd last seen her in New York. "We met at University. In Bogotá."

"Oh."

"The fucking traffic," she said. "Have you been to Bogotá?"

"The airport."

She rolled her eyes. "We have to get back. Miguel has a meeting with his advisor next week."

"Advisor?"

She looked at Miguel. "*¿La palabra correcta?*"

He nodded.

"Don't ever get a PhD, Alan," she said. "It's fucking torture."

Miguel gave a thumbs-up as he hunched over his plate and ate. In his dirty t-shirt and grease-stained jeans, he looked like someone who hacked at brush with a machete, not a PhD student.

"Thank god he's almost finished. *No más* handjobs *para mi*."

I froze, but Miguel kept shoveling beans into his mouth.

Mariana chuckled at me, touching his arm. "It's cool, Alan. Didn't you guys talk?"

I stammered. "My Spanish—"

"Miguel speaks great English," she said.

He raised his eyebrows at me, shrugging as he broke into a smile. "Sorry, man." He barely even had an accent. I stared at him, shocked.

She slapped his arm playfully. "Asshole," she said.

"He did fine," Miguel said. "He didn't need my help." Miguel reached over and patted my back. "It's cool, bro. Now you can tell everyone you made your way on your own. Big jungle adventure. *Big pimpin'*, right, my man?"

I looked at the two of them across the table. "Kind of a dick move," I said with smile.

Miguel shrugged. "Sorry, bro. I'm evolved and shit, but, you know."

"Seriously, Miguel. Dick move."

"Sorry," I said.

"No worries, bro. A buck's a buck."

"It's all good," Mariana said, and the lightness in her voice defused the tension. "It's good that you came, *parce*. Taita is the real deal. All that shit you've been dealing with—"

"Taita's a master," Miguel said. "You're in good hands."

"Miguel knows his shit," she said. "He's doing his—*¿cómo se llama?*—dissertation?"

"*Si,* dissertation." He pushed his empty plate back. "You purged good, bro," Miguel said with a big smile, possibly compensating for his prior behavior. "You shoulda seen him, *mi amor.* Puked his guts out."

I grinned, proud.

"Good," Mariana said. "Get rid of it. All that shit from the past."

"Trauma," Miguel said.

"That's what he's studying." Mariana beamed at her husband. "Fucking cool, right?"

"It's more ethnobotany."

"And psychology," she insisted. "It's like fucking magic, these plants. The world needs this shit, Miguel. People are carrying so much shit around."

"*En serio.*"

I finished my coffee. "You really think it helped?"

"Don't you?"

"I guess," I said. "I feel okay. I'm just glad it's over."

"Yeah, until tonight," she said.

"Tonight?"

They both looked at me.

"We're here for a week, *parce*," Mariana said. "We drink every night. At the end of the week, you'll be a new man."

"Jesus," I said. I pushed my chair away from the table and stood up. The boy raced past me, laughing, and then his sister followed. He looked no worse for the wear.

"*Cálmate*," Mariana shouted to the kids. Then she straightened up and looked at me. "Don't worry, Alan."

I sighed. "It gets easier?" I asked.

"No," she said, and Miguel shook his head in agreement. "I mean, maybe. Or it could get worse. Who the fuck knows. But you have to keep going."

"Christ," I said.

Mariana jumped out of her seat and chased after her kids, laughing and shouting at them in Spanish.

"She's right, bro," Miguel said. "You came all the way here."

I shook my head at Miguel one last time, and he smiled in response, and then I took my dishes into the kitchen.

My head was still spinning. I pulled down my hammock and lay in it under the mosquito netting. I'd flown three thousand miles chasing a woman who'd jerked me off for money. I'd vomited and shit my guts out with her husband in some fucked-up psychedelic ceremony with two weird old men and a fucking child, my dead Grandma told me I smelled like shit, and Mariana—who I would never get to fuck—wanted me to stay all week and do the same awful thing a bunch more times. It was all a dumb fucking idea.

And yet, what else was I going to do, try to cobble together a life in Brooklyn? Start working on my resumé? The ceremony was a hard reset, but I was still in the throes of worry and uncertainty. My brain spewed a litany of obstacles: money, job, apartment, divorce.

The hammock rocked back and forth, and I closed my eyes. Traces of geometrics spiraled in the darkness and my gut roiled with nausea. My chest thumped and I sat up straight. I hadn't seen my duffel bag that morning. I quickly scanned the room but it wasn't against the wall where I'd left it.

Any glimmer of enlightenment I'd woken up with disappeared as worst-case scenarios rattled through my brain at high speed. My passport. My money. My phone. I'd have to get back to Bogotá first. How could I even get there? I had no way to book a flight. My asshole tightened at the prospect of calling Mom for help. I had no phone service, anyway. No phone, even—it was in my bag. I seethed for a second, and then took a dizzy breath. The bright morning sun shot perfect beams across the rough wooden floor.

I took another breath and got up. The door to the small room was ajar, and I stuck my head in. A bare mattress on a chunky wooden frame took up much of the space, and the plastic folding chairs from the prior night were stacked in the corner. My duffel sat, open, on top of the chairs.

I rifled through it as my heart rattled. My passport and money were right there, and I dug through and found my phone after another moment of panic. I shoved all of them into the pocket of my cargo shorts. The bowl was missing, though. My first impulse was that I was in trouble, that Mom would be disappointed but wouldn't say a word, and that Sarah would tear my head off.

"Mariana," I shouted.

"*¿Qué?*" She came running in, breathless.

"My things—*mis cosas.*"

"What?" she said.

Miguel stood in the doorway. "Your money's missing?"

"No."

"That's good," he said. "You have your passport?"

I brushed past him and looked out the window. The horses were swatting at flies with their tails. "My bowl," I said. I dashed to the front door and looked outside. The little girl chased her brother down the footpath. I could hear her pleading with him to slow down.

Ahead of the kids, a figure crested the steep hill beside the path. It was a man, and he was carrying something. I burst out into the sun and sprinted across the grass in my flip-flops as he plodded along. "*¡Espere!*" I yelled. He turned to look at me and then dashed away, disappearing behind the hill.

I tried to catch up, slipping in the wet grass and tripping over ruts in the dirt. I yelled again. At the top of the hill I stopped and gazed out at the treeline. He was gone. The sun beat down hard on my neck. I jogged ahead and crested the next hill; he had probably gone into the nearest copse, was probably hiding in plain sight. He might have been watching me stand there, laughing.

A cool breeze whipped along the crest and a gray frontier of clouds pushed in from the distance. I shivered, and a wave of guilt came and then passed with the wind. We didn't have much that was precious in our family; the bowl was as close as we had to an heirloom. I looked back from where I'd come, but I couldn't see the shack or anything familiar. The clouds began to accumulate and darken.

Shadows passed along the far edge of a clearing, a football field away, where a craggy tree stood alone in a patch of short brush. I stood still, watching. Its branches swayed as the breeze picked up, and my eyes caught something hanging from a low bough. I jogged across the space, watching for someone to emerge, and as I got closer to the tree I could make out a dark plastic bag waving in the wind, weighted down by something that let it rock like a child's swing after each gust had passed.

I sprinted towards the old tree in panic. The sky's bright patches had faded, filled in by a grid of undulating gray. As I drew closer, the bag's arc grew. It swung towards me as if it were trying to leap into my arms, but then the wind swung it back the other way, and I ran faster and grabbed it from the tree limb as the first pings of rain slapped against my skin.

It was the bowl, and I pressed it hard against my chest as the skies opened and fist-sized drops fell, drenching me even under the leaf canopy. My body wracked with sobs as sheets of rain washed over the clearing, mist rising above the grass, and the world that surrounded me fell into a fog. I snorted and coughed, and then pulled the bowl away from my body to inspect it. It was unscathed, even as shiny rivulets of rain ran down its worn interior, down into the chopped-in small grooves, the scrape marks left by decades of school lunches, the dark winter mornings of spongy sandwiches folded into tinfoil, her cigarette-stained fingers pressing down the bread. I pressed my nose into the wood, water running down my hair-plastered skull and hunched-over back, and into the crack of my ass, and my tears absorbed into its grain, and I inhaled deeply of the carved surface and the faint traces of fish and onion and mayonnaise, layers of scent worn and worked patiently into the old bowl.

Wind gushed along the clearing, for a moment intensi-fying the storm's sweep. I pulled my phone and passport and wallet from the pocket of my cargo pants and stuffed them deep into my crotch, hiding them in my underwear to keep them dry. Patches of sky lightened, and as quickly as it had come, the torrent faded into a drizzle. I wiped the water from my face and looked out at the foggy field. In the distance, trees were shrouded in cloud, still and exhausted from the storm's violence. I couldn't see the path from where I'd come, nor was I even sure of the shack's general direction.

A sharp buzz traveled through my groin, and I slapped at it instinctively like a bug had crawled into my pants. But it pulsed again, now against my balls. I stuck my hand into my shorts and fished around to pull out the phone. It slipped away as I touched it with my fingertips, and the buzz traveled farther down. I reached past my passport and wallet but by then the phone was touching my upper thigh. It buzzed again, stuck in a fold of my cargo shorts, and I pulled the shorts down to the ground and my phone flopped into the dirt. It buzzed some more, lighting up with incoming text messages and voicemails. A single bar of service appeared on the screen. I picked it up from the mud, and as I lifted it to my face, it immediately rang and, startled, I dropped it back to the ground before I picked it up again and answered it.

"Jesus, Alan," Sarah said. "Where the fuck are you?"

Around me, birds had begun to emerge from shelter, chirping in the light rain. A patch of sky cracked open to blue, and a column of light cut through the grey, growing as the small fissure widened. I stared, pants on the ground, and marveled at the vastness.

"Alan," she yelled. "Is that you?"

I paused, and took a breath. "Sarah?"

"Oh God, Alan," she said, breaking into sobs. "I've been trying to reach you."

"Sorry, I—"

"You what?"

"I've been—"

"You've been where, Alan? Where?" Sarah's voice heaved with cries. "I told you—"

"Told me what?" I asked.

"You aren't even paying attention." The words cut in and out.

"What are you talking about? I don't even know—"

Sarah got quiet, and the grass rustled in a wave across the clearing. She caught a final sob in her throat, and then let out a breath. "Alan," she said. "Mom's gone."

Then the phone went silent.

Chapter Eleven

I lumbered through the muck, bag over my shoulder, and made it to the river in half the time it had taken in the other direction. I flew down the rickety steps to the water. No one was at the shore, but there was a slow-moving rusted freight boat in the distance, headed in the direction of Puerto Leguizamo. I tried Sarah again but there was no service. I couldn't even send a text. I had no idea what was going on, but Sarah was a panicker. Maybe Mom was in trouble. Or maybe she'd just gone to the mall.

Still, I had to get back. If there were truly an emergency, I'd never live my absence down. If it was a false alarm, then at least I got points for showing up.

As the boat came closer, my shouting and arm-waving caught its weatherbeaten crew's attention and they slowed and veered toward me. The deck was overloaded, stacked high with mismatched furniture. Stray dining chairs, some upholstered, others stripped to their bare frames, threatened to topple into the river. At the far end, heaps of old bicycles formed a post-modern sculpture of corrosion and chain.

I stood at the bottom of the steps and shouted while waving a rainbow of peso notes in the air. *¡Por favor! ¡Ayúdeme!*

A young sailor in a baggy, short-sleeved dress shirt turned to his scrawny mate and laughed. The boat wandered closer and I shoved the money in my pocket and leapt into a flimsy canoe. I thrust it out into the flat water, paddling madly with a wedge of damp cardboard until the men pulled me aboard. The little canoe floated away, spent and unneeded.

I was newly filthy, covered in sweat and mud from the sprint. The oldest of the sailors—white bristled and ropy—snatched some pesos from my hand and gestured toward a ledge near the wheelhouse. I sat down and they ignored me for the next four hours like I was another table or chair. I used up the rest of my battery trying to text Sarah, but there was no signal. She was always full of drama. Maybe Mom was fine.

We docked in town and I waved goodbye to the crew who seemed to have forgotten I was there. I dashed off the boat and caught a sputtering mototaxi to the airport where the single counter was closing up for the day. The girl working there had a mouthful of shiny braces with tiny blue brackets and glowing archwires. She grinned like she was actually happy to see me, and kept grinning as she explained the situation in Spanglish: I'd missed that day's flight, and tomorrow's was full, and the day after that, too. *Mañana, lleno.*

"Are you sure?" I asked. "*¿Estás seguro? Tengo que ir al Estados Unidos muy rápidamente. Mi madre esta en problemas. Estamos en emergencias.*" I was surprised at how quickly the words came out of my mouth. I smiled, proud of myself. "*Por favor. ¿No hay un asiento?*"

But my competence was limited; the girl launched into a jumbled soliloquy, a rapid-fire stream of Spanish that left me with the barest of impressions: *Puerto Asis*, I heard. *El muelle. Tu mama.* I gathered she was telling me that there was another flight, from a nearby city. *Muy cerca.* There was a boat, it seemed. The way she kept smiling gave the impression it was no big deal.

"*¿Puedo comprar un tiquete?*" Can I buy a ticket?

She nodded and I spelled my name three times while she typed it into the computer. I handed over a few bills from my dwindling stack of pesos. She clicked on her keyboard a few more times and pulled a page out of the dot matrix printer, folding the perforated edges to remove the tractor feed holes. She handed me the freshly printed confirmation. I stared at it. It seemed to make sense. *This is it*, I thought. *Get after it.*

I thanked her and threw my bag in another mototaxi, telling the driver I was looking for the boat to Puerto Asis. The words came out with the same ease. I embellished, proud of my competence, and explained that I had to get back to the US because my Mom was in trouble. The driver eyed me in the mirror, but said nothing. I felt like a hero.

The taxi sped toward town, dropping me near where the freighter had let me off. A stenciled sign, spray-painted on scrap plywood, was nailed to a stud by the stairs. *Puerto Asis.* I was in the right place. I climbed down the steps to the wooden platform. Nearly a dozen people waited on benches and plastic chairs, taped-up cardboard boxes and tattered bags at their feet. They chatted among themselves, watching their kids buzz about. A brightly painted motorboat was parked alongside the platform, with rows of seats that could probably fit twenty people.

I strutted up to the ticket window with a grin. A middle-aged woman sat behind the plexiglas window smoking a cigarette. She had a scratched-up flip phone to her ear, and was nodding as someone on the other end was talking. "*Claro,*" she said. I didn't know if she was talking to me or to the phone.

"*Un tiquete, por favor,*" I said, but she waved me away, putting a dent in my hubris. "*Necesito un tiquete,*" I repeated. "*Voy a Puerto Asis.*" The woman turned away from the window and I stood there for a moment, staring at her back.

"*Tenemos que esperar*," a man's voice said. I turned to look. An old man in a bold blue shirt was sitting on a plastic chair. He had a jaunty red and gold scarf around his neck, like you'd see a rich lady wear on the Upper East Side, and he was wearing a dirt-streaked trucker cap that read *Campeón del Mundo*. World Champion. "*Sientate*," he said.

I didn't want to sit, but didn't know what else to do, so I found a space on one of the benches near World Champion and left my bag between my feet. Kids chased each other around the platform like clumsy pups, nearly falling off the platform and into the water. No one seemed bothered.

"*¿Porque estamos esperando?*" I asked the old man. Why are we waiting?

"*No hay chofer*," he said, shaking his head. "*Él no se presentó al trabajo.*" Something about the driver.

"*¿Pronto?*"

He shrugged in response. "*¿Estás de prisa?*"

I didn't understand.

"You are in a rush?" he said, carefully sounding out the words.

"*Si*," I said. "*Un poquito.*"

I noticed him looking at me. Maybe he could sense my worry. "*Mi mama. No podemos encontrarla.*" We can't find her.

He placed his hand on my shoulder in sympathy. Its weight was reassuring. "*Lo siento*," he said.

"*Gracias.*"

"*Tu mama.*" His face slumped with concern. I felt a little guilty. Maybe I'd made it sound worse than it actually was.

It was afternoon already. I had a little time—the flight wasn't until the morning—but I couldn't sit still. I pulled out my phone and pressed the power button. It was dead.

An old lady in a ratty bandana was holding court, monologuing and waving her hands as the toothy women surrounding her cackled with laughter and moans of sympathy. I caught fragments—*mi hermana, estoy cansado, jodido idiota, verga, traje un sandwich.* There was no urgency to their chatter. It was filthy and everyday, and even though I only understood a little, the rhythm felt familiar, like when my grandma played cards over Parliaments and Entenmann's, surrounded by her muumuued friends. Maybe she was there, like she had been during the ceremony.

One of the ladies saw me watching and pursed her deep-red lips into an exaggerated kiss, fanning herself with a plastic fan. I smiled and felt the flush in my face, like when I was a kid and Grandma's friends told dick jokes over mahjong. *Schlong, shvantz, schmeckle.*

A skinny teen with a wispy beard leaned back in a white plastic chair, oversized headphones covering his ears. He rocked faintly to an inaudible beat, his eyes nearly closed.

Bandana lady lit a cigarette without interrupting her litany. I'd seen Grandma do the same thing a million times. Always the center of attention, happiest at the kitchen table, the crystal ashtray brim-full, a lipstick-ringed coffee cup and a fresh pack of smokes, opining, laughing.

And then Mom, straying as far as she could with her Crossfit, her Jeep. But it was not far at all.

"How long do we have to wait?" I said out loud. A couple of older people looked in my direction but continued their chatter.

"*¿Qué?*" World Champion was looking at me, confused.

I stumbled on my words. "*Cuanto tiempo,*" I said.

"*No sé.* Sorry."

Warm river air skimmed over my arms. The old ladies kept on with their conversation like I wasn't there. I had to do something. I jumped back to my feet and went to the window where the clerk was still on the phone. She saw me coming and turned away. "*Señora,*" I said, tapping on the window with my knuckles. "*Por favor. Tengo que ir a mi madre.*"

The lady glared at me through a gauzy smokescreen. She gestured to her phone before turning her back to me again.

"*Señora,*" I repeated. "*¿Cuando nos vamos?*" I tapped my hand on the plexiglas. I could smell her cigarette through the small opening.

I suddenly sensed someone behind me. World Champion was standing there, adjusting his hat, a grim look on his face. "*Lo siento,*" I said, thinking he was there to admonish me.

He shook his head. "*Hemos estado esperando también,*" he said, and he reached past me and rapped loudly on the window with a chunky gold ring. The clerk lady turned to face us, a pissed off look on her face. She saw World Champion standing there and shook her head before she began rattling at him in high-speed Spanish, muffled by the plastic. Most of it went by me like noise. I heard *no sé*, and *no hay* and *el está infermo*. She was having none of it.

World Champ waited for her to finish before he spoke. "*Sofia,*" he said, like he knew her. "*El está regresando a su mama.*"

"*¡Sofia!*" A raspy voice came from behind us. Bandana lady waved her cigarette in the air, trailing smoke. She looked determined, like she'd grown tired of waiting and was done fucking around. She started barking at the clerk faster than I could understand. Her thin beard made her more intimidating, and her liver-spotted crew gathered around her like a biker gang readying for a fight.

Sofia's face went from steely to resigned. She flipped her phone shut. "*OK,*" she said. "*Momentito.*" She shuffled past her cluttered desk and through a curtain I hadn't noticed before.

World Champ smiled at me and nodded towards the old ladies, who'd gone back to their chatter but remained standing, ready for action. "That's the fucking A-Team," he said in English. "*Qué poderosas.*"

A moment later Sofia emerged from the back, looking defeated. She gestured to the lady with the bandana who then approached the window. Sofia leaned in and whispered something I couldn't hear. Bandana lady nodded, turned to her crew and muttered something, and the women quickly fanned out and started talking to the other passengers.

World Champ pulled a few bills out of his pocket and gestured for me to do the same. "*Una propina,*" he said. I had a small stack of pesos left and handed him a few crumpled bills. He nodded. The old ladies gathered cash from whoever had it—one or two bills here and there—and handed it over to bandana lady, who took the tiny bundle from World Champ and shoved it all through the gap in the ticket window.

Sofia examined the bills and nodded. We all waited while she went back behind the curtain again. It was quiet, except for the low wash of the water and the distant putt of under-powered boats. Even the kids were still.

A crash came from the small shack, the shake and rattle of falling pots and pans, the thump of a heavy weight falling onto wood. And then a shout. *Despiertate, maldito idiota.* It got quiet again, and then Sofia came out, followed by a scrawny teen who was pulling a baggy t-shirt over his head. His eyes were barely open and he had the fuzzy beginnings of a mustache on his lip.

Sofia held out a set of keys in front of him. The boy snatched them from her hand and walked past her, pissed off, out the door on the building's side, and down the steps to the boat.

We were all standing there, watching him, until Sofia banged on the plexiglas. "*¡Muévelo!*" she shouted, and then the boat's engine began to rumble and we all rushed to board.

"Jeff died," Sarah said. She crushed out a Parliament in the ashtray and pulled another from the pack in one smooth move, and then downshifted Mom's Jeep to exit the airport and accelerate onto the highway. Sarah clicked a button on her camouflage blowtorch lighter, and a hot blue jet turned the end of her smoke to a cherry coal, despite the wind.

I watched a gray cloud come out of Sarah's nose and dissipate into nothingness. The smell was chemical and acrid, and blended into the highway's asphalt waft. I was still spinning, after a six hour boat ride, a night in a dumpy hotel in Puerto Asis, and two flights home. Sarah had paid for my ticket from Bogotá to Florida but refused to tell me anything on the phone except that Mom was still gone. "Sorry," I said. "Say that again?"

She turned to me and sounded it out. "Jeff. Died." She took a drag. "A fucking heart attack, Alan. At the animal shelter." Sarah banged on the gas and rocketed us into the left lane. A passenger jet rumbled overhead as it approached the runway. "He collapsed. It was an hour before anyone found him." Her voice started to crack. "The video is so sad. He kept trying to get up, but this big mastiff—"

"Oh, no—"

She shook her head. A tear tracked down her cheek. "It just kept humping him." She emphasized the first syllable with a grunt. *Hump*-ing. "Humping him and humping him."

"Jeff—"

"He was *helpless*, Alan. I watched it, like, eight times. It's on my Facebook if you want to see. Tons of people liked it. He had lots of friends." Sarah smiled at the thought. "I tagged him." She sniffled, and wiped her nose with the sleeve of her Lululemon track jacket, leaving a shiny streak, then reached for the dashboard and pressed a switch.

Bei mir bist do schön
Please let me explain

She lashed out at the stereo, nearly missing the power button. Ashes scattered and the music stopped. "Fuck, Mom." She turned to me. "What the fuck is wrong with her, Alan?"

The Jeep started to wander into the middle lane. I gestured to the road and Sarah rolled her eyes. "I'm sorry about Jeff," I said.

"I'm fucked," she said. "What am I going to do? Move to Bushwick?"

I paused, hoping it was an appropriate amount of time before changing subjects to our missing mother. "Carol doesn't know anything?"

"She barely even met Jeff," Sarah snapped.

"About Mom," I said.

"Carol's catatonic. She's on all kinds of meds. Anyway I just fucking got here, Alan. I don't know dick." She sniffled again. "What do you think rents are like in Bushwick?"

"I don't know, maybe—"

She waved me off. "What a fucking mess. I was counting on him." She wiped her nose again. A crust was beginning to form on her sleeve. "He gave those dogs everything. He deserved better than to die getting humped by a mastiff."

I nodded, trying not to chuckle. I didn't give a crap about Jeff but the last thing I wanted to do was to add to Sarah's drama. We'd end up spending the whole night arguing about how insensitive I was.

"Fuck, Alan. Pay attention," she shouted. "He was forty years old, Alan. It's a fucking tragedy. Jews should not die at forty! We deserve better!"

I stared at the road ahead. I knew better than to argue. We were still straddling the white lane markers, but so were half the cars on the road, possibly inspired by the endless billboards for personal injury lawyers that lined the highway. A pack of Buicks were swerving between the right two lanes, barely going forty miles an hour. The world seemed upside-down; a few dozen hours before, I was spraying vomit and visiting my dead grandmother. Now, I was passing signs for All-You-Can-Eat Shrimp.

"Now I'm going to be like one of those fucking *yoga teachers*," Sarah said. "I'll have to get a *roommate*. In the fucking *ghetto*."

Scrubby trees lined the roadside, among patches of thin grass and gravel-strewn drainage ditches. A faded brown Olds sagged off the highway's shoulder, unattended. Its hazards flashed weakly, its sun-blotched hood propped up by a metal rod. Ahead, a cloud-blue billboard read *18 days after conception, our hearts are beating*. Two round-faced babies smiled, wide-eyed, over the 800 number at the sign's bottom.

It was as if Mom wasn't even missing. Maybe I'd overreacted. At least when she turned up, she'd know I'd jumped on a plane to find her.

"Sarah."

"What?" She was fuming.

"Christ."

"Christ what?"

I took a breath. The air was humid, like in Colombia. "I'm sorry about Jeff," I said, carefully, and pausing before I continued. "But what about Mom?"

She wagged her cigarette at me. Ashes flew in my face. "That's your problem, Alan. You have no *compassion*. My fucking boyfriend died while you were off *finding yourself*." She flicked the Parliament out the Jeep's window. "I don't even know how Andrea can stand you. Where's my fucking water bottle?"

"I wasn't finding myself—"

Sarah fished around underneath her seat. "I don't even have a place to live. I'm going to have to move to fucking Queens or something. I'll be teaching fucking 6 AM vinyasa on Astoria Boulevard like a fucking—" She paused and then spat the words out. "—a fucking Queens person." She clicked the turn signal and crossed three lanes in a fast swerve, pulling right onto the Atlantic Avenue offramp as she brandished her rose crystal water bottle in triumph. The Jeep rumbled over some lane markers and Sarah gulped water before lighting another cigarette. "Do you know what that's like?"

"Teaching yoga?" I said.

She ignored me and turned under the highway overpass. Finally, she explained. She was exasperated like I'd interrupted her favorite show to ask her to take out the trash. "Mom hadn't answered her phone for like, three days, so I called Ray, who just kept shouting *hello* until I hung up. He needs to be in a home. And Carol's fucking zonked on Valium or some shit. Could barely form a sentence. I stopped by this morning, straight from the airport. She was half-awake. Said Mom took her kettlebells and left."

"Kettlebells?"

"Did I stutter?" She wiped her nose again. "And all her pills, too. Carol was sad about that part."

"Maybe we should call the cops," I said. It seemed like a suitably dramatic reaction.

Sarah shook her head. "Mom's an Oxy dealer, Alan."

"It's not dealing—"

"No cops," she said, turning into a parking lot outside a pastel-painted strip mall. Sarah whipped the Jeep past a row of oversized pickup trucks and pulled into a blue-lined parking spot in front of a plate glass window that read *Crossfit*. She reached past me and popped open the glove compartment, pulling out a blue and white disability hangtag that she hung from the rear-view mirror.

I looked at her.

"What?" she said. "We'll just be a minute." She hopped out of the Jeep. I followed her inside.

The gym was a cavernous black box with banners and flags hanging from its cinderblock walls. Matte-black bars and weight racks were fixed to the rubber-matted floor, and wooden boxes were stacked along the sides. Metal plates clanked over a Biggie remix as a pack of spandex-clad athletes grunted and jumped. It was hard to imagine Mom here, the same Mom who'd worked in the rabbi's office, her piles of receipts and off-brand condiments, her obstinance in the face of our harsh reality.

It had been a continual process of adjustment since Grandma and Pop died. First, Carol. Then the Jeep, and the gym. I'd mostly been too caught up in my own drama to say much, but standing here among the bone-rattling sounds and the sour smell of sweat, it all seemed natural. The usual agitation that came along with life's predictable changes was starting to feel petty, like I'd been playing a part I'd learned along the way but had forgotten it was something I'd learned.

Sarah was ahead of me, quizzing a flush-faced young woman wearing a sweat-patterned t-shirt that read *Coach*. Her ponytail swung back and forth as she kept an eye on the clients. A beachy landscape was tattooed on her veiny bicep in grayscale, palm trees and crashing waves against rolling clouds. It was good quality work.

"He's gone." Sarah turned to me. "He quit."

The coach nodded, holding up a finger. "Joe! Chest up!" she shouted at one of the athletes.

"Who quit?"

"Gwo," the coach said. "I think he moved back to Haiti."

"Haiti?"

"He's from Haiti," she said.

Sarah's face contorted. "Is that in Africa?"

"No," I said.

The girl shook her head. "I wish I could help you." Then her eyes brightened. "We're Facebook friends, though." She pulled out her phone and searched, and then held it up for us to see. "There they are," she said, pointing. "Your mom is so cute. We love her here."

Gwo's real name was Mackenson Sanon, according to the profile. On the screen, he had one massive arm around Mom's shoulders, dwarfing her. Both of them had broad smiles on their faces. Her skin was reddened from the sun, and her hair was hidden underneath a baseball cap with a Crossfit logo. Both of them wore oversized hiking backpacks. They were a mismatched pair, but they looked happy.

Behind them, a rocky trail wound up and into fog-covered mountains, shades of muddy brown flecked with green patches of brush and terraced planting. In the distance, I could make out several small shacks and a few nearly invisible figures leading a donkey up the path. Underneath the photo, a caption read *sou wout la nan Seguin*. I pointed at it. "What does that mean?"

"How would I know?" the coach said.

Sarah was already typing the words into her phone. "On the road to *Seguin*," she said, pronouncing the name in a French accent. "He posted it this morning." She took the coach's phone from her hand without asking and clicked through Gwo's other photos before handing it back. "They're all old."

The coach squinted at Sarah and me. "Gwo's a good guy. I'm sure he's taking care of her."

I thanked her and we left. Sarah was staring at her screen as we walked back out to the Jeep.

It had all been a waste of time. I'd sprinted to Florida to come to my Mom's rescue, but she was on vacation with her boyfriend. Another predictable failure. The bright, alive feeling I'd had after the ceremony had faded. I needed to get back to New York and start to deal with reality. "I guess I'll go home," I said.

"What?" Sarah reacted like I'd taken my dick out.

"She seems fine," I said. "She'll probably call soon. Anyway, I have shit to do."

"You are a selfish fucking moron." Sarah started the engine.

"How am I selfish? I mean, she's on vacation," I said. "She went hiking with her boyfriend."

"In Haiti?"

"I guess."

"Who goes hiking in Haiti?" She grabbed at the steering wheel and pulled the Jeep out of the parking lot.

"I don't know," I said.

"Be a man, Alan. Dad's long gone, and Uncle Ray's a fucking vegetable. This is your job." The Jeep slowed in traffic, but Sarah gunned the gas and swerved around a pack of cars like a Nascar driver.

"*My* job?" I said. Was I actually *needed*? The idea shook me.

Sarah pressed on. "She could be in deep shit. Don't you ever watch Nightline?"

I sighed, resisting. "Or, she could be on vacation."

She braked behind a stalled Buick. "We need you." She sniffled, maybe for effect. "The family needs you."

The family. I was part of it whether I liked it or not. No matter how I'd fucked up. "We don't even know where she is,"

I said, but as the words came out, a prickle of electricity rose along my arms, an aliveness like I'd felt in Colombia.

"She's in Haiti. You saw the picture. I looked it up. It's not that far."

She was right. A few hundred miles. The excitement built in my chest but I tried to knock it down. I had things to do. "We don't speak Haitian."

"Creole."

"Didn't you just ask if Haiti was in Africa?"

"Ever hear of Google?" she said, waving her phone at me. "I know how to look shit up. Anyway I took French," Sarah said. "*Comment allez-vous?*"

"In middle school," I said, knowing I'd already given in, that I would keep arguing with Sarah like we'd been arguing our entire lives, but it was all *sturm und drang*.

"We'll be fine. And I went to a yoga retreat in Jamaica last year."

"So you've been around black people before?"

"Shut up and look at the map." Sarah turned the Jeep into Mom's neighborhood, and darted past the guard shack through the residents' lane. A white-haired man in a security windbreaker waved as we passed. I wondered if he'd been around for my Bernice incident, if he'd remember me.

I'd already typed Seguin into my phone. It was somewhere in the south of Haiti. The map was shaded with mountains and tiny villages, their names written in small type. Everything sounded French. *Au Silence. La Visite. Despiseau.* It looked like there was a highway that led there from Port-au-Prince. "It looks far," I said.

"It's like, a two hour flight," she said.

Old people shuffled down the sidewalks, under the shadows of palms. The sooner I got back to Brooklyn, the sooner I could get the *what's what,* to figure out how much I owed and how I was going to start to pay it back. I gasped out one last whiny bit of opposition. "Do we really need to do this, Sarah?"

Sarah jammed on the brakes and hard-stopped the Jeep. "Can you just stop being such a pussy for once?"

The words crashed over me, an upending, choking wave. I opened my mouth to respond, but I knew whatever I was going to say was bullshit. Instead, I shut up.

"Our mother is in danger, Alan. I don't know if you've noticed this, but things are pretty fucked up right now. My fucking boyfriend died while getting humped by a mastiff. Our lesbian Mom's off in Haiti with her large black boyfriend. I'm going to have to move to *Bushwick.*" She looked at me. Her eyes were red, but she forced a smile. "And you—I don't know what the fuck's going on with you."

"Nothing—" It was more bullshit.

Sarah winced, like she knew I was full of it. "I called Andrea trying to find you," she said. She placed her arm on my shoulder, a soothing weight. "She said she moved."

The hot sun glared off the rows of cars ahead, neatly parallel in their numbered spots. Outside the pale condo buildings, old people in crisp polyester shuffled along. I watched their lips move in chatter. *Charlar.* To chat, *en español.* Probably talking about the best Early Bird special, or which cardiologist to use, or which shows they planned to see at the Clubhouse. We'd missed the Linda Ronstadt impersonator. Or tribute, or whatever they called it.

"Alan? Are you listening?" Sarah's voice softened. "What happened with Andrea? Why did you go to Colombia? You really freaked me out. I thought maybe you went looking for Dad."

It was so much worse than that. What could I tell her? That I'd been taking advice from an overpriced drill sergeant? That I'd chased a sex worker to the jungle hoping to fuck her and instead drank some disgusting magic potion? That I'd seen our dead grandmother? There were so many secrets I couldn't share, so much I was ashamed of. It felt so precarious. I was needed *now,* but if they knew the truth—then, what? I almost wished Mom was in danger and I could save the day. I wished I'd thought to lie and say I was looking for Dad. Anything but the truth.

"Was that it?" she asked.

A horn bleated from behind us. I craned my neck; a boat-like Crown Vic had pulled up and was flashing its headlights. I gestured to Sarah. "We're blocking his spot."

"Alan—"

"Can we just go?" I pleaded, gently pushing Sarah's hand off of me. It was time to stop fucking around. "I should go home, Sarah. I need to get my shit together."

She sighed, and rolled the Jeep forward. The Crown Vic kept flashing its headlights until we were far ahead. "What about Mom?" she said quietly.

"I have to work," I lied.

Sarah rolled her eyes. "I'll go by myself."

I sighed, and pulled my trump card. "I'm broke," I said.

She shook her head. "Jeff's credit card still works. And I have some cash."

The Jeep rolled up to Mom's parking spot. Bernice was getting in her Lexus, a few cars down. She was decked out in a velour tracksuit and a Slinky's worth of gold bangles, like she was headed to the five dollar craps tables in a rundown casino. She spotted us and turned away.

Sarah hopped out. She waved at Bernice as we walked by her car, but Bernice had her phone to her ear and pretended not to see us. Sarah tapped on Bernice's window with a knuckle and Bernice waved her away, pointing to her phone. I tried not to watch.

"Say hi, Alan," Sarah said. I walked past as quickly as I could, to Mom's condo. I could hear the TV blaring through the door, and rang the doorbell. Sarah busted past me like she owned the place. The door was unlocked. "Carol," she yelled. I followed her inside. The condo smelled like it always had, thick with stale smoke and spilled coffee.

Carol sat on the sofa in head-to-toe Adidas, like she was about to go to the gym, but she was sunk into the cushions like she hadn't moved in weeks. She acknowledged us with a barely perceptible blink. The TV remote was in her hand, and her hand was resting on the floral-print pillow beside her. She was watching an old sitcom with a laugh track. The picture was in black-and-white and the volume was turned so high that the laughs distorted through the TV's small speaker. The tones buzzed in my ears.

"She's in Haiti," Sarah shouted over the TV. Her voice rattled through my head like a Purim noisemaker. A *grogger*. There were always boxes of them in the Rabbi's office where Mom worked. Cheap metal toys.

Sarah waved her hand at Carol, who blinked again and coughed lightly. "Mom. In Haiti." Sarah stepped in front of the TV and waved both hands in Carol's field of vision. "Carol! Do you hear me?"

"Hi Sarah," Carol mumbled. She cleared her throat like a cat spitting up a hairball.

A loud pounding sounded from the door. Someone was yelling something. I opened it and a gaunt old man in a blue Security windbreaker came at me, his pointer finger outstretched and his spotty right hand white-knuckling his still-holstered nightstick. He was wearing a black baseball cap with stitched gold lettering letting us know he was a Korean War veteran. It was hard to imagine military gear on his frail frame.

Bernice and Marty stood behind him, their arms folded in judgment. Marty was dressed in the same velour getup Bernice had on. They looked like rappers from the late nineties, only old and white.

"You're not allowed to be here," the old guard said.

"What are you, fucking Matlock?" Sarah yelled. "Get out." The guard looked bewildered, like he hadn't expected to be challenged. He stepped back and stood in the door frame.

The TV switched to a life insurance commercial.

Bernice shouted from behind the security guard, like she was using him as a shield. "You're banned from the condo, Alan."

"Banned," Marty repeated. His mouth hung open, his tongue protruding slightly.

Help protect your loved ones in the unfortunate event you are no longer there for them.

Carol raised a finger to her lips and shushed us. "I'm watching Blondie," she said.

Plan for the unexpected.

"It's a commercial." Bernice said. "He's not allowed in here, Carol." She turned to Sarah. "Matlock's not even a cop."

"Of course he's a cop," Sarah said.

Marty shook his head "He was a lawyer."

The security guard nodded. "Criminal defense lawyer," he rasped.

Carol shushed them and turned back to the TV. *What could be more important than your family?* On the shelf above the screen, a filigreed silver frame held an old photo of the three of us—Mom, Sarah, and me. Sarah and I were kids, gap-teeth and bangs. Mom towered over us, in our black rain slickers that read *Maid of the Mist*. She had taken us to visit Niagara Falls the summer after Dad split, an attempt to lift our spirits. Sarah's long hair was matted and wet, her face crinkled and smiling like she smelled something bad.

"MacGyver, whatever," Sarah said. "Our fucking mother is missing."

"How am I supposed to feel safe? Around this *predator*." Bernice shouted past me as if I wasn't standing there. "Carol!"

Carol held up the TV remote and raised the volume. The sound distorted further, like someone was shouting into a megaphone. *Affordable options to meet your family's needs.*

The security guard barked at Sarah, his voice as threatening as he could muster. "He needs to leave."

"Now," Marty said.

"Now," Bernice repeated. "He's a sex offender. He should have to register or something."

On the screen, someone fell down the stairs. The audience laughed for longer than necessary until the TV abruptly fell silent. Carol was holding the remote in the air, her finger on the mute button. Black-and-white images played in the background.

I'd grown tired of hearing him yell at me, but Ram was right. I'd pissed my entire life down the fucking toilet. Bernice was just one more charge on my rap sheet. "You're right," I said.

"See?" she said, turning to Marty. "You heard him, didn't you?"

Sarah stood across from me, staring daggers.

"I shouldn't be here." I turned to Bernice, who was still behind the guard. "I'm sorry."

Bernie nodded to Marty and the guard. "Get him out of here," she said, waving at me. The guard hesitated, and then stepped toward me with a wince. Sarah winced, too, like I'd failed her, like I'd failed the *family.*

The old man reached for my bicep but I pushed his hand away. His Korean War Vet cap tumbled to the floor.

"We'll leave in the morning. I promise," I said. I turned to Sarah. "We're going to find Mom."

Chapter Twelve

The bike motor whined as Johnson wound us through traffic up the too-steep hill. Sarah's suitcase teetered on the tank in front of him. It had dropped off a couple of times but he'd hoisted it back into place without slowing down.

I'd slung my duffel's strap over a shoulder so I could hold on to the tiny rack at the back of the bike. Sarah was sandwiched between us, trying not to hold onto Johnson's waist. She held her hands at her sides and clutched the seat padding with her fingertips. Her squishy purple yoga mat hung between us, battling me back by a few precious inches. It matched her *Namaste, Bitches* tank top.

The mid-morning sun beat down on my head. The air was soupy. I kept my breath shallow, trying not to inhale diesel fumes. I'd slept for most of the short flight. Now, I was wide awake, my eyes alert to every detail. We'd made it to Haiti, and I was determined to make it worth our while. Mom would appreciate the effort.

We'd found Johnson outside the airport. Sarah had cried about Jeff for most of the flight to everyone in a three seat radius, including two Haitian grandmas who clearly didn't understand a word Sarah said. But once we'd landed, she became overly confident; she'd looked up a few phrases on her phone and kept repeating them to herself as we disembarked. *Bonjou. Kijan ou ye?* She picked Johnson out from the dozens of drivers. He was wearing a yellow polo shirt embroidered with his name. It looked new enough to be real.

Johnson had nodded when she said *taxi?* and grabbed our bags, dragging them through the parking lot as we scurried behind him in the steaming heat. Sarah kept repeating *n'ap ale Seguin,* reading the words from her screen. *Ok,* he'd answered with a reassuring smile, *no problem.* It wasn't until he loaded Sarah's suitcase on the gas tank that we realized we'd be going by bike. *Don't worry,* he said. Somehow that was enough for us to squeeze onto the seat. It barely looked strong enough to carry the three of us.

Now, vehicles grunted by in both directions, beaten Toyota minivans with their passenger doors ripped off, vinyl seats crammed with gaunt bodies, sputtering Isuzu pickups with painted metal canopies over their beds, windows lettered with *Sang de Jesus* and *Psaumes* and a number: 90, 124, 92. If Haitians prayed a lot, it didn't seem to be making a difference.

Out-of-place modern SUVs, a dented school bus labeled with a New Jersey school district's name. And motorcycles by the dozen: red, black, white. Music blasted in and out of earshot, unfamiliar pulses of foreign-sounding beats and words. An occasional English phrase caught my attention. *Baby girl. Love you.*

The bike rolled past trucks and cars and argued for space with other motos, leaving inches between my bare knees and wooden stalls and three foot high truck tires. The road looked like it was meant to have two lanes but at least five vehicles fit across at any given point, with groaning construction trucks, rusted out pickups and minivans, buses painted with biblical slogans paired with crude renderings of random pop and hip-hop stars: Akon, Rick Ross, Rihanna. The designs were remarkable, at once recognizable and crude, a bright and surprising assault.

And bike after bike, loaded with passengers and cargo. We passed another moto slogging up the hill with an entire family—a baby on the handlebars, a toddler squeezed between the parents, and a propane tank strapped to the luggage rack. I tapped Sarah's arm and pointed, but she ignored me and kept staring at the back of Johnson's head.

Every scrap of roadside was taken. Vendors with open bags of beans and piles of plantains sat on the dirt in front of brightly painted lottery booths. Used appliances—blenders, mixers, fans, irons—filled folding tables and laundry baskets. Elaborate and boxy sound systems stacked on tarps, some neon-lit with power and blasting distortion into the chaos.

"I need a blender," I shouted to Sarah. Johnson glared back at me and I reddened, embarrassed I'd been caught making fun of his country.

The buildings were mostly crumbling, in various stages of disrepair. Copses of bent rebar sprouted like weeds, from cracked foundations and half-built roofs. Perimeter walls were hand-painted with distorted cartoon characters to indicate a school. Goofy, Dora. Broken bottles were cemented upright at the wall's peak, a rudimentary security measure. Once I noticed it, I saw it everywhere.

And church after church. *Église Baptiste, Église du Christ, Église Évangélique,* mostly in better shape than their neighbors, painted and trimmed, even landscaped with shrubs, and canopied with trees. They were as predictable as the potholes, from tiny, hopeful storefronts to ornate, purpose-built halls of worship. Jesus and the lottery were thriving in the face of desperation. People needed hope. *Fuck hope,* Ram had yelled from the stage of the Javits Center. *Go make shit happen.* Maybe they needed Ram, not Jesus.

Although Ram also had a mixed track record.

There was garbage, from scraps of styrofoam clamshells to plastic water bags to rotten cardboard boxes. Crushed green soda bottles nestled in vegetable scraps. Goats nosed the piles with purpose, an occasional black pig too, its face buried in a glorious slurry of trash. In the intense heat, fetid notes of decay floated on the thick air. It all seemed unsafe, and no place for Mom. There was no Crossfit, no Linda Ronstadt tribute, no deli trays.

Sarah leaned forward and shouted something to Johnson. *Il est mort,* I heard her say. *Un grand chien. Je suis triste.*

He yelled his reply in English. "So you are single?"

Port-au-Prince was a world apart from Fort Lauderdale. We'd slept in the condo, over Bernice's protests, with a promise that we'd be leaving first thing. Bernice stood on the sidewalk at six AM the next day in head-to-toe velour, clutching a floral coffee mug while she watched us load our things into Carol's Camry. Sarah gave her the finger as we drove off.

The bike brushed past a street vendor in a bright blue New York Rangers jersey. It said *Messier* on the back in red letters. He had a wicker basket of bagged bread loaves solidly balanced on his head. The vendor yelled at Johnson—a guttural chatter I couldn't understand at all—but Johnson just kept his head down and pressed on.

My butt pressed into the metal luggage rack, my fingers aching from holding onto the bars. On the drive to the airport, I'd sat in the back of Carol's Camry while Sarah rambled to her about neti pots and umcka and oscillococcinum, like it was a normal day. *Toxins,* Sarah said. *Echinacea. Flush out your system.* I ignored her and tried to concentrate on my breath.

Now, my muscles cramped as the motos wove through traffic like microscopic blood cells passing through capillaries, flowing around motionless obstacles. The four-wheeled vehicles were at the mercy of traffic's flow, with no place to go, no chance for escape, constrained by size. They crawled along, inch by inch, waiting for a slot to open.

But Johnson and the other drivers maneuvered and slipped through, even in the narrow spots between trucks and fences, cars and curbs and piles of trash, like the bikes were meant for stunts, jumping curbs and climbing steps.

Johnson forced the bike into a narrow slot of free space and punched the gas. I teetered, and gravity shoved me back into place after he slammed on the brakes to avoid a car-wide crater. He turned hard left and dragged us back into the maelstrom, before swerving into oncoming traffic to pass a belching dump truck. The bike tucked into a tiny space as a downhill bus blasted past us, blaring its horn, its creaky springs squeaking only inches from our left side.

"Fuck," Sarah yelled.

Johnson craned his neck to show his gap-toothed smile. "*Anfom, anfom.*"

If we died, how long would it take for Mom to find out? We were carrying our passports. Someone would tell the Embassy, I guessed. Someone would come claim our broken bodies after they'd been plucked from traffic and our belongings scavenged. If I had one last breath, I'd make sure she knew we'd died trying to save her.

Four-wheeled traffic continued to crawl, but the bikes found gaps near the road's edge to pick up speed, and soon we were hurtling alongside stone walls and trash-strewn lots, passing slow-climbing vans and buses.

The air started to smell less of diesel and more of charcoal, and the buildings began to look more modern and substantial, restaurants and hotels that looked inviting, banks that looked open, shops that looked air-conditioned, supermarkets that looked stocked. Johnson curved the bike past a small city park and then uphill. The heat lifted almost in an instant, as if a switch had been flipped, and as we continued up and out of the city, the air became cool and rich and earthy. Large houses and expensive SUVs hid behind gates and hedges, visible for the instants we passed. Even the most stately stone walls were topped with broken glass.

Johnson pulled the bike into a modern-looking gas station where several other moto drivers were gathered. Late model trucks and SUVs were parked at the pumps, their drivers unfazed, on their phones. Johnson turned off the ignition and signaled for us to get off the bike. I hopped down and let my duffel bag to the ground. My back was a dull throb, my fingers numb with ache.

Sarah climbed off and pressed her hands into her lower back to stretch. She paced the dusty lot, groaning. Johnson paid an attendant in a dirty t-shirt with a wad of crumpled bills. He filled the bike's tank as traffic buzzed past the station.

"It's been what? An hour?" I said.

She nodded and typed something into her phone, turning to Johnson. "*Nou rive nan Seguin?*"

Johnson nodded. He was crouched down and thumbing the bike's greasy chain. "Soon."

"How long?" I asked.

He shrugged. "Maybe one more hour."

I gagged at the thought of another hour on the bike. And then we had to find Mom. Seguin looked tiny on the map. It didn't seem like it would be too hard to find an old white lady there. *Anyone seen my mother?* I hadn't listened to the Ram app for days but I could hear his voice. *Stop being such a pussy,* he'd said a thousand times. Would my trips to Colombia and Haiti have earned me a *good job, kiddo*? Hierro Acero had promised us a whole new future if we listened to Ram, but now all I wanted was air conditioning. And I wanted my Mom back. Was this the future he'd promised, mud and dirt and heat and worry? It didn't seem worth all the trouble.

Sarah had wandered to the edge of the lot, where a group of teenaged girls were gathered. They wore matching school uniforms, navy and white, dust free, shoes glowing with polish. Sarah stood among them in her dirt-streaked yoga gear, her sweaty hair pulled back into a ponytail, her washed-out skin blotched with pink and red. I could hear her trying to speak French to them. *Vous connaissez yoga?* The girls laughed in response and chattered to each other. One of them addressed Sarah in Creole and the rest of them laughed even harder.

Laissez-moi vous montrer?

"Sarah," I yelled. "Come on." Sarah had a way of making everything about her, like most New Yorkers. Here, though, it seemed like a bad idea.

She waved me away and lifted her yoga mat off her back, displaying it to the girls like it was a game show prize. Sarah untied the mat and unrolled it onto the concrete pad. She smoothed it out and, first making sure the girls were watching, kicked off her sneakers and stepped to the center of the mat, pressing her hands together in prayer. The girl who'd spoken to Sarah looked confused, like she'd never seen anything more bizarre in her life. A friend patted her on the shoulder, as if to comfort her.

Around the gas station, men stopped what they'd been doing and watched. Johnson had crouched back down and was looking his bike over when he noticed the disturbance.

Sarah bent down and placed her hands on the mat in front of her. The girl were silent, their eyes wide, and the men began to talk to each other.

Johnson hustled over to me. "Stop," he said. It was directed at me, like I was supposed to do something. "Stop her." He race-walked past me and stood at the edge of Sarah's yoga mat. "Come. Now."

Sarah stood up and looked at him, puzzled. Then she looked over to me for guidance.

"Come," he pleaded at her. "Time to go."

I shuffled over, unsure. I didn't want to set her off. "Let's go," I said.

Sarah looked back at the smiling girls, and then across the lot at the gaggle of men who'd been watching her. "Yoga's good for everyone," she said, admonishing me. "Not just rich white people, Alan."

"Okay," I mouthed.

She stared back at the girls wistfully, like she'd changed her mind, but Johnson leaned in and began rolling up her mat without asking. "We go," he said.

I sighed with relief as Sarah put her shoes back on. She meant well, but no one here was interested in her *asanas*. We stood out enough as it was, and I wasn't a ball of Hierro Acero muscle whose presence demanded respect. No one feared a doughy Jew.

The girls watched us go as we squeezed back on the bike in the same positions. Johnson started the motor and said something quickly to the attendant, who laughed as we pulled away.

"Jeff loved yoga," I heard Sarah say, as Johnson gunned the bike up the steep road.

We passed through small villages with a makeshift food stands. Battered aluminum pots boiled over. Bloated crescents of fried dough wilted under plastic fly screens. I hoped Mom hadn't eaten any of it. She had a sensitive stomach.

Soon, we reached a largish town where political banners hung over the road and signs from the Ministry of Health reminded residents to wash their hands. Lottery shacks dotted the roadside, more common than even schools or churches. Their bright color schemes surrounded the tiny sheds with an optimistic glow. A police checkpoint marked the center, where uniformed young men inspected vehicles at random. Johnson ignored the stop like it wasn't there, only slowing to crawl past the town's many speed bumps. The cops stared at us as we rolled past.

Then we were out in the country, and the houses that had lined the roadway thinned out until our view was thick with trees and a few shacks. Goats glanced up at us, moaning as if in complaint. The landscape gave way to terraced, cultivated hills and endless, lush mountains topped with veils of cloud.

The bike hummed along without effort. I loosened my cramped fingers and stretched my arms in the cool mountain air. The sun was still high and I could feel its heat on my skin but it had been softened by the altitude, its warmth calming and welcome. I could breathe.

The road was well-paved in its center, but broken into pieces at each edge. We sped past duos and trios of barefoot children in mismatched clothing, pairs of flip-flopped old women carrying giant bundles and baskets on their heads, and donkeys pulling two-wheeled carts heaped with earth-dusted onions, trailing their pungent scents. Listless men led the tired animals up the hills. Eyes followed us. I hadn't seen any other foreigners since we left Port-au-Prince, or at least I hadn't seen any other white people. We must have been a strange sight, me and Sarah on the back of the bike, pink-skinned like baby mice, clinging to Johnson for dear life.

There were still lottery booths with chalked numbers and cryptic words—*New York, Midi*—and tiny stores run from shacks, their scrap wood shelves stacked with yellow and red cans, over-sized bottles of cooking oil. *Bongu, bonlè.* Women stood among squeeze bottles of mayonnaise and pillow-sized bags of rice and bottles of *Toro* and plastic razors that hung from shiny cards.

We were getting close, it seemed. Mom and Gwo had been atop a hilly road in the photo we saw, but the shades were brown rather than green, and dry rather than lush. A little higher, I thought. It seemed safer than where we'd been. Maybe I'd been right in the first place, but I knew I'd get points for effort.

The bike rattled and coughed. Ahead, a smattering of shacks and a few unpainted concrete structures lined the road. Tattered rice bags marked with faded American flags formed a makeshift canopy over a stick frame. An old woman tended to blackened pots over open flames. A flock of motos and their drivers rested nearby. The men eyed us as we passed.

Johnson followed the road's curve and pulled in front of a cavernous shed set back on a trash-strewn dirt lot. It was painted in garish teal. A wooden sign reading *Église de Dieu* hung from the frame. He turned off the motor and motioned us to get off.

Sarah was looking around, at the other motos parked nearby, the rusted-out pickup trucks with brightly-painted canopies covering their beds, at the finely dressed women trudging to the church's entrance.

Johnson was crouched down again, inspecting the bike's motor.

"What's the matter?" I asked.

He looked up at me with a frown. "Wait," he said, and he stood up and walked down the road, in the direction we'd come from. I watched him disappear around the corner.

Muffled, overamplified voices came from inside the church. Rows and rows of pews were packed inside under shadow. From the roadside, I could see a dark-suited pastor at a podium, gesturing with his hands. The sound system marred his words with clicks and distortion. A faded banner hung in an arc on the wall behind him, but its message was a blur in the distance.

Sarah walked towards the church and gestured for me to follow her. Ahead, a group of perfectly coiffed little girls in ornate dresses followed a pack of grim old ladies inside. They were matched in number, separated by years of wear and suffering.

The pastor shouted something and waved at someone by his side. A melody began, a high-pitched synthetic sound that echoed shrilly beneath the shed's metal roof. The synthesizer's tone was from another era, harsh and artificial, but the congregation rose to their feet in response.

Sarah and I stood outside and watched. Behind the church, a hill of red earth and rocks rose at a steep angle, scrubby bushes and grass and lonely trees leading up to a plateau where a cow sat, roped to a stake in the ground. Far above, a path crossed the ridgeline and crept into the clouds.

I squinted to make out the banner. It looked like sheets of paper hung from twine, each bearing a crayoned letter. *Devenez ce que vous recevez,* it said. It meant nothing to me.

The pastor began to sing and the congregation followed, a swell of voices that filled the space, echoing out into the tiny town. Some of the words were familiar. *Christ, amour, surprise.* But most of it blended together into rising and falling melody atop a slow rhythm, snare drum and hi-hat. Voices harmonized, but some cut through the thick, catching my attention. I followed a high, feminine swell, scanning the room to identify its source, but another high harmony overtook it, and then my attention drew to the deep, gravelly rumblings of an old man. I could see him along the aisle, a crown of white hair circling his dark scalp, his short-sleeved dress shirt neatly pressed but hanging over brown slacks. He swayed as he sang, side to side. I'd seen a million Hasids pray, rocking back and forth. I'd mocked them under my breath, their heavy wool suits, their clumsy hats, plastic-wrapped for the rain.

As kids, we'd prayed at Bar Mitzvahs. We heard kaddish and Kol Nidre. We'd said blessings over Chanukah candles and Manischewitz. It was ritual for ritual's sake; to stop, to protest would have required thought and volition, even courage. It all meant *something.* Something about us and who we were. It was a context for our lives, unconnected to the syllables we spoke, to their associated melodies, and to the black squiggles on the pages of the *siddur.*

I looked over at Sarah who was moving her lips to the hymn. She caught my glance and smiled, turning her attention back to the congregation's song. Then she leaned into me and spoke quietly into my ear.

"This is nice, right?" she said.

"Yeah."

Sarah paused, and sniffed. "Did you fart?"

"No."

Other voices emerged from the myriad. Some were young and clear, resonating over the harmony like a bird's morning whistle. These were the easiest to pick out, to follow back to an open mouth and bright eyes.

The rasping voices, too, the throaty monotone moans that came from older bodies, papery skin glowing under the shed's fluorescence. Taita's voice had been like that in moments, rough and low, dragging along his melody's valleys until it leapt and soared and its energy filled the room. I had forgotten all of that; the ceremony was a blur of light and flashes of wrenching pain. Now, as the hymn crescendoed, as the drums rattled off the metal roof and concrete walls, I could hear the shake of Taita's rattle, and feel the sway of the hammock as fireworks cascaded across my closed eyes.

My near-panicked departure hadn't fazed any of them. I'd found them huddled in the kitchen and interrupted their fluid chatter with my broken Spanish. I stumbled over simple phrases I should have known—*tengo que irme, tengo que encontrar a mi madre*—before Miguel interceded and begged me to switch to English. He and Mariana translated my outbursts to the others, who sat stonefaced.

Taita had nodded as if he'd expected the news. *Bueno*, he said. He shook my hand and sang a short blessing, blowing cigarette smoke onto the crown of my head. Miguel explained that it was for my protection.

Against this Haitian hillside, the same harsh scent wafted from the church, atop the familiar charcoal notes that had hung in the background since we alit from the plane. All of it was so far from New York: the medicinal smell of chilled air under the white lights of our drop-ceilinged office, the garbagey street rot, the subway's piss-stench. I'd been trudging to work like it was a life sentence, banners to failure openly painting the office walls. No wonder I'd been failing; I was like an ocean swimmer who'd forgotten anything but treading water, exhausted but doing my best to survive, finding whatever distractions that kept me numb to the bankruptcy of my bleak existence. Ram had been right about that, even if his methodology was fucked. I'd piled lies upon lies, and the weight of them had broken me.

Haiti had its own stench, to be sure. But survival had a different meaning, here.

I guessed I owed Ram some thanks, but there was no muscle-driven Hierro Acero grind in my future. Ram's man-slogans were empty words meant to be printed on t-shirts and mouse pads: *Give Zero Fucks. Stop Being Such a Pussy. You have pissed your entire fucking life down the toilet.* I could buy the banners in Hindi, in Russian. Khakied men around the world pinning their hopes on a drill sergeant's bark. There was no salvation in muscles and veins.

But there was a kernel in there that resonated. Ram had to have known I was a cheese-driven rat winding through an impossible maze of dead-ends: a dead-end marriage, a dead-end career, a dead-end worldview, my mouth gasping lies and bourbon breath, chasing handjobs and placing blame squarely elsewhere. Ram's remedies were one size fits all, and as appealing as they'd seemed at the time, they were starting to look like cosmetic surgery on a terminal patient. A little nip and tuck, never mind that tumor.

All of the outcomes I'd wanted seemed laughable, now.

Doris gave us a fucking hugging schedule.

Mom swung kettlebells and drove a jacked-up Jeep.

Andrea moved to Whitney to live with a crossing guard.

Ram was right on one note, at least. Whatever I'd been doing wasn't working. I was ashamed, but redemption was around the corner. I was waking up.

The congregation redoubled its swell. Sarah and I stood together and watched them sway and sing. Flattened plastic water bags scattered the hard-packed ground at our feet. A little girl toddled up the shed's aisle, chased by her mom. *Re-tay, re-tay,* the woman said. Maybe it meant *come back,* or *stop,* or maybe that was the little girl's name.

You give up too easy, Ram had said. *You hit a speed bump and act like it's a fucking mountain.*

A motor purred behind us, tires crunching the dirt.

"Come," Johnson said. He was straddling the bike, his feet planted on the ground like he was getting ready to race. Johnson revved the tiny motor and wagged his thumb at the bike's seat. *"An ale."*

The air was colder, now, as we rode up through thick woods dotted with scrap-wood shacks. The bike wound around steep drop-offs. Johnson navigated the roads with ease, even as the pavement gave way to rocky patches and muddy ruts, and then quickly to unpaved pits. The bike bounced hard, stone after stone. My wrists vibrated like tuning forks, sending arrows of dull ache up through my elbows. Through gaps in the trees, fog-shrouded mountaintops lurked and ridges lined with pine forest nestled the occasional human form, antlike in the distance, traveling on foot to or from someplace impossibly far off. Beyond each crest, another mountain loomed, its own frontier.

Sarah's head was turned to the side and her eyes were closed, her dark hair sweat-stuck against her face and neck. Her lips moved; she was talking to herself, mumbling a mantra or some affirmation she'd learned in yoga teacher training. I hoped it worked, that she called the gods' favor down on us. At very least, I hoped it didn't do any harm.

Johnson shouted something and gestured to the broken road ahead. A shuttered lottery shack marked an intersection where the road forked. A faded red sign pointed toward Seguin, to the left, where any remnants of paved road had melted into the hillside, and what remained was the merest suggestion of a path.

Sarah shouted with glee. "Almost there," she said, waving her arms above her head. The bike bounced and she grabbed Johnson's shoulder to keep from falling.

The pits began to deepen, scattered with rock and mud, and the bike's motor whined as Johnson struggled to climb the hill. Each smooth rut split off into impassable barriers, mounds of stone and mud. Johnson gripped the handlebars and spun the rear wheel, still balancing Sarah's bag on the gas tank. A burning scent floated up from the wheels and motor, a mixture of rubber and fuel. Johnson gave the engine one last rev and then killed it, shaking his head.

"*Ma-shay*," he said, pointing up the muddy path. "You can walk now. Not far."

We kept trudging up the crumbling path, stepping from rock to rock to avoid the muck. Sarah scraped her wheeled suitcase over stone and dirt. Her yoga mat hung over a shoulder like a quiver of arrows and the back of her tank top bore a sweat stain in the shape of a mushroom cloud. I carried my duffel on my back and tried to project ease, but my heart hammered from the steep climb, leaving me panting. The locals sped past us without a glance, old women in flip-flops with huge head bundles leading burdened donkeys along the same rocky pathway we were using, but with an ease that made me feel foolish.

We'd begged Johnson to take us farther, but he was resolute, demanding the full fare even though he'd dropped us shy of our destination. "Go," he'd said, pointing up the mountain. He wanted sixty bucks and Sarah argued for a minute before flipping him three twenties. He looked startled, probably surprised we paid what he'd asked. He stuffed the money in his jeans pocket and raced down the hill.

Even though the air had cooled, the sun kept beating down on us since we'd begun our walk an hour earlier. My back was slick with sweat. A bike sped by, unburdened by passengers and luggage. The air quieted as the moto buzzed into the the clouds, and then all I could hear was the crunch of our footprints on rock and gravel, and the thud and tumble of Sarah's suitcase along the ground. Ahead, a few shacks signaled some life. Tired-looking women sat on boards and bricks. One of them held an infant against her chest. They noticed us, one at first, and then the whole flock looked at us in surprise. Then, from nowhere, a posse of children emerged, and began to scurry alongside us. They were all barefoot, the youngest ones in filthy tank tops and no pants, their faces webbed with snot.

I eyed Sarah, afraid she'd lay out her yoga mat again, but she'd zoned out and was just trying to put one foot in front of the other. She picked up her pace and pulled at her bag.

Blan, the kids kept repeating. *Blan*. They said it like a mantra.

"It means white," Sarah said. Her voice was a flat monotone. She raised it to shout at the adults. "Seguin?" she yelled, pointing ahead.

One of the women nodded, and then another followed suit, pointing her finger at the road.

"*Lwen?*" Sarah said.

The women looked at each other and then back at us.

We kept walking, the kids alongside us shouting *blan*, until they reached some imaginary marker and turned back. I listened to their chatter disappear as they faded down the hill.

"Johnson said it's not far," Sarah mumbled to me. We were nearing a crest, and the green roadside had mostly faded to muddy brown.

My feet hurt. Blisters had formed along both insteps and heels, making each step sting and burn. We'd rest once we found her. The sun had begun to drop in the sky, and there was no place for us to go; we had to find Mom before dark. One bar flickered on my phone since we started walking, but it wasn't enough to Google anything. The map just showed a glowing blue dot in the middle of a green patch of nothing. We had to keep going.

Sarah looked up, a scowl on her face. She grunted, tugging at her bag to get to the hilltop, a few hundred yards ahead. I scrambled to keep up. "This was a dumb fucking idea," she said. When I didn't reply, she gestured to the path. "We must be near the top," she said. "This looks like the picture."

I scanned the road. It was hard to tell if she was right, or just hopeful. Nothing looked any different. The same scrubby plants clung to the nearby hillsides, the same pocked earth, the same crumbling stones.

"Alan? Are you awake?"

"Uh-huh," I grunted.

"Did you hear me?"

"Yeah," I said.

Sarah groaned as she pulled her bag over a pillow-sized rock. "Fuck," she said. "Do you think we're close?"

I shrugged. "I hope."

She shook her head. "We better be." She looked back at me over her shoulder for a moment. "What the fuck did you do?"

"About what?" I said, even though I knew what she meant.

"With Andrea?"

"Nothing," I said, like it was a silly question.

Sarah kept walking, thumping her bag behind her. "So she moved out?"

"I mean, we're fighting. That's all."

"Did you cheat?"

"No!" I said, too quickly.

"Did she?"

I mouthed *fuck off.*

"Not even a little?"

"Cut the shit," I said.

Sarah pouted. "Lighten up. You need to do some yoga."

I glared at her. "Don't you fucking dare."

She bowed slightly as she kept walking, one hand in prayer position. "Namaste."

"My feet hurt," I said, adjusting the duffel on my back.

"Mine too," she said.

"Are you fucking someone?" she asked again.

"No."

She paused. "Is someone fucking you?"

I shook my head.

Sarah shrugged. "Fine. We're almost there." Her stride grew longer as she approached the hilltop.

I pushed ahead to try and keep up. My head pounded from the effort, and pain shot through my feet. I stopped as Sarah crested the hill. She stood at the top and gazed out ahead.

"Shit," she said quietly. Her voice was completely different, monotone and dry. I sprinted to catch up with her and dropped my bag at my feet. We gazed out at the vista. The path we were on dipped down and followed a long ridgeline before it climbed up, impossibly high, and wound around a peak, nearly touching the clouds. There was nothing between us and that peak, no town, no shacks, just miles of dirt and rocks, brush and spindly trees. At the top, barely visible, a thicket of trees stood in a long row.

"Fuck," I said. My voice caught in my throat. I cleared it and spat onto the rocks. "Fuck fuck fuck."

"Come on," she said. "We have to keep going."

I sat on a flat boulder. My eyes began to water. I turned away from Sarah and wiped my face with a sleeve.

"Alan!" she shouted.

"I can't," I said.

"You have to," she shouted. "We are in the middle of fucking nowhere. Look!" Sarah gestured to the endless rocky path ahead. "She's up there somewhere." The sun silhouetted Sarah as it began to dip toward the distant hilltops. She dropped her bag's handle and turned away from me before sitting down on the roadside a few yards ahead of me. "It'll be dark."

I looked at my phone. Zero bars, but who would I call? Sarah and Mom were all I had left. Andrea was probably fighting with Joe over Doritos. *I want Cool Ranch! I want Jalapeño!* What would she say to me if I called? *Where are my fucking headphones?* I hoped she choked on a pierogi.

"Come on," Sarah said. "Stop being such a pussy."

I looked up at her. "What?"

"You heard me." She stood up and stretched her arms over her head. "Shake it off, bro." Sarah propped a leg up on a rock and leaned forward to touch her toes.

Stop being such a pussy.

Fuck her. Fuck Joe, and Andrea, and Mariana. And fuck Ram Hardy and Hierro Acero. Fuck Gene. Fuck Miguel. Fuck Gwo. And Carol. And Bernice and Marty, too.

Fuck Sarah and Mom for that matter.

"I'm out," I said. "I'm going back."

"No you're not," she said. "You're not leaving me here alone. You'll die. I'll die. Mom will be furious."

"Fuck Mom," I shouted.

"Fuck Mom?" Sarah looked shocked.

"It's pretty selfish, Sarah. She knew we'd be worried—"

"Alan—"

"It's irresponsible." I spat the words. "I need to get the fuck out of here. I need a fucking miracle."

"Alan, stop—"

"She ran off with her Crossfit coach, Sarah. She didn't give a shit about us. Why should we give a shit about her?" I sniffled, and wiped my nose with my sleeve. "We have terrible parents. Look at us." I gestured to her and lowered my voice, the words catching in my throat. "We're barely functioning."

"We're fine," Sarah said.

I shook my head. "You're delusional." I sniffled again, and choked back a sob.

Sarah rolled her bag over and sat down next to me. She leaned her head on my shoulder and put her arm around my waist. "Mom did okay," she said.

"She took off."

"It's not like that," she said.

"She just disappeared," I said.

"It's not the same. We're adults."

"I'm her kid."

She paused. "You're almost forty."

"That's not the point," I said.

"Then what is the point?"

I took a breath. There was no point, really. What could I tell Sarah? That I was only interested in how things impacted *me*? That I loved the story I'd constructed for myself, that I was an abandoned child, even approaching forty? That life was unfair, and all the unfairness was directed at me?

I didn't give a crap about what Mom wanted, or that Sarah had lost Jeff, or my failed marriage—or even how Andrea felt—and whether I'd participated in something unjust or immoral with Mariana or any of the other women I'd been paying. I was aggrieved, and no amount of yoga was going to change that. "I just—she should be thinking of me. Of us. One phone call. *I'm going hiking.* A text, even."

Sarah looked away. "She told me," she said.

"What?"

She paused. "She called me from the airport. Said she was going with Gwo to visit his family. I told her not to go."

The sun sank lower and touched the far treetops. A faint breeze kissed my skin. The blisters on my feet burned and throbbed. "She didn't tell Carol?"

"Who the fuck knows," Sarah said. "Carol's half dead." She pulled herself closer to me, hugging me firmly. "I needed you."

The sky softened. Its glow suffused the rocks and mud, and the scrubby plants along the roadside. The low clouds swirled and luminesced and blanketed the far mountaintops, lit from within like the last remnants of a campfire.

"You could have told me," I said.

"No, I couldn't," Sarah said. She pushed herself to the edge of the rock and turned to face me. She spoke quietly, over the low wind and the distant rustle of leaves, and the rich charcoal air. "You would have told me to fuck off. You would have told me about all the important things you had to do, all the things that were more important than me or Mom. Work. Another seminar. It had to be an emergency, Alan. That's about the only thing you'd respond to." Then she coughed, and cleared her throat forcefully before spitting a big wet wad into the dirt. It sparkled, a glistening bubble of phlegm. "I love you, but you're selfish as fuck."

All the reasons she was wrong spun in my head, but instead of spitting them out, I took a breath. She knew me: I never would have come had she not guilted me into it. I'd be back home, trying to rearrange the deck chairs on my sinking life.

"Fine," I said, getting to my feet. I eyed the copse of trees ahead, impossibly far away. "We'd better move, then." I reached out my hand to Sarah. She took it and stood up.

"Thanks," she said.

I nodded and we started walking. "I *am* sorry about Jeff." I paused. "Sorta."

She shrugged. "Sure," she said, and she dragged her bag along the stones and led the way up the hill.

Chapter Thirteen

The sun dropped, setting the trees aglow in shades of emerald and coral. The muddy, rocky climb had turned to a flat gravel path, bordered by pine and grass and lined with flattened plastic water pouches. The landscape turned in an instant, from tropical to temperate. Looking straight through the scattered forest verticals, its beds of needles and rough pine bark, its endless and disorienting patterns of thick and thin, it was as if we were in Vermont or New York, in some state park close to a highway's edge, a short drive from a Stewart's or a Cumberland Farms, a tank of gas and an ice cream sandwich.

But there was no short drive to anything, just limestone gardens spat from treeless fields, and plastic detritus dropped bag by bag, wrapper by wrapper, until the pristine forest was tied in braids and ribbons that would stay intact for a thousand years after we'd passed by.

Sarah's bag tumbled along the rocks. We hadn't seen another soul for a mile or two. Up until then Sarah had stopped each of the few people we'd passed. *Seguin?* was all she said, pointing the way. They mostly nodded in response, probably shocked to see us. We were a sight: a couple of ill-prepared Jews trudging up a Haitian mountain. Sarah had picked up a few phrases and used them liberally, to incredulity. *Bonswa,* she said to everyone. *Ki jan ou ye.* How are you? A few people smiled. A few others responded in kind. *Anfom, anfom.* Fine. My patterns with Sarah ebbed and flowed. Her constant chatter was annoying, and then endearing, and then infuriating. The same scheme applied to my view of my own life. It was going to be okay, and then it was not, and then it didn't matter, and then it did. I was embarrassed and relieved, worried and elated.

The road curved. Another limestone field burst from the ground alongside the road, grey teeth in crooked rows pointing to the sky.

"I hope this is right," she said. "I feel like we've gone too far."

We'd had this conversation ten times already.

"It's going to get cold." Sarah clutched at herself with her free hand to emphasize her point. "We could die up here."

"Just keep going."

She kept going.

We passed underneath a canopy of trees that overlooked the road, and as the sun began to lurk in the distance, the daylight turned to deep dusk.

"This was a dumb idea, wasn't it?"

"Yes."

"Did you bring a flashlight?"

"No," I said. "I have my phone."

"Me too," she said. She was ahead of me by a few yards. In the fading light she began to blend in with the trees, a blur that merged with the forest's edge.

"*Blan.*" The voice came from down the path. At first I thought it was Sarah putting me on but then it repeated, high-pitched and pleading. "*Blan.*"

Sarah stopped. I came up alongside her. A figure popped from the woods onto the path, a small boy in a tattered blue sweater and underwear. He looked about five or six, and he stared up at us with his mouth open. *"Blan,"* he repeated. He held out his hand. *"Mwen grangou."*

I looked at Sarah. "What's he saying?"

She shrugged. "He wants something. Money, I guess."

"Mwen grangou," the little boy repeated, and then he glanced into the woods. Another boy tumbled out onto the gravel, rushing. He was even smaller than the first, wearing a tiny wool vest with no shirt underneath, and piped gym shorts.

"Mwen grangou," the other boy said, holding out his hand.

Sarah held up a finger. "Wait," she said. *"Tann. Souple tann."* She tapped on her phone and looked up at the boys. *"N'ap chèche yon vye fanm."*

The boys looked at each other. *"Blan?"* the older one asked.

Sarah nodded vigorously.

The boys smiled and gestured for us to follow but then the older one turned and held out his had. *"Ba'm kek goud."*

Sarah instinctively reached in her pocked and handed him a coin. He took it in his hand and examined it.

"It's a quarter," she said.

"Quarter," the boy repeated.

Sarah nodded, and the boy smiled and ran up the path, looking back to make sure we were coming.

"Come on," she said. "They know where Mom is."

We stumbled through the dimming woods with our bags, between wild gangs of trees, over camouflaged traps of fallen logs and deep ditches. The boys stopped and took our hands like we were the children, helping to guide us over the most precarious spots. Strips of white cloud slid by the sliver of moon as dying gasps of sunlight faded behind the mountains.

Sarah struggled with her suitcase, thumping over rocks and branches. She grunted and whined with each step. I shrugged my duffel higher on my shoulders as it slipped. My feet burned with ache and stabbing heat.

I'd run through more woods in recent days than in my entire life, in the hands of strangers. And now, kids. I wanted to make it mean something: I was stupid, or brave. I was reckless, or loyal. It came in waves, from apogee to perigee.

The boys were chattering with each other in Creole and every once in a while Sarah would interject with one of her few phrases. *Pa lwen?* I heard her say, and the older boy responded with a rat-a-tat of sounds that made the younger one laugh.

Ram had promised change and he had delivered, but I didn't like it. I was carving a new path, along a cliff's edge. It was hard to enjoy the scenery while I was worrying about tumbling into the dark. The tea I'd drunk in Colombia had dislodged something, but nothing had settled, and I was rattling around in panic. I thought of listening to Ram on my phone but the idea of his yelling made me feel sick. Everything that had been familiar was gone. Except Sarah. And Mom, too, if we could ever find her.

My toe caught a root and I tumbled forward before catching a tree trunk to halt my fall. My duffel fell to the ground and I leaned over to pick it up, and the boys' chatter fell to a hush.

"Oh," I heard Sarah say, and I looked up.

We were at the edge of a thicket, facing a tiny shack behind a scrap wood fence. A small fire glowed on the ground. Two women sat next to it, against the shack. In the dark it was hard to tell their age. The boys ran inside the shack.

"*Bonswa*," the bigger one said, in a raspy singsong. Her few yellow teeth glimmered.

"*Bonswa*," Sarah replied. She stepped forward into the firelight, startling me. Her face was caked with sweat and dirt from our scramble through the woods. She swatted at a bug and thrust her suitcase in front of her. "Say something, Alan."

"Hi," I mumbled.

Sarah looked at her phone and repeated what she'd said to the boys. "*N'ap chèche yon vye fanm.*"

The bigger woman mumbled something back to Sarah that I couldn't understand. Sarah looked at me, clueless. The other one laughed and then the two of them snorted and cackled with abandon.

"What's so funny?" I said. Sarah shushed me.

"*Bonswa*," a voice boomed. The fire flared up, revealing an old Haitian man who stood in the door frame. He wore a maroon striped short sleeve dress shirt that ballooned over his small figure. His dress slacks were baggy, too, and hung over his polished loafers. It was as if he'd lost weight but kept wearing the same clothes.

"*Bonswa*," Sarah repeated.

A shadow filled the door frame. It was a young man, his tank top distended by dysmorphic pecs and traps, like a cartoon superhero. He stared at us, stone faced, and then curled a plastic jerry can up to his chest. His bicep gleamed.

"Hello," I said.

He grunted in my general direction and dropped his can with a thud. The kids dashed out from the shack, running towards us. The boy in the sweater tugged at my duffel with a smile. I let it go, and he dragged it inside. The smaller boy followed with Sarah's bag.

The skinny old man grinned. Muscles whispered something into his ear and both of them cracked up laughing, and then the women joined in, and then the young boys came back out, laughing hard. Then Sarah was laughing, too, and she sat down next to the ladies and took off her shoes. I just stood there, my feet throbbing.

"*Chita*," the bigger woman said, gesturing to a rock by the fire. I sat down and looked up at the group surrounding me. There was no sign of Mom. They were probably going to rob us, but my worry had subsided. I was too tired to run, and Sarah had already settled in, trying out her few Creole phrases on the ladies, the same *vye fanm* that she'd used on the kids, and a few others I didn't recognize.

Where would I go, anyway?

I untied my shoes and pulled them off, and then my sweat and blood-caked socks. The cool night air made my blisters tingle and thrum.

The younger boy in the wool vest had unrolled Sarah's yoga mat. He sat on it, smiling, and pressed his fingers into its squishy and unfamiliar surface. Then he lay on his back and stared up at the sky before bolting to his feet, too excited to rest.

The old man threw a chunk of wood into the fire, geysering sparks into the night air. He sat next to Muscles on a splintered board suspended between cinder blocks. The firelight brightened and Muscles straightened and stretched, revealing a kettlebell design on his tank top.

I gestured to Sarah but she didn't notice. She was repeating after the ladies, who were giving an impromptu Creole lesson, pointing to body parts and saying the appropriate words.

Cheve. Nen. Bouch. Jenou. Zòrèy.

Each time she said one, the whole group laughed. Then the older boy chimed in, suggesting words.

Pye. Janm. Bra. Zepòl.

Sarah repeated all of them.

"Do they know where Mom is?" I asked Sarah.

"I think so."

"Did you see the kettlebell on his shirt? Maybe he knows Gwo."

The old man saw the concern on my face and smiled. A long scar ran from his hairline down to his chin, like his face was comprised of two distinct parts, puzzle pieces that nearly fit together.

"We're looking for our Mom," I said.

He stared at me blankly.

"Our mother."

He turned to Muscles and murmured something. The big man laughed and slapped him on the back. Then they both looked back at me. "*Manman ou*," Muscles said.

He nodded and said one word in English. "Soon."

Sarah noticed the boy standing on her yoga mat and got to her feet.

"Sarah, no," I said, a swell of worry rising in my chest. She ignored me and hustled him off the mat and the wave subsided.

"Watch me," she said. Then she got on her hands and knees on the mat and curled her toes, pressing her fingers into the squishy foam. She checked to make sure he was looking and then pressed her butt up to the sky. Sarah's dark hair hung around her face in sweaty clumps, but there was an elegance to her pose, a fluidity that seemed *right*. "*Adho Mukha Svanasana*," she said to the boy. There was no strain in her voice. "Now you try." She got to her feet and stepped off to the side.

The little boy adjusted his wool vest and stepped to the center of the mat, staring straight ahead for a moment as if in meditation. Then he got to his hands and knees.

"*Adho Mukha Svanasana*," Sarah repeated.

"*Adho—*"

"*Mukha*," Sarah said.

"*Mukha.*"

She drew the last word out slowly. "*Svanasana.*"

"*Svan—*"

"*Svanasana.*"

"*Svanasana,*" the boy repeated, smiling .

Sarah nodded at him and the boy pressed his fingers into the mat and lifted his butt into the air, but unlike Sarah's elegant angle, the boy looked like he was doing some kind of bear crawl, his back arched and his feet wide apart.

She adjusted him, pulling his hips back until his arms straightened naturally. Then she stepped away and he held the pose for a moment before looking to us for affirmation, his smile wide and proud.

"*Adho,*" the boy said.

"*Mukha—*"

"*Mukha,*" he repeated.

"*Svanasana,*" Sarah said, and he shouted the word after her and collapsed on the mat, laughing.

The women laughed, too, and so did the other little boy and the grown men. I smiled but held back a laugh, until it came out like a snort, which started another round of laughter that ended with coughs and shouts.

The old man lit a joint and passed it to Muscles, who took a hit and passed it to me. I inhaled deeply and let my exhale blend into the fire's ashy fumes. I took a second hit before passing the joint back. The fire crackled and a cadre of dogs began to bark in the distance.

Sarah was trying to get the boys to balance on one leg, with little success. Muscles handed her the joint and she placed it between her lips before floating her foot up to her thigh and placing her hands in prayer. The tip glowed orange as she inhaled, and then she let out a huge cloud through her nose, holding the pose with precision, a stone carving in the feeble light.

The Haitians cheered her on, laughing, and the boys looked at her in awe. I hopped to my feet and grabbed the joint from her mouth and took another hit. Then I lined up next to Sarah and pressed my blistered sole to the inside of my leg, before raising it to my thigh. Joint in my mouth, my sore foot wobbling, I pressed my hands into prayer next to her. The shack's scrap wood wall was straight ahead, and I fixed my gaze on a knot, trying not to fall, and then I swayed a little bit, caught myself, and teetered and collapsed to the dirt.

The world swirled around me and I crawled over to Sarah's mat, shooing the boys. "*Savasana*," I said, the one Sanskrit word I remembered, and I lay down on my back and stared up at the sky.

Sarah took the joint from my mouth and took another hit before handing it back to the old man. Then she lay down on the earth, next to me.

The tall conifers encircled us. We were in a little oasis. The few clouds ambled away, leaving the night sky awash in stars. As my gaze focused, the dozens of pinpricks turned into hundreds and then thousands, a carpet of sparkle of varying sizes and intensities. Patterns emerged, constellations I recognized and others that formed anew in my imagination, warriors, princesses, houses and dogs, roaring suns on opposite ends of galaxies, countless lifetimes apart.

The shapes melted away, and I saw at once that there had been no shapes to begin with, that it was all my invention or inventions I'd inherited, that it was all matter—elements and particles, the hot and cool dust from which we'd been formed. It was all energy. Even time was a conversation someone had devised, and everything I saw, heard, and felt was given by impressions from the past, and in the absence of all that, there was only the Infinite.

I turned my head towards Sarah. "None of this is real," I said.

Sarah faced me and closed her eyes as if she was straining to think. Then she farted, a long, low blast, hesitant and halting at first. Then her face relaxed and the fart strengthened and smoothed out, revving like a truck engine before it ended in a sharp uptick squeak. She raised a fist in victory.

The Haitians cheered. "*Bon bagay*," the old man shouted.

"*Bon bagay*," a familiar voice chimed in.

I sat up. Mom was standing over us in her regular spandex, a kettlebell in each hand. She muttered something to the old man in Creole—*ba'm*—and he stuck the joint in her mouth like he did it all the time. She took a huge hit without dropping the weights. "Hey, kids," she said out of the corner of her mouth, exhaling, and a huge column of smoke rose into the sky, hiding the stars.

Gwo was skipping rope on a stone slab outside his house, a few hundred yards from the shack down a narrow footpath. The cord thrummed as it snapped across the ground, two ticks for each jump. Bugs buzzed around the harsh white light hanging from a beam. Gwo looked up and grinned when he saw the beam from Mom's headlamp, but didn't break his stride. His face glowed with sweat.

The two boys greeted Gwo with a whirlwind stream of Creole. They stood for a minute, watching him in awe, and then dumped our bags alongside the house and before running back home. Mom had pressed her kettlebells overhead for the

entire walk, grunting and lunging as she filled us in: the boys
were Gwo's nephews, and Muscles was his little brother, named
Ti. One of the women was Ti's wife, the other was an aunt,
and the old man was a cousin. The whole area was filled with
Gwo's family.

"*Mesi*," Mom shouted after them.

"Your Mom speaks Creole now," Gwo said.

"*Tou piti*," Mom said.

"Glad you guys came to visit," Gwo said. The jumprope
thwacked against rock, and as we came closer I could hear the
quiet patter of his sneakered feet.

"Fucking detectives," Mom said. "Cagney and Lacey."

"Which one am I?" Sarah asked.

"You're a Jewish Tyne Daly," I said. I hobbled over to a
chair alongside the house and kicked off my shoes. Gwo put
down the rope and wiped his face with the front of his tank
top. He seemed even bigger than when I'd seen him last, but I
was still a little high. He looked down at my feet.

"Yuck," he said. "We should clean that up."

"Yuck?" Mom said. "Did they teach you that in med
school?"

"It's the first thing they teach you," Gwo said. "Yuck and
ewwww." He went inside, where I could hear him rattling around.

"Med school?" Sarah mouthed to Mom.

"I'm a doctor," Gwo shouted from inside. He came out,
carrying a metal pan filled with soapy water and a clean cloth.
"Here in Haiti, anyway." Gwo knelt down in front of me and
washed my feet. "In Florida, I'm Coach Gwo."

I clenched, determined not to moan.

"We're here for clinic," Mom said. "He comes down every
month. I've been collecting meds from all the *alter cockers*—"

"*Gezunt zolstu zein*," Gwo said to her.

"Yiddish!" Sarah said.

"A *bissel*," he replied. He squeezed some ointment out of a packet and wrapped gauze around my feet. "I try to come down and help the people who live around here. My family, all the locals. The nearest hospital is a long way."

My foot looked like a baby's in his huge hand. He finished bandaging me and stood up.

"You just—help people?" I asked.

He looked at Mom, puzzled.

"Some people do that," she said.

"Oh. Well, thanks."

"*Mesi* is what we say here," he said.

"*Mesi.*"

It got quiet for a second. Mom settled down in a metal chair and lit a cigarette. The tobacco's familiar scent floated toward me over the earthy air. Mom was Mom. No spandex, no kettlebell could change her.

"You guys walked all the way up here," Gwo said, shaking his head. "I'm impressed."

"Sarah was worried," I said.

"He wasn't going to come," Sarah said.

"I came—"

"Barely," she said. "Bernice and Marty called security on him—"

"Will you stop?" I said.

"Alan was jerking it—"

"Cut the shit," Mom said, dismissing us with a tiny gesture. She softened her smile and the tone of her voice, but there was no mistaking she was serious. "You two need to get your heads out of your asses." She paused, and shook her head. "I'm glad to see you both, but I'm not a fucking idiot."

"Sorry," I said, embarrassed.

"I don't need you to save me."

"I was worried," Sarah said.

"I told you what I was doing."

"Old people get robbed and murdered all the time," Sarah said. "I figured he was scamming you or something." She looked over at Gwo with a thin smile. "No offense. It is kinda weird."

"It's not."

"You're *Jewish*," Sarah said, like she was talking about an alien race. "He's *Haitian*."

Gwo rolled his eyes. "A *shonda*."

"You watch too much Nightline," Mom said. "And I'm not that old."

"You have cataracts," Sarah said.

"*Had* cataracts," Mom said. "And I back squat two and a quarter."

"She's telling the truth," Gwo said.

"Then that settles it," I said. A well of sadness rushed into my chest. Mom and Sarah's bickering hadn't changed in thirty years. It didn't matter that we were atop a Haitian mountain, or that Sarah and I had come on foot to try and be heroes. It didn't even matter that I was broke and jobless, that Andrea was fucking a crossing guard. There was nothing more familiar or comforting than their sniping. "Mom." My eyes welled and the words spilled out. "I fucked up," I said, surprised at myself.

"It's not that big a deal," Mom said. "I'm not mad—your sister's always been racist—"

"I am *not!*" Sarah barked.

"No, no," I said. I coughed. "I've been a shit—"

"Alan—" Mom interrupted.

"It has nothing to do with race," Sarah said. "I phone banked for Obama."

"For Obama!" Gwo said. I couldn't tell if he was serious.

"Stop it!" I shouted. Mom looked at me like I was crazy, but everyone quieted. "I lost all our money." My cheeks were wet. I sniffled, hard.

"How much?" Mom asked.

"A lot. Thousands. Tens of thousands," I said. "Our savings. Credit cards."

Mom sat back in her chair and took a drag from her cigarette. The smoke luminesced around her, a halo.

I shook my head. "Dumb shit."

She creaked to her feet and came next to my chair, placing her hand on my head like she'd been doing all my life. I reached for it and held it.

"Andrea left. And I got fired." I choked back a sob. "Everything's a mess."

Mom nodded and shushed me. Gwo leaned against the door frame, still. A moth dive-bombed the light, thumping and then bouncing away for another attempt.

I turned to my sister.

Her eyes gleamed and she sniffled, and she leaned down and gave me a hug. "I never liked Andrea."

"Sarah!" Mom glared at her.

"She was cunty," Sarah said, sticking her tongue out at Mom. "The truth hurts." She whacked me on the shoulder. "You fucking stink."

"Go wash up," Mom said, looking to Gwo for agreement, but he held up a hand as if to say *leave me out of this*. She shrugged. "You smell terrible."

"Seriously," Sarah said.

Mom glared at her. "You're a little racist, Sarah." She held up a finger. "Don't argue."

I got to my feet and wiped my nose with a sleeve. "The truth hurts," I said, smiling through my tears.

"Clean up, get some rest. We'll get the *what's what* to-morrow."

"Okay."

"It's not so bad," she said. "Just don't go running off. It doesn't solve anything."

"Okay."

Gwo placed his massive arm over my shoulder and guided me to the house. "You should get a kettlebell," he whispered, and for once, I agreed.

I stood in the bed of the pickup truck stacking cartons of medical supplies, as Mom and Sarah ferried them from inside the house. It was early, and still cool. Gwo worked underneath the truck's hood. It was an old Isuzu, held together by duct tape and paint, with a crack down the center of its windshield and smashed side mirrors hanging limply against the doors .

He jumped in the cab and turned the key. The truck coughed to a start, belching black smoke as Gwo pressed down the gas pedal. "Wooo!" Gwo shouted. The truck rattled and settled into an uneasy rhythm.

Ti buzzed down the pathway on an old moto and pulled up in front of the house. Dance music buzzed from a speaker bungeed to the handlebars. Ti turned off the bike and the music stopped. He was wearing the same tank top from the night before, a kettlebell on the front, a Crossfit logo on the back.

"Ti will take you to Jacmel," Gwo said. "You can get a bus to Port-au-Prince. It's a lot easier than the way you came."

"You sure you want to go?" Mom asked.

"I should," I said.

"You can stay here for a while," she said. "Help out in the clinic with me and Sarah. I'll be here for at least a couple of weeks."

I shook my head. "I need to get home," I said.

Mom nodded. "It's not so bad, Alan. Go clean up your mess." She pressed a stack of Haitian goud and American cash into my hand. "Get a job."

"Okay."

"You don't need a guru, Alan. Just quit doing stupid shit."

I stuck the money in my pocket and hugged her and Sarah. I took my bag over to the bike. Ti presented his fist for a bump and I complied. I stuck my headphones in my ears for the ride, and Ti hoisted my duffel onto the gas tank. I climbed on behind him as he started the motor. The engine whirred. Ti pressed a button, and the music came back on. He turned a knob, raising the volume until the sound was distorted and the beat buzzed through the seat.

Ti pam nan li fè m depale

Li fè tout san m mache

Li fè m fè sa li vle konsa

Li jwen m tankou 'on bongo

L'ap fè m danse tango

I didn't know what any of it meant, but it didn't matter. I wasn't going to let it matter. I had all the advice I needed—*quit doing stupid shit*—and there were at least two people on the planet who cared whether I lived or died. That was enough, for now.

I stuffed my headphones back in my pocket and pulled my phone out, and I found the Ram app and deleted it.

Ti rolled the bike down the path, away from Mom and Sarah and Gwo. I held onto a metal rail beneath the seat with one hand and turned to wave goodbye with the other. They were already back at work in the truck. The moto bounced along the rocky trail for a few minutes, through the canopy of trees and past Ti's shack, where I waved at his kids—they shouted *orevwa* and ran alongside the bike for as long as they could—and finally we reached the gravel road and picked up speed.

The grade steepened. We descended past limestone gardens and terraced fields. The pines disappeared and tiny villages began to dot the terrain. We wound through them, past shouts of *Blan! Blan!* I waved to toddlers and teens in twos and threes, past lottery shacks and tiny churches, clusters of homes and makeshift stores, donkeys and goats. We rounded a long curve, and as we emerged, Ti shouted over the music.

"*Ga-day!*" he said, pointing.

Endless miles of valley laid in front of us, patches of trees and farms, shacks and livestock. In the distance, the Caribbean glowed a hazy blue, framed by cascading hills. Ti cut the engine and let the bike roll down the bumpy road, and then he cut the music, so that all I could hear was the crunch of the tires and the wind's whistle in my ears. I stared out at the landscape and breathed the hints of salt in the air.

We picked up speed, and my mind began to spin. I wondered what would be next, whether things would be different and how I would manage to dig myself out from under the mess I'd made. Everything had come unglued, and my heart fluttered with worry. But then the breeze began to warm, and I felt the sun on my arms and my face, and I smiled.

Acknowledgments

If this book is any good, or even readable, it's because of the amazing people who have surrounded me. My extraordinary graduate school advisors: Darin Strauss, Helen Schulman, John Freeman, and Matthew Thomas. All my grad school classmates who so graciously told me when I went too far. Galt Nieder hoffer, Keith Hollihan, Jonas Goodman and Leslie Nipkow who all read the damn thing and liked it. Richie Jackson who encouraged me to start writing again. Paul Calderon who taught me about books. Maestro Alberto Torres Davila and Maestro Hamilton Souther, and all the other amazing Maestros and staff at Blue Morpho who I would trust with my life, anytime. Luis Gutierrez, the best Spanish teacher ever. My incredible clients, who would probably prefer not to be named— thank you for your support and flexibilty, even when I was calling you back from the side of a mountain in Haiti or from an Amazon riverbank. Carla Elfeld, Joh Benichou, Amy McLaughlin, Jo Anne Davidian, Anne Weiss, Shaun Mader, Amy Allison, Mary Ellen Kramer, Ernest Biscardi, Darrick Richardson, Emanuele Ancorini, Joyce Pike, who were always there with love. Heather Rae and Mari Kornhauser, who had my back when I needed it. Freddy Tovar who showed me what commitment looks like and who helped me pull my head out of my ass more than once. All of you have made the most enormous difference for me, but especially: Lily and Eli, who inspire me every day and make me so proud, my mom Lorraine who would be proud of me no matter what I did, my late grandparents Sid and Doriss, who thought I was the shit, my sister Jenn, my brothers Micah and Josh, and my beautiful Suzzanne, who makes me feel loved everyday. Thank you.

About the Author

Jon Rubinstein has spent the last thirty years working with some of the world's top actors in film, television and theater. His clients have included Oscar, Emmy, Tony and Golden Globe nominees and winners. He is the CEO and founder of Authentic Talent and Literary Management, one of the industry's top firms, with offices in New York and Los Angeles.

Jon produced the award-winning film HIGHER GROUND, released in 2011 by Sony Pictures Classics after premiering at the Sundance Film Festival.

He has long been deeply involved in nonprofit projects around the world, working to provide prenatal care for rural women in southern Haiti, English language instruction to adults in Port-au-Prince, as well as projects working with children and teens in Guatemala, Kolkata India, and Brooklyn.

Jon has led leadership training programs to hundreds of people, he's participated in dozens of shamanic ceremonies in the Peruvian Amazon, and he's repeatedly hiked across Haiti's mountains.

He is a graduate of NYU's MFA program in Creative Writing. Jon speaks Spanish, his French and Haitian Creole are fading a bit, and he can hardly remember any Italian.